NICE DRAGON

Now it has been wi... ...s, when sleeping, disp... ...ty that makes them lo... ...d vicious grizzly bear... ...m as warm and playf... as a cocker spaniel; the most sadistic warrior, when dozing, appears as innocent as a child, and even vermin such as toads and snakes take on a kind of cute, toylike appearance.

This is not true of dragons.

This dragon, in fact, looked even nastier than most. It was curled in a loose ball with its nose resting on its tail and a thin trickle of drool emanating from the side of its mouth.

(Dragons tend to drool a lot. In fact, the worst thing about fighting dragons is that when they first open their mouths to flame you, you are likely to be showered with dragon spit. All knights really hate this part and it's the sort of thing that doesn't get mentioned during those romantic evenings of bragging by the fireside.)

Charming reflected on all this while watching the dragon from the doorway with the sword Endeavor in his hand. He breathed quietly and shallowly while he took in the dragon, the room, the location of all the entrances and exits, the position of the furniture, the windows, the light, and the various obstacles scattered about that could trip up a man if he wasn't watching where he was going, like if he was preoccupied with fighting for his life. "Okay," he told himself silently. "This is not such a problem. He's asleep. I'll walk over there very quietly, being very careful not to disturb him, and put this sword through the eye socket before he knows what hit him. It's been done."

At that point, the dragon awoke.

"Time to fall back on plan B," said the Prince, but unfortunately the dragon seemed to have the same plan and charged. . . .

SLAY AND RESCUE

JOHN MOORE

BAEN

SLAY AND RESCUE

A Baen Books Original

Baen Publishing Enterprises
P.O. Box 1403
Riverdale, N.Y. 10471

ISBN: 0-671-72152-6

Cover art by Stephen Hickman

First printing, January 1993

Distributed by
SIMON & SCHUSTER
1230 Avenue of the Americas
New York, N.Y. 10020

Printed in the United States of America

Thanks to the members
of the Houston Ritual
Society, for their support
and enthusiasm

THE WIZARD WAS evil. Really evil. Truly evil. Evil with no redeeming qualities. He created plagues that fouled the air of the surrounding countryside. He created pestilences that poisoned the water of the villages downstream from his castle. He murdered lonely travelers, grinding up their bones for his powders and boiling their blood for his potions. He tortured small, furry animals in bizarre necrotic experiments. He pulled the wings off butterflies. Not for any magical reasons. Just for fun. He never wrote his mother, not even on her birthday. At the marketplace he always squeezed the fruit too hard, leaving it unfit to sell. He welshed on bets. When he stopped at a local tavern (in disguise, of course), he drank freely of others' largess but would never buy a round himself.

The Princess Gloria, on the other hand, was sweet, pure, chaste and innocent. She was also chained to a wooden table in a locked room in the highest tower of the Wizard's castle. The Princess Gloria was not crying. She had cried continuously for four days and eventually decided that it wasn't going to do her the least bit of good. Her only hope of survival lay in being rescued by an outside party. In which case, it certainly wouldn't do to be found with her eyes red and puffy. If she was killed, well, it wouldn't matter.

Also present were the Wizard's two henchmen, dim-witted thugs and ugly to boot, but effective enough in the physical violence end of the business. Now that the actual job of kidnapping was over, they weren't really needed, but the Wizard felt safer with a couple of bodyguards around. Besides, seeing a beautiful naked girl in chains was a treat for them. They were kinky that way.

The wizard Magellan bustled around the small room, setting out knives and beakers and flasks. His plan was to drain the blood from Gloria's living body, the blood of a virgin princess being very useful for all manner of dastardly spells, particularly if taken between midnight and sunrise. It was a warm night and he opened the small window. A faint breeze made the candles flicker, throwing dancing shadows against the stone walls.

"It's not that I like hearing children cry. Oh no, far from it. I'm a soft-hearted man and crying really bothers me. Sets my teeth on edge. And the screaming! Between midnight and dawn, that should give us nearly five hours of screaming. You scream, don't you? Don't shake your head like that. I can tell you're a screamer. My nerves are jangling already. I'd much prefer to stuff a gag in your mouth, but it throws off the dynamics of the magic." Magellan had a tendency to babble when he was doing something really nasty.

The Princess cringed. The wizard laughed evilly. The two thugs chuckled. The stage was now set for the entrance of Prince Charming.

He timed it beautifully.

The clock, a tacky ornate thing of copper and brass, chimed the midnight hour. Magellan did not hurry. He always set his clocks a little bit fast so he wouldn't be late. He picked up a knife, a slender, curved blade whose wicked gleam bespoke a past filled with torture and mutilation. (The knife had actually been designed for cleaning fish and, in fact, the handle was marked off in inches so you could measure your catch.) Magellan tested the irons on the girl's wrist with a short tug (she cringed again) and slowly, gently, lovingly, placed the blade against her skin. The Princess Gloria closed her eyes. The two thugs leaned in for a better view. There came a knock at the door.

They all stopped and looked.

The knock wasn't a knock exactly. It was louder and more forceful. More penetrating. It was the sound made by a heavy blow on an oak door with a double-bladed ax. The tip of the ax was even protruding through the door, as if to remove any doubt. As the conspirators stood dumbfounded, the blade was withdrawn. Seconds later it struck another shattering blow that left the door hanging in splinters from its hinges. A mighty kick followed the blow and, with a confidence fortified by virtue and righteousness, in strode a tall, well-muscled figure.

"It's Prince Charming!" cried Princess Gloria, combining adulation and relief with recognition.

"It's Prince Charming," echoed the two thugs, though not with the same joy as the Princess.

"Oh, shit," said Magellan.

Prince Charming gave the Princess a smile that was meant to be reassuring and it was. He had a great smile. She warmed right down to the tips of her toes. The Prince was young, just seventeen, and his golden hair hung in loose curls to his shoulders, the result of an hour with an iron curling wand. His boots gleamed—hard rubbing with pig fat. His right hand lay negligently on the hilt of his sword, his left hand displayed a gold ring with the royal seal. His silk shirt was open to his chest, just enough to display a light growth of blond hair and clearly defined pectoral muscles, while his silk-lined cape hung from his broad shoulders. His beardless face was bright with boyish charm and enthusiasm, but his eyes were gray as a winter's sky and just as cold when they set on the Wizard.

"Well, hello, Maggie. What are you up to?"

"Don't call me Maggie," snapped the Wizard and immediately got angry with himself for letting this kid get him angry.

"You know you'll never get those bloodstains out of a white pine table."

"What are you talking about? That's beechwood. I paid forty shillings for it." Magellan got even angrier for letting himself get sidetracked into this stupid digression.

"Pine," said the Prince. He walked over casually and scraped the table with his dagger, revealing a faint white streak. "See. It's been stained." He winked at the Princess. She giggled.

This was quite enough for Magellan. He was a great and powerful wizard, feared throughout the land, and no young punk was going to make a fool out of him in his own castle. Prince or no prince. "Kill him," he snapped.

Reflexively his two henchmen drew their swords and descended upon Charming. Almost immediately, however, discretion got the better of valor and they both stopped after one step, each with a foot in the air. "Uh, Boss," said one. "It's, uh, you know. It's *Prince Charming*."

The Prince breathed onto his nails and buffed them against his shirt. His sword still rested in its scabbard.

"Oh, get him," snapped the Wizard. "He's not so much. There's two of you, after all."

His minion nodded, gulped, and leaped forward, sword raised to strike. His stroke never fell. The Prince moved like quicksilver. His arm swept in a fluid arc, blindingly fast yet completely relaxed. With one liquid motion, he drew his sword and sliced a thin red line across the henchman's throat. Then he stepped aside. The thug lunged past and collapsed against the table, his neatly severed head following his body to the floor by only a second.

The Princess Gloria was totally grossed out.

The dead man's partner opted for a sudden career change. He dropped his sword and bolted for the door. The sound of his boots could be heard clattering down the long spiral staircase. Then there was silence.

Magellan and Charming considered each other. Magellan knew a dozen spells that could have vaporized the young prince instantly. He knew spells that could have left him in constant agony for a year before letting him die. He knew spells that did things far worse than death. Unfortunately, all these spells had one thing in common. They required advance preparation. Some required only a little, but none could be inflicted right now. The Wizard had been too busy setting up the bloodletting, relying on his now departed cohorts to provide security.

The Prince was holding his sword at shoulder height. The tip was angled slightly down, straight at Magellan's heart. It was not a friendly gesture. Magellan decided that a strategic withdrawal was called for.

"You haven't heard the last of me, Charming," he said menacingly and immediately decided that it sounded hokey, which it did. "I'll be back," he added, which sounded even hokier. "Fuck it," he finished, and dove out the window.

"Oh," said the Princess.

The Prince calmly sheathed his sword and leaned out the window. Magellan was falling quite slowly, his cloak streaming up behind him. Then suddenly his clothes seemed to collapse inward. Then they separated, the robe, boots, socks, and hat floating to the ground of their own accord, while from their midst a large black bird appeared. It beat its wings and flew off into the cloudless sky.

The Prince was unperturbed. He called, "Wendell!" and a boy appeared.

His page was eleven years old and staggered under the weight of a huge knapsack. The fully packed duffel bags he held in each hand didn't help either. He piled the gear on the floor, glanced disinterestedly at the Princess, and sat down on the knapsack, breathing heavily. He said, "One hundred and eighty-one steps."

"Peregrine," said Charming.

"Right." In spite of his fatigue, Wendell got right to work. He untied the knapsack and removed a small, covered cage. The cage proved to contain a falcon, which he handed to the Prince, exchanging it for Charming's sword. Charming removed the bird's hood, stroked it twice, and brought it to the window where it disappeared into the night. He then turned his full attention to the Princess Gloria.

The Princess Gloria was occupied with two conflicting trains of thought.

One. She was going to live.

Two. She was going to die of embarrassment. He was standing right there beside her, the brave, the handsome, the legendary *Prince Charming* (wait till she told the other girls) and he was looking at her *body*. And she was totally naked. Not only that but her hair was a mess, she had no make-up on, and (oh my God) her toenails were dirty. She wished she were dead, right now.

The Prince was not, however, looking at Gloria's nubile body. With a great effort of willpower, he kept his eyes fixed firmly on her face. Then in a gesture of theatrical chivalry, he swept his cape from his shoulders and covered her from feet to neck. The Princess Gloria gave an audible sigh of relief. "Thank you."

"It is my pleasure to be of service, dear lady," the Prince said solemnly. "Wendell!"

Wendell finished wiping down the Prince's sword with an oily cloth and rummaged through one of the duffels for a hammer and chisel. With these he attacked the princess's chains. Charming, meanwhile, came up with a silver-backed hairbrush and mirror. As soon as her hands were free, he passed these to Gloria. It wasn't the first such rescue he'd performed and he was getting to know the ropes. First, though, he gave himself a surreptitious glance in the mirror to make sure his own hair was still perfect.

There was a beating of wings at the window. The falcon returned bearing a dead bird in its talons. A raven. The Prince examined it without surprise, dropped it into a leather bag, and fed the falcon a piece of meat.

Wendell had freed the Princess Gloria's arms and was making short work of her leg irons. When he was finished, she stood up. Although she was small, her regal bearing impressed the two boys. With the cape wrapped around her, her hair brushed back, and her chin held high, she was the very picture of good breeding. She curtsied once and then spoke to Charming. "Your Highness, may I speak to you in confidence?"

"Wendell!"

"On my way out," said Wendell, vanishing down the stairs.

Charming gave the girl what he hoped was his most dazzling smile. "Proceed, dear lady."

The girl returned Charming's smile with a weak smile of her own. Then she cast her eyes downward and twisted her hands. "Your Highness, you have saved my life."

"Well, I'm glad I was able to arrive in time." Charming did not mention he had scouted the place out and waited in a nearby wood for three hours just to make a dramatic last-minute rescue.

"I owe you a debt of gratitude that I can never repay."

The Prince let his eyes flicker to her breasts. "Oh, I wouldn't say that," he said hopefully.

"I come from a small kingdom, your Highness, and although I am a true princess, I am the last of many sisters whose dowries must be established before mine. I have no jewels or treasure to offer you."

Charming's pulse beat faster. "Think nothing of those. The knowledge of your happiness is reward enough."

"Still, I have been taught since birth that a debt of honor must be paid, that a favor accepted must be reciprocated, and that courage and"—she blushed— "virtue should be rewarded."

"Sounds good," said the Prince. "I mean, if that's the way you feel, I won't argue with you." A slight beading of sweat broke out on his upper lip. He moved closer to the Princess. She looked up at him with limpid eyes. Her breathing now came fast and shallow.

"Still, there is but one favor I can offer you."

"Oh, yes." The Prince took both her hands in his and looked deep into her eyes.

"Honor demands that honor be sacrificed," she murmured. "Do you understand what I mean?"

"Yes, darling," breathed the Prince, pulling her close. "I have long waited for this moment."

"Good." And with that word the Princess Gloria screwed her eyes shut, clenched her jaw, stood up on tiptoes and kissed Prince Charming.

On the cheek.

She quickly ducked out from his arms and scooted over to the stairs, giving him the satisfied look of one who has just completed a noble deed. Then she blushed deeply once more and giggled.

Not a word of disappointment escaped the Prince's lips. Not by the slightest frown, not by the merest twitch of an eyebrow did he show that he had hoped for something more substantial than a single chaste kiss. No, neither by word nor deed did he ever betray the expectation that the Princess Gloria was anything but sweet, pure, chaste and innocent in every way.

After all, they didn't call him Prince Charming for nothing.

The sun rose on a land verdant with green fields and lush pastures, a land whose swollen streams swam with trout, whose tall, deep forests ran with deer, a land whose cobblestoned roads and well-tended hamlets bustled with trade and the cheerful activities of a happy populace. It was the Kingdom of Illyria, not the biggest, but certainly the most prosperous of the many kingdoms that lay along a broad corridor between the mountains and the sea. It was, as were all the twenty kingdoms, an ancient land replete with history and legend. There were families with lines of descendency unbroken for a hundred generations, wells that had given water for a thousand years, castles whose very stones were crumbling with age. They were lands steeped in tradition whose people much valued honor, justice, and family. They liked men who were strong and brave, women who were beautiful and loyal, kittens that were warm and fuzzy, maidens who were sweet, pure, chaste and innocent, and dogs that didn't drool too much. Anyway, Illyria was, above all, an enchanted land, a magic land (as were they all in those days), a land brimming with the strange and wonderful. And it was a land that made heroes.

For despite Illyria's general prosperity, its cheerfulness and good humor, its strong moral code, its close-knit fabric of family and social ties, there were still citizens of evil intent. There were those of sick minds and deviant behavior. There were those who let a lust for wealth and power overcome them. And there were those who were just kind of pissed off at the world.

Prince Charming harbored no evil intent, but this morning he fell into the category of pissed off at the world. His boots echoed against the polished oak floor of his father's castle and his leather game bag slapped against his side. He was preparing to have an argument with his father and, in his mind, he was already rehearsing the bitter retorts he would make to the king's refusal of his request. For the moment, however, he made what he considered a valiant effort to keep the conversation light and pleasant. "Did you see the mammaries on that girl, Wendell? They were perfect. And the way they held their shape when she walked! I'll bet they're firmer than my biceps. And my God, the way her nipples stood out! They practically poked right through the cloak."

"Sire," said Wendell, "may I speak frankly?"

"Sure, Wendell. Go ahead."

"Shut up! You have spoken of nothing but the Princess Gloria's breasts the whole four-day ride back to the castle!"

"They were great breasts, Wendell. When you're older you'll appreciate breasts like that."

"Yuck," said Wendell. "I hate girls."

"Not for much longer."

"They always want to muss my hair. I hate that."

"You'll change your mind."

"Hah! Anyway, let's talk about something interesting. Like fishing. Or eating. Peaches are coming into season. I'll bet Cooky makes a peach pie for dessert tonight. What do you think?"

"Speaking of ripe peaches," said the Prince in his best deadpan, "did you see the . . ."

"Oh, Lord," said Wendell. "Just stuff it, will you?"

They reached the end of the great hallway and were faced with a massive carved oak door, with a smaller, newer carved oak door in its side. The big door was decorated with deep relief scenes of a hunt in progress. There were men on horseback, dogs, archers, stag, boar, and bear. The smaller door showed either a cannon and a stack of cannonballs, or a mermaid eating a sea turtle; it was hard to tell which. There were pieces like this scattered throughout the castle. Charming had once commented on them to the castle decorator and had been rewarded with a forty-minute lecture on "non-representational art." It had taught him to keep his mouth shut about art.

Now he turned the knob in the smaller door and pushed through without knocking.

There was more of a reception than he anticipated. Six men, almost half of the Council of Lords, rose when he entered. "Prince Charming!" they said in tones of awe and respect. The King remained seated but beamed at Charming with fatherly affection.

"Welcome home, son. Hello, Wendell."

"Hi, Dad. Good morning, gentlemen. I believe I have a little present for all of you." Charming tossed the game bag carelessly on the table. Lord Isaac Stern, the most powerful of his father's vassals, shook it out on the table. A large dead bird rolled across the deeply waxed wood. The six Lords examined it carefully.

"Magellan," they said happily. "At last we are rid of that scourge."

"Good old Maggie," said the King, prodding the bird with a thick forefinger. "A raven, eh. Must have been trying to flee."

"That's right."

"I'm surprised he didn't turn himself into a magpie. Maggie the Magpie. Has a nice ring to it."

"I guess he just didn't have a sense of humor. Fact is, he seemed a bit upset about something. He didn't even offer me a drink."

The Lords exchanged glances and smiled knowingly at this attempt at self-deprecating humor. It proved, they were sure, that the Prince was even braver and more noble than he appeared.

"Did you save the Princess?"

"Don't I always? She's a little shook up but none the worse for wear, now safe and sound in the arms of her loving family. That's why we took so long getting back. They had a victory feast in my honor."

"They roasted a whole ox," said Wendell reverently. "They basted it with this sauce made with honey and raisins. It was awesome. But then." His voice darkened. "All these families invited the Prince to tea and we went to every one of them. And we had to wear our best clothes all the time."

"Thank you for that assessment, Wendell," the King said gravely. "You may go out and play now."

Wendell was off like a shot. The Prince shrugged. "It was a good gig, Dad. We definitely scored some diplomatic points down there."

"Prince Charming," said Lord Stern. "I know I speak for all the noble families and, indeed, for all the people of Illyria when I thank you for your service to this kingdom. Your bravery, your honesty, and your devotion to the cause of justice and mercy reflect an ideal unmatched in the history of our beloved country."

"Well, thank you, Sir Isaac. But I'm just doing my duty."

"And doing it magnificently, your Highness. But I shall speak no more of this, for I can see I am embarrassing you. Besides, words alone cannot express the gratitude with which we are filled." Around him the other noblemen nodded. "That is why we come today bearing a gift. All the noble families have contributed to its manufacture. We hope you will honor us by accepting it."

"Aw gee, guys. You shouldn't have. What is it?"

"Sir Tyrone," said Lord Stern.

Sir Tyrone Boldstroke stepped forward, cradling a handsomely carved walnut case in his arms. The other Lords parted so he could get through to the table and there he set the wooden box. Carefully he snapped the gold-plated latches. Gently he folded back the top. A hush filled the room as Charming looked into the box.

"Um," said the Prince. "It's a sword."

It was indeed a sword. It lay in the case, thirty-six inches of gleaming blade, gently curved steel leading to a jewel-studded hilt. The grip was knurled from aged maple, then wrapped with oiled lambskin leather. The handguard was intricately engraved and gold-plated, and a full month had been spent honing the edge so that it "bit" at the slightest pressure.

"It is named," said Lord Stern, "*Endeavor*. The finest craftsmen in the twenty kingdoms have labored a year in its making. It has been specially designed for your height, weight, reach and grasp. There is none equal to it anywhere in the world."

"Nice," said the Prince. He picked it up. "Got a good feel to it. I like a sword with some weight."

He glanced up at the circle of noblemen and saw a tinge of disappointment in their faces. Clearly "nice" was not the reaction they were expecting. He took a deep breath.

"Gentlemen, this sword is the most magnificent I have ever held. Or even beheld. From this day forth I shall bear no other." The noblemen smiled. With a dramatic flourish the Prince tore his old sword from his belt and cast it, clattering, to the stone floor. He held the new sword up high, tilting it toward the window, so it caught the light of the morning sun. "Endeavor," he told the blade, "from this day forth you shall be my constant companion. From this day forth we will fight together to protect the weak, defend the innocent, smite evil wherever it lurks, and further the cause of justice and decency." He lowered the sword and thrust it into his scabbard. The nobles burst into applause.

"Well said, son," said the King. "And I know I speak for everyone here when I say that our hearts and our prayers go with you on each and every one of your quests." The nobles applauded again.

"Thanks, Dad. And thank you, gentlemen. Dad, may I speak with you privately? You know, man to man."

"Certainly. Your Lordships, if you'll excuse us."

The noblemen filed out, each one pausing to shake the Prince's hand. Stern gripped his shoulders. "God be with you, young Charming."

"And with you, Sir Isaac."

Boldstroke was the last to leave. "If that sword gives you any trouble, your Highness, you bring it right back and I'll have it taken care of. It's guaranteed for one year against defects in material and workmanship. Just fill out the warranty card and return it in the original box."

"I'll remember that, Sir Tyrone."

When the room had cleared, Charming closed the door, locked it, and shot the bolt. He turned to his father. The King was filling a glass with wine from a hidden tap built into the arm of his throne.

"Endeavor?" said the Prince. "The Endeavor? I've got a whole room full of these pigstickers and now we're going to start naming them?"

"Something the PR department came up with," said the King. He passed the glass of wine to the Prince and began filling another for himself. "Fancy swords with names are great for catching the public imagination. They love that stuff. Think of Excalibur and all those old stories. Anyway, you only need to carry it a few times. After you've slain a dragon or something with it, we'll put it on public display and charge people tuppence to see it."

"But *Endeavor*? It sounds like a battleship."

"Count your blessings, it could have been worse. They originally wanted to call it *Dragonskewer*. They were going to have master engravers etch little scenes with dragons charging up and down the blade. I told Isaac I thought it sounded a bit garish. Form follows function, that's the ticket. Come on, my boy. What's really bothering you?"

Charming was pacing up and down, two fingers drumming methodically against the hilt of the sword. "Dad, it's this hero trip. You've got to take me off of it. I just can't handle it anymore."

The King choked on his wine. "But why? Charming, you've been doing a wonderful job. Superlative! The people love you. *Your* people. And every time you rid the countryside of some evil influence, your popularity increases even more." The King pulled a paper scroll from under his robes. "Just look at the results of these polls."

"I don't care about the polls! I've had enough! Slaying and rescuing, rescuing and slaying, that's all I ever do anymore. I'm sick of it. Every two-bit sorcerer, every renegade knight, every dragon, troll, or ogre that sets up shop around here, the first thing he does is grab himself a piece of ass. And then everyone says the same thing. 'Oh, let's call Prince Charming to the rescue. He'll save her.' And I do. But do I get any thanks for it? Nooooooo!"

"The Princess Gloria didn't thank you? I'm sure

she'll send a note. She's very well bred." The King sipped his wine again.

"No, that's not what I mean. She thanked me. She even kissed me."

This time the King choked and sputtered for a full minute, not getting his words out until Charming pounded him on the back. "She did *what*?"

"On the cheek."

"Ah. On the cheek." His Highness tapped his fingers against the arm of the throne. "Well, I guess that's all right then."

"No, it isn't. Look, remember that little Duchess I rescued last month? I had to fight my way through a nest of giant serpents just to get to her. And then I had to answer a bunch of stupid riddles from some lion-type thing. And that dragon at the end nearly turned me into toast. And after all that, you know what she did when I finally freed her? She punched me on the shoulder."

The King chuckled. "Hillary always was a bit of a tomboy."

"I mean, I'm laying my life on the line for these babes and I think I deserve a little something extra."

The King instantly grew stern. "Like what?"

"Well, you know."

"I think I do know. And I think I don't like what I'm hearing."

"Gosh, Dad. A man has his needs."

"Are you seriously suggesting that you are entitled to defile the fairest daughters of the twenty kingdoms just because . . ."

"Okay, okay. Forget the fairest daughters. Just give me a couple of nights off. I'll head down to Madam Lucy's and . . ."

"Prince Charming! The scion of our royal family, the symbol of virtue and purity, the epitome of everything that is good and noble in young manhood, does *not* go around rutting in brothels like a common sailor!"

"Aw, Dad."

"That's quite enough, young man! As a public figure and a member of the royal family, it behooves you to set a good example for the nation's youth. Premarital intercourse would totally destroy your image. And I shudder to imagine the character of any young woman, royal or common, who would consent to such a sordid liaison. Now report to the Minister of Intelligence for your next Slay and Rescue mission."

Defeated for the nonce, the Prince gave a resigned shrug and started for the door. "All right, Dad, but I think you're letting this popularity thing get out of hand. What are you going to do when people start demanding that I usurp your throne?"

He left just in time to miss the uneasy shifting of the King's eyes.

Wendell fell into step beside him as he trudged across the courtyard. The page was eating a large apple and carrying another one, which he offered to Prince Charming. The Prince took it and bit into it half-heartedly.

"He didn't go for it, huh?"

"No," said Charming.

"No red-hot weekend?"

"No."

"Did he take you off the hero mission?"

"No."

"Ah, well," said Wendell. "The reluctant hero. Reluctant heroes are actually the best kind. If you wanted to be heroic, people would just think you were a show-off."

"Mmmmph!" said Charming. He swallowed a bite of apple. "What are you talking about? I'm always trying to be heroic. I have to watch every word I say, dress like a costume-party warrior, keep in practice with the sword, lance and bow, and be courteous and helpful to everyone I meet. You think that's easy?"

"Well . . ."

"Okay, it probably beats the hell out of plowing a field or pounding an anvil, but still, it's a full-time job. I'd much rather be lying on a mossy bank somewhere with a fishing pole."

"That's what I mean," said Wendell. "People pick up on that. They think you'd prefer a quiet life, so they appreciate you going out on these adventures. It's the same thing with being Prince Charming. If it were easy for you to be charming, it wouldn't command respect. It's the effort you put into being charming that makes it so, well, charming."

The Prince had to smile. "You're getting awfully philosophical for a kid your age, Wendell. Have you been hanging out with Mandelbaum again?"

"Yeah, I was just up to see him. He said I'm precocious. He's working on a spell to keep the frost off strawberries. He thinks it will make him big money."

"I ought to ask him for a love potion."

"He has them. He only gives them to married couples, though."

"Figures."

"Where are we going?"

"To see Norville. We have another assignment."

"We just got back!"

"Now who's reluctant?"

They waited for Norville in the small library which led off from the big library. The big library was usually inhabited by the court lawyers, who spent hours each day poring over musty tomes. The small library, however, was bereft of books, containing instead a great many maps. The walls were covered with maps and hundreds more were rolled up and stacked in glass fronted map cases. They ranged from simple, quick battlefield sketches, hastily drawn on paper in india ink, to elaborate illuminated maps of the twenty kingdoms, drawn with painstaking detail on parchment or vellum. Such a map of Illyria was posted on the wall; the Prince amused himself by picking the smallest towns he could find and piercing them with his dagger at twelve paces. Wendell sat cross-legged on the floor, taking the edge off Endeavor with a piece of ebony. The Prince didn't like a sword that was too sharp. He thought a cut from a blade that was slightly dull had more shock value.

"This is neat. This is really neat," said Wendell. "This is the neatest sword you've ever had."

"Too gaudy. First chance you get, Wendell, pry those rubies out of the handle, sell them, and give the money to the poor."

"All right. Hey, look at this blade. It's got little dark lines running right through the metal. They won't polish out."

"That means it's Damascus steel." Charming had to admit he was impressed. "That's a really good steel."

"And look at this handle. All this other stuff folds out. Look, here's a corkscrew, and a nail clippers, and a file, and a leather punch." He opened up the last blade. "What's this?" The final accessory was a short piece of springy round wire, slightly pointed, with a gently curved hook at the end. "Is this one of those things for taking stones out of horses' hooves?"

The Prince looked at it curiously. "I don't know. I think it's one of those things for splicing rope."

Minister of Intelligence Norville entered. He was dressed in black, as befitted the nation's number one spy, and carried a thick dossier with him. He extracted some papers from the dossier and passed them to Charming, then sat at a table and made a few notes upon a slate. "Good morning, your Highness. You know about the situation in Tyrovia?"

"Vaguely," said Charming. He slouched in a chair, one leg dangling over the armrest, looking out the window.

"The Wicked Queen Ruby treats her daughter most cruelly. Her stepdaughter actually. She is quite vain and extremely jealous of the daughter's beauty."

"Forget it. I don't get involved in family squabbles."

"Our information is that the Queen dresses the girl in rags and forces her to work as a scullery maid."

"Good. I'm a great believer in vocational education."

"Prince Charming, I really wish you would make more of an effort to live up to your name. The Wicked Queen is capable of powerful magic. She poses a security risk to this kingdom. This provides us with just the excuse your father has been looking for to eliminate a dangerous rival. And when the young princess inherits her throne, we gain a pliable and easily manipulated ally to the west."

"Excuse me?" said Charming. "Security risk? Allies? I'm into political assassination now? I think not. I'm a hero, not a hit man."

"Your job is to rescue maidens."

"I rescue maidens from fates worse than death and deaths worse than fate. I protect the weak, defend the innocent, support the downtrodden, and, um, all that stuff. Protecting young girls from household chores is not exactly in my job description."

"Ah," said Norville. "But the Queen has made an attempt on the girl's life."

"Why?"

"Why not? Popular princess, unpopular Queen. When the girl comes of age, there will certainly be competition for the throne. We heard the story from a woodcutter. He said the Queen offered him a substantial amount of money to cut the girl's heart out."

Charming gave him a skeptical look. "This Queen has all this magical power and she has to hire a wood-cutter to stab someone for her? And the guy she picks just happens to be one of our informants?"

"I admit it sounds rather haphazard," said Norville. "But such situations do occur. Come now, good sir. The Little Princess is young, she is beautiful . . ."

"The Little Princess?"

"Called so by her people as a term of affection," said Norville, "and reputed to be of breathtaking beauty. Skin like cream, lips like cherries, that sort of thing. Her name is Ann. Consider, good sir. Here is a sweet and innocent young girl, whose life may be in danger. Surely your noble soul is inspired to feats of gallantry?"

"Huh," Charming grunted. He pointed out the window. "See that milkmaid out there? The one with the big knockers? Her little sister fell down a well once. I plunged in and pulled her out. It was my first rescue. I was thirteen. The milkmaid was crying and hugging me and kept telling me over and over again how grateful she was and how she was going to do something that would show her appreciation."

"And did she?"

"She sent me a box of cookies."

"They were good cookies," put in Wendell.

"That sounds like a very nice gesture," said Norville. "I am glad to hear that the commoners are maintaining a high moral standard. Why, I recently undertook a fact-finding mission to some of the lands across the sea. I was much dismayed at the level of degeneracy there. Women walking the streets unaccompanied, young girls showing their ankles, some even cutting their hair short like a boy's."

"Sounds awful," said Charming. "Why don't you schedule me a rescue there and I'll check it out myself?"

Norville made a noise that sounded like *harumph*.

"All right." Charming swung his foot down and sat forward in his chair. "I'll take a ride over and scope out the situation. But I'm not promising anything. I've told Dad many times I'll not be a part of any expansionist schemes. As long as this Queen Ruby keeps her nose clean, I'm walking away."

"Well then. I suppose we'll have to be satisfied with that. But hesitation may put your life at risk."

"Yeah, well, I'll be the judge of that. What sort of defenses does she have? Any dragons in the kennel? Soldiers on the payroll? Knights?"

"Not according to our information. She seems to rely solely on her magic for protection."

"Hmmm. Wendell!"

"Yes, Sire?"

"We travel light. Pack the new sword . . ."

"Endeavor," said Wendell, holding it up.

"Yeah, yeah. Pack Endeavor, the Sheffield sword, the Nordic sword, and the crossbow."

"Check."

"The new shield with the crest, the ax, and the oak lance with the bronze handguard."

"Got it."

The Prince thought a minute and turned back to Norville. "You say this Ann babe is a real looker?"

"Our information is that she is very fine, yes."

"Wendell, bring along a dozen roses, a box of candy, and a bottle of wine."

"Check."

"Also a large stuffed toy animal."

"Right."

"It never hurts," said the Prince, "to be prepared." He pushed off with his boot against the table and his chair slid back along the polished hardwood floor. He had once asked the castle decorator why all the floors were bare wood or stone, while the walls were hung with tapestry. The castle decorator had taken a deep breath and the Prince had beat a hasty retreat, before another lecture could be forthcoming.

Now he stood up, received his sword and belt from Wendell, and buckled it on. "We leave at daybreak, Wendell."

"Yes, Sire."

"Good luck, your Highness," said Norville.

"Thank you." The Prince paused at the door. "Ah, Count Norville?"

"Yes, your Highness?"

"Any progress on the slipper thing?"

"We are working on it, Sire."

"Okay, then. Well, I'm off." He shut the door firmly behind him, but Norville could still hear his bootsteps echo on the polished wood floor.

"There are kingdoms where I wouldn't have to do any of this." They were walking their horses along the cobbled path that led west from Illyria. Leafy trees, oak and hickory and yew, overhung the road. The ground was dappled with sunlight. "Over the ocean, the girls will line up around the block to sleep with a prince. They wouldn't care if he never slayed a horned toad."

"Girls," said Wendell. "Yuck."

As instructed, Wendell had awakened the Prince in the dark hours of the morning. By daybreak his hero was ready to depart, dressed smartly in highly polished, black riding boots, black pants, a white silk shirt, a light armor breastplate, and wearing his sword and buckler. The two young men strolled boldly through the castle halls, across the courtyard, and over the moat, capturing the admiring glances of the female servants up for the early morning chores, and the respectful looks of the men. They rode through the center of town, Wendell carrying the royal banner on a short staff. Those townspeople awake came out of the shops to line up alongside the road, the women waving the Prince on with their handkerchiefs, the men saluting, the girls starry-eyed, the boys envious. The Prince rode tall in the saddle, morning sun glinting off his highly polished armor. (Wendell applied a light coating of clear lacquer to give it that extra shine.) His horse, a white stallion (Wendell dusted its coat with flour), was prancing and chafing its bit, tossing its head from side to side and then straining forward, as if eager to see where this adventure would take him. Beside him, his young face stern with responsible thoughts, Wendell rode a sleek black stallion and led two pack horses, each burdened with camping equipment, gifts and weaponry. At the city gates, the Prince turned his horse and dug his spurs into its side. The horse reared; from the saddle, the Prince waved once to the assembled throng. The crowd cheered. Charming and Wendell trotted their horses into the soft golden haze of the morning sun.

Once out of sight, they immediately turned off the road, tethered the horses, and stretched out under a thickly foliated shade tree for a two-hour nap. In no particular hurry, the Prince changed into more casual clothes, then watered the horses, while Wendell laid out a midmorning repast of cold chicken, brown bread, cranberry salad, and cider. The sun was well along its arc by the time they resumed their journey. "The way I see it," said Charming, "is that there is trouble pretty much everywhere we go, so there is no point hurrying from one place to the other. If we're too late to rescue one princess, another will be snatched before too long." Wendell, not a morning person either, did not argue.

At this pace it took almost a week to reach the edge of the kingdom and enter Tyrovia. It began at the foothills of the mountains and extended up their chill and fog-shrouded slopes. High above the trees grew thick, with black and gnarly limbs, and strange forms lurked in the shadows beneath, or skulked from trunk to trunk with a quiet rustle of dead leaves. Down in the foothills, however, tracts of land had been cleared for neatly tended farms, studded with small thatched huts and laced with gaily running streams. The sun was still shining and a cool breeze coming down from the mountains made the day altogether pleasant. The Prince should have been in a good mood. But instead he was preoccupied with thoughts not uncommon in seventeen-year-old boys.

"Do you think the girls really show their ankles in foreign lands, Wendell?"

"I don't care," said Wendell crossly. He had been listening for a solid week to this sort of speculation. But his erudite reply was interrupted by a rough bass voice booming through the trees.

"None shall pass!"

Charming and Wendell quickened their horses. They broke out of the woods where the road led to the banks of a river. Spanning the river was a narrow wooden bridge, just wide enough to walk a horse across. Astride the bridge, legs apart, hands boldly on hips, was a tall, broad-shouldered figure. He was made more imposing by the fact that he was dressed head-to-toe in black armor. An evil-looking sword swung from his right hand, while his left held a crested shield. The crest was pretty much illegible since it was painted in black on a black shield; still, there was little doubt that this was indeed the infamous, much feared, and little-respected Black Knight.

"You great metal-covered sod," snapped a woman. She was carrying two buckets of milk on a yolk across her shoulders. "How am I going to get this to market, then? With the sun so high it will turn in a matter of hours."

"None shall pass!" roared the Knight again. His sword whistled as it cut the air an inch in front of her nose. She scrambled backwards, milk sloshing on her clothes as she retreated. "None shall pass."

"How does he get his sword to make that noise?"

"He's got a whistle built into the hilt," explained Charming, as he handed Wendell his reins. "An old trick. Kind of juvenile, I think." He dismounted and shouldered his way through the crowd, coming to the front with his hand resting casually on his sword. "Yo, Blackie. Good line. Think it up yourself?"

"It's *Prince Charming*," cried the peasants as one voice and the milkwoman finished, "*He'll* teach that asshole a lesson."

"Be off, young prince," said the Black Knight. "I guard this bridge for the Wicked Queen. Step one foot on it and you die."

"Great," said Wendell. "Norville steered us wrong again."

The Prince considered the river. Though swift, it was shallow and would be easy enough to wade across were he to go a little upstream, out of this jerk's sight. But the peasants were watching and he *did* have his rep to consider. "You made me a similar challenge last spring, Blackie. I seem to remember I kicked your ass."

"Don't call me Blackie," muttered the Knight.

"What?"

"I was drunk last spring, Charming." Cold fury underscored his words. "Besides, I've been practicing. And furthermore, although you may be quick with a sword, I am fully armored this day and you are not."

"Ah." The Prince smiled. "But for how long?"

"What do you mean?"

Slowly and carefully, his arms now well away from his sword, the Prince stepped onto the bridge and approached the Black Knight. The peasants and

Wendell watched curiously as he stopped only a sword's length away. But he leaned forward and spoke in a confidential tone that only the big man could hear.

"I mean sooner or later you are going to have to take a leak. And when you remove your codpiece, you will leave yourself open for—how shall I put it—the unkindest cut of all?"

The Black Knight's knees drew together a fraction of an inch. "You wouldn't dare."

"Mmm." The Prince folded his arms. "Yep, I'll bet it gets pretty hot standing in this sun all day. Especially in black armor. Why, I'd have drained half a dozen canteens by now, were I in your place."

Behind his visor, the Black Knight's gaze shifted involuntarily to an empty wineskin hanging from the bridge railing. "I can hold it," he said hoarsely.

"Sure you can. And I admire you for it. Guarding a bridge like this, where you have to listen to the sound of this rushing water all day long."

The Black Knight became suddenly aware of the river's gurgle. "Shut up. Just shut up!"

"Trickling over the rocks, flowing between the stones, the constant sound of running water hour after hour . . ."

"Damn you." The Knight lunged forward on wobbly legs. The Prince danced nimbly out of the way.

"Gosh, I didn't mean to upset you. I'll shut up then. You won't hear another word out of me." He put his elbows on the railing, crossed his legs and leaned back, smiling benignly at the Black Knight. The Knight scowled back. In the silence the sound of rushing water seemed to grow louder and take on a musical tone. Charming drummed his fingers silently on the rail. From beneath the bridge a dripping noise began and added itself to the din.

Sweat broke out on the Black Knight's forehead. He looked at the peasants, staring at him in mystified silence. The old woman set down her buckets and the milk made a sloshing sound. Wendell took a canteen from his pack and drank from it. Several of the men began passing a wineskin back and forth. The Knight looked at Charming gazing across the stream, and wondered if he could leap suddenly and slice the kid's head off.

Charming began humming an old sea chantey. The Black Knight gave one more mighty effort at concentration and then his nerve broke. "All right, you can pass, you little twerp. I'll catch you on the return trip. Just get out of my sight."

"Many thanks."

"And don't call me Blackie."

"Sure thing."

Charming winked to the crowd, collected the reins from Wendell and remounted. The Prince and his page crossed the bridge at the head of a procession of baffled but admiring peasantry. They looked back but once to see the Black Knight disappear behind a tree.

"What was that all about?"

"Tell you later," said the Prince.

They reached the castle of the Wicked Queen the next day.

It was a hard ride. The road grew narrower, then steeper, and they had to dismount and walk the horses. A chill rain started, turning the already muddy road ever muddier. Twisted, storm-tortured trees lined their path, trunks dank with moss, tangled branches reaching out to snag the weary travelers. In the mountains the shadows fell suddenly and unexpectedly, fogs hung in the clefts and valleys, defying what pale sunlight penetrated their damp realm, and the uneasy snorts of the horses echoed strangely from the black rocks. The road terminated at a small plateau which held an even smaller village of a dozen or so dismal, rain-streaked huts and shops. It was late evening when they arrived. They rode down the single, deserted street with only the occasional gleam of a tallow candle showing through the tightly shuttered windows. Perched on a crag overlooking the village was the castle.

It loomed before them, grimly black and foreboding. Rain slicked the crumbling stone; condensation clouded the cracked and dirty windows. From the moat arose a fetid mist. A cloud of bats circled the southern tower from which a single red light gleamed like a bloodshot eye. The north tower dissolved halfway up into a jumble of scorched and shattered stone, as if it had been torn apart by an explosion. There was a crackle of lightning and a low rumble of thunder. The rain coursed down harder.

"This," said Wendell, "is the spookiest place we've ever had to attack."

"But it's close to the school and to the shops," Charming pointed out. "In real estate, location is everything." He glanced into the moat, noted his reflection in the slimy waters, and finger-combed his wet hair.

A sudden cranking and grinding made Wendell start. The Prince merely glanced around calmly. The noise came from the drawbridge which hesitantly, in fits and starts, tried to descend. About a third of the way down, it broke free of whatever was obstructing it and fell, hitting the ground with a teeth-jarring crash and a rattle of rusty chains. Then silence reigned once more.

"Well," said Charming. "That seems like an invitation."

"Sire, perhaps we should scout the place out before we cross that bridge."

"We've already scouted it out."

"Perhaps we should scout it out again."

"Oh, come now," said the Prince. "They're probably keeping dinner waiting for us. Mustn't be rude." His tone was light, his manner was not. With great care and an even greater show of uncaring casualness, he stepped onto the drawbridge.

But before he could advance, the castle door was flung open and a young woman appeared, silhouetted by the light from within. The Prince stepped back and motioned Wendell to move closer. "A babe!" he whispered. "Now listen. She's going to say, 'It's *Prince Charming*!'"

"You must leave immediately," said the girl.

"Nice call," said Wendell.

"Hey," said Prince Charming. "I'm *Prince Charming*."

"I know exactly who you are," said the girl. Coming closer, Charming could see that she was quite beautiful. Her hair was a long, deep, lustrous black; her eyes dark and liquid, framed by heavy lashes; and her lips were red, full and pouting. Her pale skin was smooth and without the slightest flaw or blemish. Her simple, low-cut blouse showed plenty of cleavage and the slit in her skirt ran clear up her thigh. Even the Prince, who had seen plenty of beautiful girls in his day, was momentarily dazzled.

"I know exactly who you are," said Ann. Her voice, though concerned, was clear and musical. "Word of your arrival has preceded you. I have already heard the tale of how you defeated the treacherous Black Knight and slew a dozen of his minions on your way here."

"Oh, that. It was nothing."

"True. It was nothing compared to the danger you face from my stepmother. Her power is enormous and she has spent the last three days doing nothing but preparing horrible ways for you to die."

"Say, you don't mind if we get out of the rain, do

you?" Charming and Wendell slipped past her into the castle.

"No!" said Ann. "I mean, yes, I do mind. You can't come in!" It was too late. The Prince was already striding down the entrance hall, shaking water off his cloak and glancing incuriously at the tapestries that adorned the walls. They were spotted with mildew, for the inside of the Wicked Queen's castle proved, if anything, to be only marginally less damp than the outside. Ann hurried after him.

"Your Highness, I appreciate your efforts to rescue me, but it is of no use. You cannot defeat Queen Ruby's power and if you took me away she would only bring me back. You must leave now and save yourself."

"Nice dress. Make it yourself?"

"Yes." Ann looked down at herself and a tinge of pink appeared in her cheeks. "This isn't really me."

"Of course not. Who is it?"

She tried to explain, awkwardly. "Your Highness, even before my father died, I longed to get away from these mountains and this isolation. I dreamed of the day that some gallant knight errant would carry me off to a distant and more, well, cosmopolitan city. I even made some clothes that I thought would be more, um, *inspiring* to such a knight. But this was a mistake. An error in judgment. Rest assured your Highness, that I am as sweet, pure, chaste and innocent as any princess should be."

"Yeah, great," said the Prince, with a noticeable loss of enthusiasm.

An uneven grinding noise filled the air. Ann swung her head around nervously. "She's pulling up the drawbridge! She has sealed the castle against exit! You are trapped!"

"Guess we'll just have to stay for dinner then."

The grinding noise stopped, then started again.

Then it stopped again. The drawbridge crashed back down. Charming raised his eyebrows.

"It's those round things with the teeth on them . . ." explained Ann.

"Gears."

"Right. I knew that. Some of the teeth are broken. She has tried to repair them but there's only so much she can do with her magic, especially to iron gears."

"Mmm," agreed Charming. "I tend to find that most magic is only good for rather impractical things."

"Like killing people in horrible ways."

The talk of killing was making Wendell a bit uneasy. Lacking the Prince's appreciation of pulchritude, he was concentrating more on his surroundings and he didn't like what he was seeing. The entrance hallway was lit by torches, not the more even light of the lanterns he was used to, and they flickered in the draft and threw dancing shadows on the walls. The ceiling was high enough that its corners remained in darkness. He could have sworn he saw movement there. The portraits on the wall were not exactly uplifting, either. The subjects were grim and slightly pop-eyed, as though staring in horror at some ghastly sight. And faintly, high above, almost at the limits of his hearing, he could hear the sound of heels on stone.

A flash of lightning lit up the windows; thunder crashed outside. Wendell and Ann jumped. Charming glanced at the windows, where the rain was coming down in sheets. On the walls, the torch flames fluttered and threw off oily black smoke. When the thunder faded away, the sound of footsteps could be distinctly heard.

Ann pointed to a staircase. "The south tower. My stepmother descends even now. Oh, Prince Charming! May you die as bravely as you have lived."

"Thanks."

"Uh, Sire? Maybe we just ought to leave a business card and take off?"

"Don't be silly, Wendell. It's raining cats and dogs out there. See if they have a place to stable the horses."

"I'm not deserting you until this is done," said Wendell. He dropped the duffel bag he'd been carrying and started pulling weapons out. The Prince ignored them.

They listened to the ringing of metal heel caps on stone, echoing from the dark stairwell. It grew steadily louder, closer. Ann was twisting her hands together and Wendell was staring into the staircase like a hypnotized rabbit when the sound suddenly stopped. There was a final flash of lightning, a penultimate crash of thunder, and all the torches in the hall went out. At the same moment a figure, bathed in a red glow, appeared on the stairs.

"Nice entrance," murmured Charming.

The late King Humphrey, it seemed, had married young. The Wicked Queen was only twenty-six years old. The red glow came from a fist-sized ruby that she held in, of course, her fist. It cast a sphere of eerie light that accented the blood red of the lips and nails, and reflected from hard, black eyes that glittered like anthracite. Her dark hair, redolent with sickly sweet perfume, gleamed and writhed about her shoulders. She stood at the top of the final flight of stairs, fixed her gaze on the Prince and said, in a voice that dripped with venom. "Prince Charming! So, you dare to take away my stepdaughter?"

All eyes switched to Charming, who was dusting his boots with a handkerchief. He glanced up, as if surprised to see anyone there, and looked the Queen up and down. "Your stepdaughter? Why, I would have sworn you two were sisters."

The thunder died away. There was dead silence in

the room for the space of ten heartbeats. Ann closed her mouth with a snap. Wendell held his breath. Charming continued to favor the Queen with his most dazzling smile.

Then the Wicked Queen raised a hand to her head and patted a stray hair into place. "Oh, do you really think so?"

"Absolutely. I really like your outfit, too. Black leather goes so well with your eyes."

"Why, thank you, Charming." The Queen descended the last few steps and came into the hall. "You don't think the spiked heel boots are a bit too dressy?"

"No, they're perfect."

"Good grief," muttered Ann. Ruby shot her a hostile look.

"Well, I do try to keep myself in shape. Eat a proper diet, you know, and stay out of the sun. Still." The Queen pointed to a large mirror that hung against the wall. She realized it was barely visible in the dim light, so she waved her hand and the torches flared back on. They revealed a huge slab of ancient plate glass, heavily silvered on one side, surrounded by an ornate wooden frame covered with gold leaf. "The magic mirror says that *she* is more beautiful than I." The was no doubting who *she* was. Ann stuck her chin defiantly in the air.

"Oh, I wouldn't trust those magic mirrors," said the Prince. "They always have to be recalibrated. Besides, the light in this hall is so bad."

"Well, that's true. Perhaps it would see things differently in the morning sun. In fact, I've been intending to move it. But it's so heavy."

"It would be an honor to assist you with it." The Prince flexed a bicep.

"Well," the Queen looked at the young man's well-muscled form, particularly noting the tightness of his breeches. "I was thinking, perhaps, it would be much more suitable in the master bedroom."

"I couldn't think of a better place for it," said Charming. He lifted the mirror off the wall and moved forward with it. "Say, Wendell, this might take a few minutes. Don't wait up, okay?"

"I don't believe this," said Ann. The Queen glared at her and then smiled sweetly.

"Ann, my dear, why don't you get that nice young page a glass of milk and some cookies? And then you can amuse yourself until bedtime."

"Why don't you jump . . ."

"She's such a darling child," the Queen told Charming, linking her arm in his as she led him away. "You don't think this red nail polish makes me look cheap, do you?"

"On the contrary, I think it's very classy," lied the Prince. "It really suits your—ah—theatrical style." The rest of his patter was lost as the couple negotiated a turn in the hallway and their voices were swallowed by the thick stone.

Ann stared after them in astonishment. Then she looked at Wendell. Wendell shrugged. "They don't call him Prince Charming for nothing."

Although the castle of the Wicked Queen had huge, echoing hallways, the rooms were rather small. This was made up for by the fact that there were a lot of them. The Queen's bedroom was, in fact, a small suite with a sitting room in front and two dressing rooms flanking the actual bedroom, which was completely filled by a four-poster bed. "Here you go," said Charming. "We can just set this up in front of the bed here."

The Queen gave him a look of cool amusement but led him back out to the sitting room. "Silly boy. No woman wants to lay in bed staring at her own hips. I think it will do just fine out here. Why don't you set it up while I slip into something comfortable?"

"Um," said the Prince. "Okay, I guess."

The Wicked Queen patted him on the rump. "Don't worry, the high heels stay on."

"Righto," said Charming with more enthusiasm. As soon as she vanished into her dressing room, he laid the mirror down on the carpet and flipped it over. On the rear side, concealed among the intricate carvings of the frame, were four tiny set screws marked "BRIT," "CON," "VERT," and "HOR." Charming examined them carefully, then made some small adjustments with the blade of his knife. He took down a painting and hung the mirror in its place. After adjusting it to hang straight, he stood back and surveyed his handiwork. The mirror, although slightly dusty and showing a few finger smears, nonetheless presented him with a perfectly adequate reflection. The Prince waved a hand dramatically.

"Mirror, mirror, on the wall," he said. "Who's the fairest of them all?"

The image on the mirror shimmered and grew cloudy. Light and dark billows swirled across the glass, as in the bottom of a muddy well. Abruptly the turbulence ceased and faded away to reveal the sparkling image of—Prince Charming. The Prince smiled broadly. "Thought so."

"Is the mirror working, darling?" called the Queen.

"Works perfectly," said Charming.

"Then do come in."

Charming pushed the door open and let himself into the bedroom with all the coolness he could muster. But his suave facade abruptly disintegrated when he saw the Queen. She was wearing a push-up bra, the kind that only covered the bottom of her breasts, leaving the erect nipples straining outward. A dozen candles bathed her skin with a warm, gentle glow. Her taut thighs were encased in fine black mesh stockings, held up with a garter belt, and, true to her word, she had kept the spiked heels, giving her legs the illusion of incredible length and slimness. She presented a vision like nothing the Prince had ever seen—indeed, there were few men in Illyria who could claim such a sight—an erotic figure so compelling that only Charming's long experience with stressful situations and his carefully honed ability to manifest grace under pressure, kept his hormone-pumped teen-age instincts from overriding his brain.

"Nice stockings," he told her.

It was a stupid thing to say, even to Charming's ears, but considering he was on the verge of swallowing his tongue, it wasn't that bad a line.

"Thank you," said Queen Ruby.

There was a longer pause. Ruby shifted her hips, causing a dozen gentle curves to ripple like water on a calm sea. A thin sheen of sweat broke out on Charming's forehead.

"Well?"

"Hmmm?"

"Aren't you coming to bed?"

"Bed?" said the Prince. "Bed. Oh, yes. What a great idea. This one here looks good."

The bed did indeed look good; it looked even better when the Queen stretched out on it, turning away from Charming and then looking back over her shoulder in an attempt to be coy. It was a futile attempt since the Wicked Queen's normal expression of predatory intelligence would have shown through a mud mask, but it was good enough for Charming. He wasn't looking at her face anyway. He fumbled with the buttons on his shirt with sweating hands, and eventually ripped it off and tossed it in a corner. He followed this with his boots, hopping around on one foot in a positively antic way while he tore the opposite one free.

"Are you nervous, darling?"

"Who me? Of course not."

"Your hands are shaking."

"Well, it's drafty in here. I feel a slight chill." The Prince was fumbling furiously with a recalcitrant belt buckle.

"But you are sweating, also."

"Must be those peppers I had at lunch." Charming finally got his pants off, leaving only his underwear, and hopped into bed alongside the Queen. She turned to meet him, opening up her arms and he seized a breast in each hand and locked his lips to hers in a lubricious kiss that lasted a full two minutes before he had to come up for air. The Queen, panting, said, "Take it slowly, darling. I'm not going anywhere. You don't have to act as though this was your first time."

"Who's acting?" said the Prince, just before taking one nipple into his mouth.

The next moment he was lying on his back on the floor. "Ow!"

He sat up on the rug, where the Queen had flung him with the force of both arms and legs, and gingerly rubbed a tender spot on the back of his head. He looked up to see the Wicked Queen towering over him, and when she wanted to tower, she could really tower. She pointed a long red fingernail at him. "Say that again."

"Um . . ." It took the Prince a minute to clear his head. "Who's acting?"

The Queen's eyes narrowed and glittered. "You are pure?"

"Pure? Well, I'd hardly say that. I've had a lot of impure thoughts. About a minute ago I was having them in bucketfuls. In fact . . ."

"Are you a virgin?"

"Yeah, I'm a virgin, okay?" the Prince shouted back.

"Tell the world, will you! Does that bother you? You want a certificate of prowess or something?"

The Queen sat down on the edge of the bed and crossed one knee over the other. Her face was a study in concentrated thought, and when she looked at the Prince, it was with the speculative air that one uses when choosing a calf for slaughter. Charming had only to look at her face to reach three conclusions:

(1) She was up to something.

(2) It was not something fun.

(3) Once again, he was not going to get laid.

These thoughts, particularly thought number three, did not make him happy. "I knew it," he muttered. "I should have gone after the stepdaughter."

"Get dressed," said the Wicked Queen. She tossed him his pants. "I've got a proposition for you."

To put it in the most understated terms, Princess Ann was miffed. As a young girl, she had long and vivid daydreams about being rescued by a handsome prince from some terrible danger, like being eaten by a dragon. When she got a little bit older, she had decided that the danger part was probably not necessary, and messy besides, and that being carried off by a handsome prince was more than adequate. A few years later she decided that she didn't really care about being carried off, either. Should a suitably romantic rendezvous be arranged with a handsome prince, she would be more than happy to meet him halfway or even all the way. Alas, the severe dearth of handsome princes passing through Tyrovia forestalled her putting any of these plans into action.

Now the most famous, most regal, most handsome prince of all was within the very castle and what was she doing about it? Well, right now she was cooking oatmeal for breakfast. "Great," she thought. "Oatmeal. He's probably used to pheasant under glass."

"Does his Highness like oatmeal?" she asked Wendell.

"He doesn't care. He's not really into food."

"Do you like oatmeal?"

"No. Do you?"

"No."

"Does your mother like oatmeal?"

"She's my stepmother. No, she doesn't."

"Then why are you making oatmeal?"

"We don't have pheasant."

"Ah."

Ann had not spent a restful night. The sight of her stepmother leading the Prince to her boudoir, after having spent the last week railing against him and plotting his demise, had quite astonished her. It had also left her with a feeling of profound rejection that was not relieved one whit by the crying of hot tears onto the shoulder of her favorite stuffed animal. Then, just at the time that she imagined the two of them involved in the most sordid undertakings, there arose a furious altercation. The stone walls of the castle effectively muffled the sound so that it was impossible to discern the actual words, but there was no mistaking the heat in the young Prince's voice, or the cold calculation in her stepmother's reply. Then came the sound of steps on the stair. When she arose this morning she found the Prince sleeping on a couch in front of the fireplace. For some reason she felt immediately cheered.

He was still sleeping when she went back. Asleep, he looked very boyish, but there was a hint of cragginess to his features that spoke of impending maturity. "He will age well," she thought. "When he loses his prettiness, he'll look distinguished." She touched him on the shoulder.

"He came to carry me off on his white steed. He'd take me back to his castle in Illyria, there to live in splendor as his bride and, later, his Queen." Ann let the daydream linger only a moment longer. She knew she wasn't going to leave Tyrovia. The peasants had been loyal to the old King. When he died, Ann knew it was her responsibility to repay that loyalty. To leave now would be to abandon them to the rule of a mad sorceress.

Charming stirred and rubbed a hand across his eyes. He focused them on her. "Hmmmm?"

"You didn't have to sleep down here," said Ann. "We have plenty of empty rooms. I would have fixed one for you."

"I thought you were asleep. I didn't want to trouble you."

"It would have been no trouble."

"Well." The Prince sat up on the couch and reached for his boots. Ann sat down beside him and demurely crossed her hands in her lap. Charming watched her from the side of his eyes. She was, he decided, quite cute. In fact, she was really beautiful, particularly if you went for that pure and innocent look. Charming didn't. He rather preferred the down and dirty sort, but what the heck. If pure and innocent was the hand you were dealt, pure and innocent was the hand you played.

Aloud he said, "Is your stepmother up yet?"

"She's my stepmother. I mean, yes, she's up. She didn't go back to bed. After you came downstairs, she went to her laboratory."

"Ah." The Prince did not like the sound of this. "Any idea what she was doing there?"

"Well, I'd say she was either laying more curses and spells on you, or she was lifting the spells she already laid."

"Hmmm." Charming considered this. "If I'm lucky, it's the former. Okay, Ann, what's the story? I was sent to check out the situation because I heard you were in trouble. I came, I saw, I slept on the couch, now I'm leaving. You seem to be doing okay. The

Queen seems kind of bitchy, but frankly, I really don't see any problem here that couldn't be solved by a cold bath."

"What do cold baths have to do with anything?"

"I'll tell you later."

"Excuse me, I think the oatmeal is done."

The Prince followed her toward the kitchen, but peeled off when he saw Wendell. He took the page aside. "Hi, Wendell. Seen the Black Widow around?"

"Yeah, she's in the library. She's been there all morning. And wow, you should see the library she's got. Packed to the max with books and scrolls and old, old maps. Mandelbaum would flip over this place."

"At least I know what they've been spending their money on. It sure hasn't been maintenance." The Prince and Wendell looked around. In the daylight, the castle looked even drabber and more depressing than it had looked the night before. Paint was peeling from the door frames and there were cracks in the ceiling. The tapestries were moth-eaten and full of holes. Stuffing leaked from the sofa. Broken windows were patched with oiled paper. In spite of the air of impoverishment, the furniture was free of dust and the floor was swept clean. Ann's doing, Charming guessed.

"What sort of books does she have?"

"Magic books. All sorts of magic books. Here, I grabbed one." Wendell showed him a well-thumbed volume, which the Prince recognized.

"*Modern Organic Alchemy,* by Morrison and Boyd. I've seen this in Mandelbaum's lab." He leafed through it. "This woman has really studied it."

"How can you tell?"

"All the important formulas are highlighted with yellow ink." He snapped the book shut and set it casually aside as the Wicked Queen entered. Although the rain had disappeared, to reveal a morning that was merely overcast, Queen Ruby's presence was enough to create a mood of dramatic tension. She was not wearing the vicious leather outfit of the night before, but her appearance in a tight black sweater, with scarlet lips and nails, was only a little less striking. "To breakfast, boys," she said briskly. "We've got business to discuss."

Wendell followed Charming to the dining room. "What business?"

"A quest. She wants me to go on a quest."

"Did you tell her you don't do quests?"

"I told her. She thinks I'll change my mind."

"Oh, come on." Wendell seated himself before a bowl of oatmeal. "You're Prince Charming, heir to the wealthiest and most powerful throne in the twenty kingdoms. What could she possibly have to offer you?" He noticed the Prince flick his gaze to the Queen's sweater-clad bosom and sighed. "Never mind. Forget I asked."

"Specifically," said the Prince, "a grail quest."

"Oh, not again. Every knight who ever lived has searched for the Holy Grail."

"We are not looking for the Holy Grail," said the Queen. "That is but a fantasy."

"There's another one?" asked Ann.

"Dozens of 'em," said Charming. "The ancient fertility cults were very big on grails. Every two-bit druid who ever put up a couple of standing stones had to have a magic grail. There's grail legends all over the place and knights have been tracking them down since time immemorial. None of them came up with spit."

Said Ruby, "It is the very ubiquitousness of those legends that convinces me they have a common basis in fact. I have researched this subject thoroughly, examining the common threads among them, till at last I, and I alone, have deduced the location of the Fisher King's castle."

"Ubiquitousness?" said Wendell.

"Who is the Fisher King?" said Ann.

"The mythical Fisher King had the grail, which made his land fertile and his people prosperous," explained Charming. "The grail is hidden in a chapel. According to the legend, the Fisher King gets mortally wounded and land becomes barren as a result. The knight who survives the dangers of the Chapel Perilous gets the grail and becomes the new Fisher King."

"Well," said Ann doubtfully. "I suppose it's better than looking for a magic sword."

"It's not much of a legend, but at least it's to the point."

"It's an excellent legend," said the Wicked Queen, eyes gleaming. "The full text contains all the clues needed to locate the Grail Castle."

"Yeah, sure. And no one has ever figured them out except you, right?"

"Many have figured out the location of the Grail Castle. Of that I am certain. And yet none have recovered the Grail. Of that I am certain also. For the ancient texts make it quite clear. Only one who is pure can hope to survive the Chapel Perilous."

"Pure?" asked Ann.

"Chaste. Virtuous."

"This doesn't sound like anyone I know," said Wendell.

"Must I spell everything out for you?" the Queen demanded of Ann. "Only a virgin can brave the Chapel Perilous."

"All right," said Charming. "You don't have to make a big deal about it."

"You've never . . . um?" Ann stopped and blushed.

"I've been saving myself for the right girl."

Wendell made a choking noise, but Ann looked at the Prince with new respect.

"Well, I think that's very nice. I don't know why you think it's something to be embarrassed about."

"That's because you're a girl. You'd think differently if you were a boy."

"If we could return to the subject at hand," said the Queen.

"Look," said the Prince. "I told you last night. I don't do quests. Slay and Rescue, that's my line. Quests are not in my job description. Find someone else. In fact, I can refer you to some knights who do good quests. Grails, the True Cross, magic swords, enchanted rings, hidden treasure, philosopher's stone, fountains of youth, a breakfast cereal that tastes good and yet is good for you, if it's out there, they'll look for it. I'll bet there's a couple of virgins among them, too. There's an epidemic of it in the twenty kingdoms. Besides, some of them are pretty ugly."

"You are the best for the job," said the Queen. "You are young, strong and incredibly brave. Your swordsmanship is without parity. You are too rich and high born to be easily bought off. You are respected throughout the twenty kingdoms and can easily raise reinforcements, if they should be needed. And finally, you are, of course, *Prince Charming*. You may even be able to talk your way to the grail."

"You flatter me. But flattery is not enough to persuade me to undertake this silly and futile quest."

"You will do it," said the Queen, "because you are Prince Charming. You have seen this land. The forests are dying and the game is disappearing. The rain is washing the topsoil away. The corn grows shorter each year and the cows are barren. The lambs are sickly. The orchards are bare. These people need a fertility grail. They need you to bring it to them. You will not ignore their plight."

"It is pretty bad," admitted Wendell.

Charming looked at the ceiling, then at the floor, then at the walls. "They're not my people," he said guiltily. "I've got my own kingdom."

"If this land is dying," said Ann to the Queen, "it's because of you and your sorcery. You are constantly spraying noxious potions into the air and into the water, for one thing. And for another, the evil influence of your sorcery spreads from this castle like a poisonous cloud."

"Shut up," snapped the Queen. "You are not qualified to make judgments on the complex art of sorcery. The spells I cast upon this land were for the good of its people. My intent is to raise them from their squalor and poverty and make this into a great and powerful country."

"Under Daddy's rule the people led simple, pastoral lives. There was no squalor and poverty until you took over."

Said Wendell, "Do you have any brown sugar to go with this oatmeal?"

"No!"

"All right," said Charming. "Here's the deal. I'll check it out, okay? I'm not making any promises. I'm not saying I'll get the grail. But I'll take a look around."

"Very well," said the Queen. "I'm sure we can reach an agreement after you have assessed the situation."

"You don't have to do this," said Ann.

"Be quiet!"

"One question," said Charming. "If this grail thing is so valuable, what makes you so darn sure I'll bring it back to you?"

"The integrity of Prince Charming is known throughout the twenty kingdoms."

"Good point."

"Furthermore," said the Queen, "Ann is going with you."

"Hey, I'll tell you what," said Charming, as he saddled up a horse for her. "We'll take a little side trip to the marketplace at Alacia. You can go shopping. It's right near the wharf and they have a lot of imported perfumes and spices and silks and other girl stuff."

"Don't patronize me."

"Well, you don't have to look so dour about this. You don't really believe this grail thing, do you?"

"Don't you?"

"No. I think your stepmother is a nut."

"She's very wicked. But she's not stupid. I think she wants to get me out of the country while she cooks up some other scheme."

"Hmmm. Why wouldn't she just banish you?"

"The peasants would not stand for it. They've tolerated a lot, but they are still loyal to my father's memory and will only stand so much."

"On the other hand," Ann continued, "she would not have nearly as much trouble if I were away on a quest and were to meet with some sort of accident. . . ."

"Hey," cut in Charming. "Don't worry about that. Anyone comes near you, I'll slice him to ribbons."

"Yeah," chimed in Wendell.

"Thank you," said Ann. "I appreciate that."

These noble sentiments were interrupted by a small crowd of peasants who approached the courtyard. "Excuse me," said Ann. "I must talk to them." The Prince followed within earshot.

As he drew closer he saw that the peasants comprised one of the most sickly and depressing groups he had ever seen. Charming had traveled all over the twenty kindoms in his search for wrongs to right, but most of his travels had been in the fertile lowlands and prosperous trading port kingdoms. He was used to fields fat with grain, contented cattle, heavily laden orchards. He had dealt with jovial farmers and happy, well-fed children. He saw none of that here.

The crowd was dressed in rags. Some had rags

wrapped around their feet, most were barefoot. Their haggard faces were streaked with mud and their backs were stooped from long hours in the fields. Their farm implements were worn and rusted. Several of the women carried small children, and in their large eyes the Prince saw a despair that chilled him to his very bones.

The crowd stopped. The eldest of them limped forward. Ann stepped forward, also. "Yes, Cumbert?"

"Little Princess," said Cumbert. "It is rumored that you are leaving us."

"I shall be gone only for a little while, Cumbert."

"Do not leave us, Little Princess. Without you to intercede, we will be at the mercy of . . ." The man stopped. He looked past Ann and his eyes grew round in his head. "It's *Prince Charming*!"

Charming smiled and shrugged. A murmur of awe went up from the crowd. Ann smiled also. "Yes, Cumbert. It is he."

Cumbert's next words held pure panic. "It's Prince Charming come to marry our Princess. He'll carry her off to Illyria and we'll never see her again!"

A great wail rose from the crowd. The men and women hesitantly shuffled around for a minute and then, motivated by the same instinct, moved forward to form a protective circle around Ann, defiantly separating her from the Prince.

"Oh, for goodness sake," said Charming. "I've heard of chaperones, but this is absurd."

"Your Highness, why don't you speak with my stepmother while I talk to these people?"

"Good idea," said Charming. He retreated across the drawbridge while Ann engaged the peasants in agitated conversation. "Terrific. If I try any moves on this babe, I'll have a lynch mob waiting when I get back." Inside the castle Ruby was putting the final touches on a hand-drawn map.

"Here," she said. "At the edge of the Black Oak Forest, in the foothills of the Craggy Mountains. Travel south from Sojourner's Hamlet and hang a left at the waterfall. You can't miss it."

"Uh huh." Charming looked over her shoulder. The map showed an X inside a circle. There were some tiny notes, written in a crabbed hand, next to the X. "What do the notes mean?"

"Oh," said the Queen airily. "That just mentions the thorns."

"What thorns?"

"There may be some thorn bushes growing around the castle."

"Well, I can handle a thorn hedge. What's that other word there? Starts with a D."

"Oh, nothing."

"D," said the Prince. "Now what starts with D? Hmmmm. D, D, D. Let me think. Why, golly, dragon starts with a D!"

"Well, yes. There may be a dragon there."

"Maybe, huh? You can't use your magic mirror and take a look?"

"Unfortunately, no. It only has a range of fifteen miles. King Humphrey wanted to put an antenna up on the tower and pull in the jousting matches, but the tournament directors got their own magicians to scramble the signals." The Queen rolled up the map and slapped it in Charming's hand. "Oh, come on. A big strong man like you isn't afraid of an itsy, bitsy, little dragon, is he?"

"A big strong man like me isn't afraid of ridicule, either. Especially from itsy, bitsy, bubble brains who have never gone up against an attacking dragon. If one of them is there, you're going to have to give me a big, strong incentive to take it on."

Ruby took Charming's hand and placed it against her left breast. "Have you ever had a woman drip warm honey all over your body and then slowly lick it all off with her tongue?"

"Oh, hell," said the Prince. "What's one dragon more or less?"

"Exactly. Now then, are you three ready to go?"

"As soon as Ann is finished talking with her fan club."

The Wicked Queen glowered. "That little bitch. It's disgusting the way they adore her. I'm the Queen. They owe allegiance to me. They should be willing to grovel at my feet. And they will. When I have the grail I'll crush . . ." She saw Charming staring at her. "Ha ha, just kidding. When I have the grail, I'll bring peace and prosperity and subsidized dental care, and all that good stuff to the kingdom."

"You're at peace now."

"Right. And we'll stay that way. Certainly."

"Yeah, well, I can see this country is in good hands, so we'll just be off then."

Ruby followed him out to the courtyard and watched the trio mount up. "Farewell, young prince. May good fortune follow you in all your endeavors. Goodbye, Wendell." To Ann she said nothing, nor did Ann acknowledge her.

Outside the gate the townspeople stood aside to let them pass. Some had tears in their eyes. "Goodbye, Little Princess."

"Goodbye, good people. Goodbye, Cumbert. I'll be back, I promise."

"Sheeesh," said Wendell. "Let's get out of here."

They rode southward out of the mountains. It was a relief to Wendell to get away from the sterile crags and deserted forests of Tyrovia, and down into the lush valleys of Alacia where spring was whipping along at an open rein. Newborn lambs cavorted in the fields, colts and fillies pranced on wobbly legs, and fingerling trout danced just below the surface of the streams. The horses were in fine humor and soon fell into an easy step along the moist, loamy earth. The weather graced them with sunny skies and warm breezes. It was, all in all, an ideal time to travel and Ann couldn't help voicing her opinion that they could have been making better time than they were.

The Prince ignored her. "Quests are supposed to be long and filled with travails," he explained. "You can't just nip out and back, like you were running out to the fish market to pick up a bass, and expect your people to be impressed. If you come back with this grail thing too soon, you'll just cheapen it for them."

Ann thought this theory was, to put it mildly, stupid. But she didn't want to be objectionable this early in the trip. She had plans of her own to put into effect. She hadn't quite formulated these plans yet, but she knew she had them. So after the first few objections, she held her tongue while the Prince and Wendell took a few hours off each day to explore a side trail, do a little hunting or fishing, swim, climb trees or just nap. "Rome wasn't built in a day," Charming would explain laconically, bunching his jacket under his head for a pillow. Wendell, knotting a fishhook onto a piece of thread, would nod. Ann bit back her impatience.

Another thing bothered her. When he was away from the towns and villages and not likely to run into anyone influential, Charming would pack away his silk shirts and royal blue cloaks, and dress in plain gray homespun. There was nothing really wrong with him wanting to dress in comfortable clothes, Ann knew. Riding could be hot and dirty work and she, after all, had mere housemaid's clothing. Still, it just made him seem so much less, well, *princely*.

"Are you sure this is the right way?" she asked. "You haven't looked at the map since we set out."

"All roads lead to Rome," replied Wendell with a

scholarly air. He baited his hook with a minnow and dropped it in the stream.

"What does that mean?"

"I don't know. It's just a saying I heard. But this road goes to Briar Rose Village which is right near the spot your stepmother marked on her map. It's a good-sized village."

"But if there is a village nearby, surely someone would have found the grail chapel by now."

"So? Maybe the map's wrong."

Ann gave up on the subject. "When in Rome, do as the Romans do," she reasoned and tried to force herself to match the Prince's easy rhythm of life. She stretched out next to him under an apple tree, letting the warm sunlight caress her face, and fell into a prolonged daydream. Fluffy white clouds passed overhead and she incorporated them into tales of virtuous, beleaguered maidens, brave and noble knights in shining armor, gleaming castles, and elaborate weddings with multitiered wedding cakes, dozens of bridesmaids, and a full orchestra for the reception.

"You've rescued lots of maidens, haven't you?" she said to Charming, who was peeling an apple with his dagger.

Charming shrugged. "Somebody's got to."

"Don't you like doing it?"

"Oh, sure. I mean, it beats working for a living."

"You're so brave. Even the dragons must shake with fear when they see you coming."

"Huh?" said Charming. He bit into the apple. "Dragons fear nothing."

"I hate dragons," said Wendell.

The Prince nodded. "Nasty, vicious creatures. Tough, too. With that scaly armor all over, they're virtually indestructible."

"And they're fast," said Wendell. "Over rocky ground they can outrun a horse."

"They can get up on their hind legs and run like blazes. That's not the big ones, of course. Once they get bigger than about, oh, fifteen feet they stay down on all fours. Still, fifteen feet of dragon towering over you, claws extended, smoke and flame spewing from his nostrils, is plenty enough dragon for me."

"Then how do you slay them?"

"Charge straight at them. A fast, brave horse and a sharp lance. When he opens his jaws to roast you, put the lance through the roof of his mouth and into his brain."

"But that means you charge right into the flames!"

"Well, if it were easy, everyone would be doing it."

"Good Lord!"

"The beauty of this method is, if he opens his mouth, he's vulnerable. If he doesn't open his mouth, you have no problem. Except for the claws, of course. But basically, all it takes is a steady nerve. And a good horse and lance, as I said. And you have to get him on a flat, open stretch of ground where your horse can get up some speed. It's not really that big a deal."

"What if you're attacked and you're not on a horse and you don't have a lance and you're not on open ground?"

"Then it's a big deal."

"Then you have to go for the eyes," said Wendell. He paced the ground excitedly, making stabbing motions with his fist. "Pierce the eye socket with your sword. Zounds! Right through the eye and into the brain. Skissshhh!"

"Ah," said Ann, amused. "You've killed a dragon, I see."

"No," said Wendell. "I *could*, though. I know I could. But his Highness thinks I'm too little."

"I didn't say that. I said you weren't ready yet."

"You go at him from the side, see, 'cause the dragon's eyes are on the side just like a horse's. That way you can keep out of the flames. You have to keep moving fast, though, to stay to the side of his mouth." Wendell danced a half circle around the base of the tree, jabbing and thrusting at an imaginary adversary. "Yah! Tchah! I drive in my mighty sword Challenger to the hilt. Take that! Gotcha!" He stood back, hand triumphantly on hips, and watched the invisible foe collapse thunderously to the ground.

"So perish all our enemies," quoth the Prince solemnly. Ann's eyes were laughing.

"Then," continued Wendell, with an air of noblesse oblige, "I offer my arm to the beautiful princess that I've just rescued. She takes it and I swing her on to the back of my horse . . ."

"You don't have a horse, remember?"

"I leap on to the back of her horse," said Wendell, not missing a beat, "and then sweep her up and take her back to her kingdom, where she is so grateful that she . . ." He paused.

"Yes?" said the Prince.

"Yes?" said Ann.

"She throws an enormous banquet in my honor. And the food is all dessert. Cakes and pies and whipped cream and ices and puddings and candy. So there."

Charming and Ann applauded. "A noble spectacle, good sir."

"It does seem as though dragons are always carrying off maidens young and fair," said Ann. "I will have to be careful."

"Everybody carries off young maidens around here," said the Prince. "And then the call goes out for— um—some dumb sap to risk his life rescuing them. Why a dragon should prefer to eat young girls instead of a goat or a cow is beyond me. Or why they carry them back to their lairs instead of devouring them on the spot."

"Oh, but it's so romantic. A beautiful girl in the delicate flower of youth snatched away from the arms of her loving family by a hideous, snarling monster, a monster no doubt drawn to her by her aura of innocence, as a moth to a flame. Then . . ."

"Also dogs," interrupted Wendell.

"Dogs?"

"Dragons love dogs," explained Charming. "Beautiful maidens and dogs, that's their two favorite meals."

"Dogs," repeated Ann, with diminished interest.

"We used to have a dog that hunted with us," said Wendell. "But a dragon got him."

"Scooped him up with his tail and popped him right into his mouth," said Charming. "Two bites and he was gone. He was a good hunting dog, too. That's another thing you have to watch out for when fighting dragons—the tail. Knock you right on your ass, um, bottom."

"Girls and dogs, just great," said Ann. "Centuries of romantic epics told, hundreds of beautiful ballads sung, scores of tapestries woven, dozen of murals painted, all inspired only by the fact that there weren't any dogs around that day."

"Oh, I'd hardly say that. Dogs are a lot harder to catch than girls."

"You are a jerk," said Ann, and stomped off to tend to her horse.

"What's her problem?" said the Prince. Wendell could give no reply.

But Ann's sour mood was no match for the delightful spring day and the spirits of the whole party were in full fine fettle as they approached their destination. They passed through the thriving village of Briar Rose without stopping, as the Prince did not want to be delayed by admiring throngs, and entered a dense wood about a dozen miles beyond. Although they had to dismount and walk their horses, the woods were not particularly hard going, and enough of the sun showed through the trees to keep an accurate idea of direction without resorting to compass. Charming removed Ruby's map from his saddlebags and the three travelers consulted it. "Any time now, according to this, we should start running into some thorn bushes," said Ann.

"Mmm," said Wendell. He pointed to the ground where a stand of mushrooms grew in a perfect circle. "This is a fairy wood."

Charming was examining the trunks of the trees. He scraped some of the moss with his fingernail. "This *was* a fairy wood. I think most of the magic has gone out of it. It happens sometimes." He shrugged and they pressed on. A few hundred yards later, they found thorn bushes.

"Oh my," said Ann.

It was not a descriptive comment, nor a particularly helpful one, but it did seem to sum up the situation as well as anything else that could have been said. What they found was a solid, impenetrable wall of thorns some thirty feet high. There was no way to judge how thick it was, but it stretched out of sight in both directions, with a slight curve that indicated it would completely circle the castle within, if indeed there was a castle within. The thorn bushes were unlike any Ann had ever seen, for they followed no one style or species. Some were long, gleaming stilettos, iron-hard spikes that could pierce all the way to a man's heart. Others were the softer hair-type thorns, thin almost-invisible pins that stuck to your clothes, penetrated your fingers when you tried to brush them off, and were nearly impossible to pluck out because they were so hard to see and even harder to get a grip on. In between lay thorns of between one and three inches long, and plenty of them. They grew of oily dark wood, were needle sharp, and seemed to shine with an evil gleam. The bushes themselves were of the flexible cane type, almost a vine, the kind of branch that could wrap around and cling should you have the misfortune to fall into it. All in all, it was a most disturbing sight.

"A few thorn bushes," said Wendell. "I think the Wicked Queen was slightly misinformed."

"That's my stepmother. A mind like a steel trap rusted shut."

"Hmmm," said the Prince.

"Hmmmm what?"

"This is not a natural formation. Someone went through a lot of trouble to grow this hedge. That's pretty tough magic."

"Is that what drained the magic out of the rest of the wood?"

"Maybe. I don't know. But whatever is behind it must be pretty worthwhile. Now what's the best way to get in?"

"I know," said Wendell. "A bag of smoke."

"Say what?"

"Mandelbaum told me how to do this. Do you ever watch the smoke from a fire?"

"Sure."

"And it always goes up, right?"

"Get to the point, Wendell."

"Okay, okay. Mandelbaum's idea is to get a huge silk bag and let it fill up with smoke. If the bag is big enough, the smoke will lift up the bag and also a passenger hanging beneath it. You can fly right over anything. We start upwind and then, when we cross the thorn barrier, we let out some smoke and gently descend."

Wendell waited expectantly. Charming and Ann stared at him. Finally Charming said, "Mandelbaum thought of this?"

"Doesn't it sound great?"

"Good old Mandelbaum. Wendell, that is the craziest idea I've ever heard. I can't believe you took this seriously."

"Who is Mandelbaum?" asked Ann.

"Dad's royal magician. The best wizard in Illyria, which means the best wizard anywhere. When I was a kid he was constantly coming out with new spells and enchantments. He wrote a whole bunch of papers on integrated magical systems."

"What happened to him?"

"Same thing that happens to all court magicians. Once he got tenure he kind of slacked off. Anyway, thanks for the suggestion, Wendell, but this looks like a problem that can best be solved by the classical methods of brute force and ignorance."

The Prince pulled Endeavor from its scabbard and ran his thumb once along the blade. He paced back and forth along the wall of thorns, choosing a likely-looking spot for his assault. Eventually he concluded that one spot looked no better than another and simply whipped the sword forward and down in a rapid slicing motion. Thorny branches parted neatly beneath the flashing blade and fell to the ground. A few more chops and he had cleared a man-sized opening in the hedge. He stepped back and looked at it.

"Well, this isn't so bad. We still have a few hours of sunlight left. I'll see how far I can go."

"Would you like some help?" asked Ann.

"No, I can handle this. You just relax. Wendell, why don't you unsaddle the horses? This is going to take a while."

Ann settled herself back against the trunk of a tree while Charming hacked and slashed some more, creating a tunnel into the thorns. Wendell hobbled the horses and set them loose to graze, after rubbing their noses. It was very quiet, the only sound was the quiet buzzing of a stray bee, the occasional snatch of bird song, and the swish and chop of Charming's sword. Ann watched as he worked himself deeper and deeper into the hedge. She could see his arms working as he switched the sword from hand to hand, sweat beginning to trickle down his back. As the tunnel grew deeper, he worked himself into shadow until she could only discern a dim movement. It was strange, she thought, how the shadows made him seem bigger. Suddenly she realized that he didn't look bigger at all. It was the tunnel that was shrinking.

"Prince Charming!" she screamed. "The entrance is closing!"

It took Charming a few seconds to understand her meaning. He was ten feet into the hedge when he turned around and found himself in a barbed wooden cage. Fresh branches were sprouting from the tunnel floor, new thorns were growing from the cut walls. He started for the opening and a branch snagged his foot, the needle sharp thorns piercing right through his high boots. "Damn it." He slashed his foot free and stumbled forward. Another branch dropped from above and wrapped itself around his sword arm. Cursing, he drew his dagger and sliced through the tendril, leaving a bracelet of thorns around his forearm that burned like fire.

Wendell reacted instantly to Ann's cries. He was combing the horses when he turned and saw Ann beating at the thorn hedge with a tree branch, saw the Prince hacking his way through the vicious brush. "Sire!" He dropped the comb and ran for the baggage, instantly removed a brace of spare swords, and raced furiously for the hedge. "I'll help you!"

"No!" yelled Charming, sword and knife flashing like an eagle's talons. He was still a half dozen feet from the entrance, with a score of thorny tendrils wrapped around his arms and legs. Wendell paid no heed. Swords swinging left and right, he chopped through the closed entrance.

"Get back, Wendell!" But Charming spoke too late. A tangle of fresh branches sprouted beneath the page's feet and instantly wrapped around his legs and waist.

"Aaah!" Wendell screamed as the needles drove into his skin. He looked down, but only for a second. More branches were coming at him from the sides and overhead. He kept both swords moving, lopping off the branches as they came near him, but had no time to deal with the branches from below. Rapidly the tendrils climbed up his chest, across his shoulders, pulling down his arms. In only a few more moments, the boy knew, he would be immobilized.

Charming was still fighting his own battle. His skin was crisscrossed with a myriad of deep scratches and his clothes were torn and spattered with blood. Ribbons of thorn branches, resisting every movement, wrapped both legs and arms. Beyond his struggling page the Prince saw the gap to safety narrowing. The entire hedge was shifting to close off the entrance.

With a final mighty effort, Charming drove his arms forward, tearing loose the branches that held them, driving the thorns deep into his flesh. Diving to the ground at Wendell's feet, he used the dagger to cut the stems that held the boy to the ground. "Drop your swords, Wendell!" When the page stopped struggling he lifted the boy up and, drawing on his last reserves of strength, hurled him through the small opening to freedom. Wendell hit the ground in a mass of twisted thorns and, with a great crashing of underbrush, the hedge closed in on Prince Charming.

As soon as Wendell cleared the hedge, Ann ran to him and helped him tear the thorns off. Her own hands quickly became scratched and bloody, but she paid no mind to them, ignoring the minor wounds in the crisis of the moment as Wendell ignored his. When the last twig had been cleared away, they both cautiously approached the hedge.

"Sire?" called Wendell hesitantly.

"Prince Charming?" said Ann.

"Your Highness?"

"Yo," came the whispered reply.

Ann and Wendell peered into the thicket. Charming was only a foot into the thick brush, but was nearly impossible to see because of the thorns wrapped around him. His arms, his legs, his entire torso, were tightly wound with branches and his head seemed to be encased in a woven, wicker mask through which his blue eyes could still be seen searching alertly forward. His hands still gripped sword and dagger, but the blades, too, were wrapped with thorny tendrils. Blood slowly ran down his arms and dripped to the ground.

"I can't move," whispered Charming. "There are thorns right up against my throat."

As soon as this was over, Ann promised herself, she was going to have a good cry. Half a dozen long, black thorns were jabbed tightly against Charming's jugular, as though directed there by a malevolent force, the thin points pricking the flesh and drawing bright drops of red liquid. The Prince was breathing in slow, shallow draughts, his chest constricted by the vines and more needles. "Wendell," he whispered.

"Yes, Sire?" Wendell whispered back.

"You don't have to whisper. I'm only doing this so the thorns don't tear up my face."

"Oh, right," said Wendell in a normal voice.

"Don't get too close. Try cutting a branch and see if they are still growing."

"Right." Wendell got another blade from the packs. Gingerly he approached the hedge, with Ann taking a firm grip on his tunic to yank him away if the thorns should make a grab for him. The hedge remained motionless. He chose a hefty-looking branch at eye level, where Charming could see it, and took a swipe at it. The sword sliced neatly through the wood and the branch broke free. Almost immediately, the severed end sprouted, and within seconds the barbed vegetation had replaced itself. "Darn. We'll have to do some fast cutting."

"This is hopeless," said Ann. "We must ride back to the village and get help. We'll pour salt water on the ground and poison the plants. That will keep them from growing back. Then we'll cut you loose."

"Forget that idea," said Wendell. "I'm not riding off and leaving him."

"You stay here and I'll get help."

"Hold on," murmured the Prince. "Let's try something else first. Wendell, build a fire and get some torches going. Ann, you'll take a torch. As soon as Wendell cuts a branch, hold the flame to the severed end and cauterize it. Be careful not to get too close."

Wendell and Ann nodded. It took an hour to put this plan into action, but the results were gratifying. This time the cut end, once scorched black, remained inert.

"All right," said Charming. "Cut my hands free first, but don't get into the hedge. It might be another trap."

"Got it," said Wendell, much relieved to have a plan of action and greatly reassured by Charming's calm tone of voice. He and Ann went at it industriously, but it was slow, careful work made difficult by the close proximity to the Prince. Several times Wendell dealt him nasty cuts as he strove to remove the intricate web of twigs, and Ann raised blisters with her torch more than a few times before Charming's arms were free. But the Prince bore this stoically. When his left arm bearing his dagger was at last loosened, he cut the thorns from his neck and gave Ann an encouraging smile as she burned the tips of the branches.

"There's your right arm," said Wendell. Charming flexed it and pulled out a few of the largest thorns, wincing as he did so. Ann moved in with the torch and cauterized the cut ends. As she did so, she jumped back with a little cry.

"What?" said Wendell and Charming together.

"Look." She pointed to one of the first branches to be cut. A small bud of green was showing through the charcoal. "It's growing back."

Charming looked it over. "Okay, it's growing back. No need to panic. We have plenty of time." He had Endeavor tucked under one arm and was quickly, but methodically, stripping the branches from his legs with his dagger. "You two stand back, out of the way. Wendell, keep passing me fresh torches as they burn down." His page drew back, obedient, but reluctant to retreat. Charming took a torch from Ann and burnt the branches in a circle around him as he cut himself loose.

It was a near thing. It took the cauterized branches a while to get started, but once the new buds pushed out of the burned area, they grew enormously fast. But Charming was close enough to the edge that he had only to cut his legs free and step clear, and this he did manage, although probably with less than a minute to spare. Wendell hugged him and Ann wanted to, except that he still had so many thorns sticking in him, it would have been a painful gesture at best.

Charming bent down and put his mouth close to Wendell's ear. "She didn't hear me swearing, did she?"

"I don't think she noticed. She was pretty upset."

"Good. Got to watch my reputation, remember."

Although his reputation may have been intact, the Prince was in a sorry state. His clothes were punctured and rent, stank of smoke, and were spattered with bloodstains. His skin was crisscrossed with scratches, some of them deep and still bleeding, and his whole body was dotted with pricks and puncture marks. Dozens of thorns remained embedded in his flesh, some of them broken off beneath the skin. It took Ann the better part of two hours to pull them out with a pair of tweezers she carried in her bags. Wendell had more than a few thorns himself, and Ann had badly scratched her hands and forearms. Dusk had long since fallen by the time they got each other cleaned up, bandaged, smeared with salve, into fresh clothes, and were sitting around the fire in the clear star-lit night.

"What do we do now?" asked Ann. "Are you still on the quest?"

"Sure," said the Prince. "Okay, we can't chop through the hedge and it doesn't look like we can burn through it, either. We can still try your idea of poisoning it. Right now, however, we are going to fall back on plan B."

"What is plan B?"

"Wendell, tell the lady what plan B is."

"We eat dinner," said Wendell.

"There you go," said the Prince. "In a situation like this, we always try plan B next. Things look a lot better when your stomach is full."

The Briar Rose Inn was the only hostel in the village of Briar Rose and thus was not imaginatively named, but nonetheless it was warm, well lit, and comfortable. It boasted a large public room that was filled with a cheerful and boisterous lot; mostly the young couples of the village, off for an evening away from the watchful eyes of their parents, and a dozen or so of the village elders, regular customers who drank steadily, moved dominoes around a table, and kept a grandfatherly eye on the younger crowd. Charming and Ann were able to slip in and find a corner table without fanfare, leaving Wendell to stable the horses. The proprietor, a cheerful smile on his round face and beads of sweat on his bald head, promised that slices of roast beef and bowls of potato soup would soon be forthcoming, and his equally cheerful and round-faced wife served them with great tankards of ale. Ann, who was not used to crowds of strangers, edged her chair a little closer to Charming's. The Prince was agreeable. Wendell bounced back in. "Sire! Look who is here."

He was leading an elderly gentleman who was the tallest, skinniest, and at once the most imposing man Ann had ever seen. A full beard of salt-and-pepper gray framed his face, gray curls sprang from his forehead, and a pair of alert and penetrating gray eyes stared from deep, narrow sockets. His nose was large and hooked; his fingers long, gnarled and crooked. His clothes, though well-made, were plain and simple except for the black cloak he wore over his shoulders. It was lined with red silk and held around his neck with a short gold chain. He smoked a long, curved Meerschaum pipe that gave a faint, strange odor Ann had never smelled before.

"Mandelbaum!" said Charming. "Speak of the devil and up he pops."

"Your Highness," said Mandelbaum, bowing slightly from the waist. "Little Princess," he said to Ann, bowing again.

"Sit down, sit down," continued Charming. "Have a brew. You're just the man we needed to talk to. And here you are. Funny coincidence, that."

"It's not a coincidence," said Wendell. "Mandelbaum came here to join us."

"I figured that, Wendell. I was being sarcastic. But,

Mandelbaum, what could bring you down from your ivory tower?"

"Wait a minute," said Ann. "Illyria is farther from here than my own castle. You would have had to leave before we knew ourselves that we were coming here!"

"That's right. A magic mirror showed me your destination." Mandelbaum took the pipe out of his mouth and sat down.

"You have a magic mirror, too?"

"Saw it in the marketplace at Yobindia and I couldn't resist. Only thirteen hundred royals. Actually, I paid a little more, but it was worth the extra royals to get downward compatibility with my crystal ball."

The Prince nodded. "And they always want to charge you extra for the cable, too. But what about this grail thing? Is this a load of codswallop or what?"

Mandelbaum drew on his pipe and reflected. Eventually he said, "Grail rituals were an important aspect of ancient fertility cults. And some of the ancient priests commanded an impressive power, though in those days it could be but crudely used. But, young sir, the legends by which the Wicked Queen is attempting to trace this grail descend to us through the mists of antiquity. Even should one of these relics still exist, it would contain but a faded trace of its magical power."

"You mean," said Ann, "if we found this grail, it would be useless?"

Mandelbaum thought again. Gentle puffs of smoke rose from his pipe. "Perhaps not. It could exert a subtle influence on a land. You couldn't make a wasteland bloom, but the cumulative effects, over the long term, could be beneficial—providing the grail were considerately used and by the right man."

"Or woman," said Ann and then bit her lip as though she had revealed an important secret. Mandelbaum gave her a knowing smile.

"I'm afraid not," he said. "There are symbolic connotations to a grail that are specifically female. Thus, only a male, the Fisher King, can master the grail and release its power. Now, a magic wand, say, or a staff of power, would be a male symbol that would be wielded by a woman."

"I don't get it," said Ann. "Why?"

"Symbolism," said Mandelbaum. "The basis of all magic. We are talking fertility symbols here. The cup is the female. It requires a male to release its power. The staff is the male. It requires a female to release its power."

"But that just begs the question. Why should a cup be a female symbol and a staff be a male symbol?"

"Oh, for goodness sake," said Mandelbaum with exasperation. "The cup is female because it represents the, uh, that is, it holds the man's, um . . ." Ann was staring at him. "The staff symbolizes the man's . . . oh, for goodness sake. Wendell, you know what I'm talking about, don't you?"

"No, but if you say it's true, I believe you," the page said stolidly.

"Prince Charming, surely you understand why a cup symbolizes a woman and the staff symbolizes a man?"

"Er, to be perfectly honest, no. But look here. That hedge grew like a wildfire. It nearly ate me alive. There must be plenty of magic left in that grail, to maintain that hedge alone."

Mandelbaum had been muttering something about the decline of the liberal arts. He looked up and said definitely, "There is no way an old grail could generate a hedge such as you describe. That is strong magic and fairly recent, too. Certainly well within the memory of some of the people in this tavern. I suspect we have merely to ask around to discover the solution to this problem."

"Prince Charming!"

A thunderous voice bellowed the name across the hall, cutting conversations short throughout the room. All heads turned and all eyes focused on Charming's table. The Prince sighed. "Looks like it's time to sign a few autographs."

"So, you're the great Prince Charming." The voice came from a huge bear of a man, swarthy and dark-eyed, clad in furs and leather. He wore a Roman-style short sword at his waist and carried a crossbow over his shoulder, a vicious-looking affair of dark wood and black-painted metal. His boots were tipped and heeled with copper bands; they left scars on the wooden floor as he swaggered across the room. The rest of the crowd suddenly decided to edge closer to the wall, out of the way, yet with a good view of the impending fight. The village elders stacked their dominoes and leaned back in their chairs, eyes watchful under thatches of white hair. "The great Prince Charming," repeated the interloper, his voice fairly dripping with challenge. "Well, you don't look like so much to me."

"He must have forgot his autograph book," said Wendell.

"Just as well," said Charming. "I don't have a quill." With an easy smile, he rose and approached the man, his right hand absolutely nowhere near his sword. Charming was by no means short, taller than average, in fact, and powerfully built; but the braggart towered over him by a full six inches and had shoulders like an ox. Had this been a betting crowd, Charming would not have been the odds-on favorite.

"Oh, Wendell," whispered Ann. "They're not going to fight, are they?"

"I hope not," said Wendell. "I hate it when the Prince kills someone just before dinner."

"Bear McAllister," said the Prince.

The big man started. "You know my name?"

"I saw you in the tournaments last year. You were pretty good with that crossbow, as I recall."

"I'm the best there is," bragged Bear. "I was the best then and I've gotten even better now. I can defeat any man alive in single combat, armed or unarmed. I've kicked ass in every kingdom from Illyria to Arondel. And yet, still, people refuse to accord me the respect I deserve. Even here in my home village, I constantly have to beat people up for not getting out of my way. Do you know why?"

"Because you're a jerk," muttered Ann.

"Because I haven't got a reputation," sneered the Bear. "Because I don't have a bunch of namby-pamby scribes running around pushing my name in every corner of the kingdom, or a hired bard to sing tales of my exploits that I've written for him. All I've got is the true fact of my own greatness. And facts don't travel as well as fancy."

"Life is tough."

"On the other hand," the Bear continued, "suppose I was to run into one of these puffed-up papier-mâché heroes. And suppose I was to defeat him in single combat. Now *that* would be a tale that would be told and retold." He grinned slyly, revealing a mouth full of yellow teeth. Fists the size of hams clenched and unclenched.

"Have you got an apple?" asked the Prince.

This was not the reply the Bear was expecting. Nor, for that matter, was anyone in the room. Even Wendell was nonplused.

"Does anyone have an apple?"

"No," said the Bear. The rest of the room stared in silence.

"Wendell."

Wendell shrugged and got an apple from the kitchen. He gave it to Charming with a questioning look. Charming winked. He walked across the room, turned, placed the apple on top of his head, and leaned back against the wall, hands crossed negligently at his belt buckle. "Okay, Bear, let's see just how good you really are."

The Bear chewed the inside of his cheek. He unslung his crossbow. "This?"

"That's right. Should be an easy shot for you."

"I don't believe this," said Ann. "Somebody stop him."

"You want me to shoot the apple off your head with this crossbow?"

"Well, if you don't think you're up to it . . ."

The Bear was working his jaws. He knew this was a trick, but he couldn't quite figure the angle. He looked around the room. Every eye was on him. He slipped a wooden bolt into the crossbow and slowly cocked it. The crossbow had a ratcheted cocking lever that made a slow grinding noise as he pulled it back. "I'm up to it. But you're an awfully cocky young punk, aren't you?"

"Oh, I wouldn't say that. At the tournament, I saw you nail copper coins at four times this distance."

Several of the bystanders nodded. Ann grabbed Mandelbaum's sleeve. "Mandelbaum! He's going to kill him."

"He can't. If McAllister shoots Charming, he'll appear to have missed an easy shot. He'll get his reputation all right. A reputation for killing a prince by *accident*. A reputation for being a bungler. It's the last thing he wants. But he can't draw his sword and attack, either. It will look like he refused Charming's test."

"But what if he tries for the apple and really misses?"

"He won't miss." But Mandelbaum did not say this with certainty. He was not proficient in the military arts and the apple seemed an awfully small target. The room was long, and the lamps provided a flickering, uneven light.

The Bear put the crossbow up to his shoulder and sighted along its length. He glowered at the Prince, realizing that somehow, he wasn't quite sure how, he was being duped. Then he fired.

You couldn't actually see the bolt in flight. McAllister's weapon had over a hundred pounds of tension on it. You heard the twang of the bow and the hiss of the bolt through the air, but your eyes leaped immediately to Prince Charming.

Who moved so fast that to this day some of the villagers claim it was one of Mandelbaum's illusions. One moment he was standing negligently against the wall, looking faintly ridiculous with an apple perched on his head, a look of polite boredom on his face, and his hands folded in front of him. In the next instant he moved. The eyes caught a flash of lamplight on steel, the memory retained a blurred impression of fluidly shifting muscles, and Prince Charming's sword neatly cleaved the speeding bolt in midair, the two halves of the wooden arrow separating and piercing the apple a quarter inch apart.

"I don't believe it," said Ann. Mandelbaum shook his head in wonderment. Wendell only shrugged.

The Bear stared dumbfounded. Charming stood stock still with both hands wrapped around Endeavor's hilt, the gleaming blade still held in front of his face. Slowly, he allowed his shoulders to relax. He took the apple from his head, glanced at the two half-bolts protruding from it, and tossed it to the Bear. There came that fluid shifting of muscles again, and Endeavor disappeared back into its scabbard. Only then did the audience begin to clap.

The Prince nodded at them and walked forward, extending his hand to McAllister. The Bear took it with some degree of nervousness, noting that charming's other hand was still resting on the hilt of his sword.

"You were saying?"

"Huh?"

"You were talking about reputations, as I recall. Something about my reputation being made by hired bards."

"Uh, right," said the Bear. "Bards. Great for a man's reputation. Um, you wouldn't happen to know where I could hire some, do you?"

"No."

"Right. Well then, I'll just be off."

"No, no, stay and have a drink with us." Charming clasped the big man by the shoulder. "As a matter of fact, I was just looking for a man who could fill me in on some of the local folklore."

"Uh, well, as long as you're buying, I guess I can't refuse." McAllister sat down and introductions were made all around. "That's a pretty nice piece of steel you carry, Charming. Your own armorer made it?"

"No, it was a gift." Charming unbuckled his scabbard and passed it to the Bear. The big man examined it respectfully. "Very nice, very nice indeed. Excellent balance." He unfolded some of the gadgets from the handle. "What's this curvy thing? Some kind of nut pick?"

"Um, I think that's for splicing rope."

After a few moments' chat about weapons, the local tournaments, hunting, etc., Charming questioned his adversary about the thorn hedge, with Ann and Mandelbaum chiming in. In response to their questions, the Bear ran his fingers through his coarse hair for a while and shook his head. "There's magic in that woods all right, but I don't recall I've ever heard of no grail. These old timers,"—he gestured at the village elders, who had resumed their game of dominoes— "would surely have mentioned it if there was. But those thorn bushes surround the castle of Princess Aurora."

"Never heard of her."

"It's a strange story. That forest, you may have noticed, is a fairy wood and those are no ordinary thorn bushes."

Charming, Ann and Wendell exchanged looks.

"We did notice."

"See, the old King Stephen built his castle in the center of that wood and he never got along too well with the fairy who controlled it. She was a bitchy little thing named Esmerelda. On the day of Princess Aurora's wedding, she put a curse on the whole castle and cast Princess Aurora into a deep sleep. The legend goes that she can only be awakened by a kiss of a prince."

"Oh, that's terrible!" said Ann.

"What's terrible?" said Charming. "That she was cast into a deep sleep or that she can only be awakened by a kiss?"

"That she missed her wedding. Do you realize how much work goes into one of those?"

"Think of her poor fiancé. He missed his wedding night."

"Shut up."

"Then this hedge of thorns grew up around the castle and the whole thing was lost to sight. And that's the last anyone ever saw of the King, the Princess, and strangely enough, Esmerelda too."

The innkeeper came back with a platter of beef and refills of ale all around. The Bear and Wendell began to feed while the other three leaned back and pondered this story.

"Think of her," Ann said dreamily. "Still sleeping, year after year, while leaves turn color and fall, and the seasons change, dreaming of the day her prince will come and awaken her." She sighed. "Think of those unopened wedding gifts."

"I wouldn't put too much stock in that story," said Charming. "A fairy's magic isn't *that* powerful. There are plenty of guys around who could break a spell like that. Like Mandelbaum."

"In all modesty," said Mandelbaum, "I am compelled to say there are not many sorcerers who are my equal. Nonetheless, Prince Charming's assessment is largely correct. A grail may be too obscure and esoteric to waste much time on, but with an entire castle at stake, that wall of thorns should have been breached within hours."

"You're forgetting something," said the Bear, stabbing at a piece of gristle. "All the nobility of the kingdom was at the wedding. They're all inside. As well as all the leading merchants, tradesmen, and moneylenders. It was a big wedding, you see. Everyone who was anyone was there. That damn fairy wiped out the entire leadership of this kingdom. Only peasants remained on the outside. There was no one left with the cash to hire a first-rate magician, or the leadership to take action."

"Seems to me that left a pretty substantial power vacuum. Why didn't the neighboring kings try to move in?"

The Bear looked surprised. "Your Highness, they did. Your grandfather, King Charming, declared Alacia a protectorate."

"Illyria owns Alacia?"

"You didn't know that?" said Ann.

Charming shrugged. "I don't keep up with the political end. I deal more with tactical matters."

"I know. Slaying and rescuing, right?"

"Right."

"But didn't the people remain loyal to their own king?"

The Bear studied the bottom of his glass. "Well, they had a choice. They could pay taxes to the King and then more taxes to the nobles who held their land. Or they could just pay taxes to a new King. Figure it out."

Ann didn't like the idea at all.

"Mandelbaum, what do you think? Is there a Princess in there or what?"

"On the one hand, your Highness, local folklore is a very unreliable source of information. On the other hand, throwing up a hedge like that is not a piece of cake. I daresay there's *something* important behind there."

"All right then. I was ready to blow off this grail thing, but if there is a princess to rescue, then my duty is clear. I'm going in tomorrow."

"Ah, Sire, it will take me three or four days to analyze that hedge spell and devise a counter to it. If I have to send for equipment from Illyria, possibly several weeks."

"Leave the hedge alone. I've got an idea."

Mandelbaum brightened. "No, wait, I've got just the thing. Have you ever noticed how the smoke from a fire rises up the chimney . . ."

"Ride over in a bag of smoke? Forget it," said Charming.

Mandelbaum looked at Wendell. "Perhaps it wasn't explained to you clearly. It will work."

"I'm sure it will. I've got a better idea. Remember that time the army was chasing those bandits and they crossed the Lassendale River and burned the bridge behind them? Well . . ."

Charming sketched out his plan. Mandelbaum stroked his beard and nodded.

"I can do it, Sire. I can make the preparations tonight and be ready at dawn."

Wendell jumped up. "I'll help you, Mandelbaum!"

"Okay," said Charming. "Get some rest, too, Wendell. There's no telling what we'll find on the other side."

"Then if you'll excuse us, we will get to work." Mandelbaum rose and bowed once to Charming, once to Ann. "Good night, Little Princess." He left with Wendell in tow.

"What a nice man," said Ann.

The Bear rose also. "Guess I'll be pushing off, too. Thanks for the dinner, Charming. You're a right good sort." He grinned. "Pretty neat trick with the sword."

With the table clearing out, the innkeeper saw his cue to come over. "Prince Charming, I can't tell you what an honor it is to have you staying in my humble inn."

"Why, it is not humble at all! I find it to be excellent."

The innkeeper puffed out his chest. "Thank you, your Highness. You will find I have put you in our largest and finest room, and supplied you with a goose-down mattress. Your retinue will occupy the room next to you. Your maid can sleep in the kitchen with the other girls." He beamed at Ann. "My wife has prepared a place for her right next to the stove, so she will be quite warm."

"Um," said the Prince. He glanced at Ann, waiting for her to announce that she was, in fact, of royal blood and would appreciate a room befitting her status. Instead she simply returned to him a cool stare and said nothing. "Actually, uh, I will need my maid to do some, uh, mending, yeah, mending, and she'll have to consult me on things and will be up pretty late so why don't you just put her, uh, in the room next to mine."

The innkeeper was shocked into speechlessness. A wave of angry red started up from his neck and climbed quickly to the bald circle of his scalp. Ann was certain that it was only the threat of *lese majesty* that prevented him from striking the young prince. Then the man came to a sudden realization and his anger disappeared as quickly as it had grown, to be followed by a roar of laughter. "Of course," he bellowed. "Your Highness is making a joke. Ho, ho, ho. Certainly you would never expect us to lodge an unmarried woman in the same wing with the men. How foolish of me to get caught by your little jest."

Charming glared at Ann. Still she said nothing. He forced a smile. "Right, right. I was just being flippant. Sure, put her in the kitchen. And if she gives you any trouble, throw a bucket of cold water on her."

Ann rose and curtsied. "Whatever his Highness desires," she said meekly. "But I must come up to your room this evening to bring you your milk. The Prince always has a glass of warm milk and an oatmeal cookie before he goes to bed," she told the proprietor.

Charming ground his teeth.

"Eh?" said the innkeeper. "Cookies?" He looked at Charming and then back at Ann. "Well, I guess that's okay. One of the married women will accompany you. And now, by your leave, Sire, I must attend to the other guests."

Charming saluted him off. Ann smoothed her dress. "And now, by your leave, Sire, I must be off to attend my place in the kitchen."

"Wait a minute! Why don't you tell him . . ." But Ann had already flounced away, leaving Charming alone at the table in a rapidly emptying room. "Girls," he muttered.

Eventually he went up to his room. Wendell had neatly unpacked the bags but was nowhere to be found; presumably, he was still out with Mandelbaum. Charming pulled off his boots and lay down on the bed. The goose-down ticking was every bit as comfortable as promised, but he found himself unable to relax. He thought about Ann. She had a really pretty face. But the girl drove him crazy. She showed no appreciation for the fact that he was *Prince Charming*, for goodness sake! What did she want from him anyway? He rolled over on his stomach, then rolled over on his back again. She had great tits, too. Those maid's uniforms really showed them off. He rolled over on his stomach and pounded the pillow. Then he fluffed it up again. Then he rolled over on his side. "This mattress is too soft. That's the trouble."

The door burst open and Wendell popped in. "This is great! This is going to be a great spell." He grabbed some candles from the bags and ran out again.

"Well, good for them," Charming said to the empty room.

Charming had a great deal of respect for Mandelbaum and he admired the magician's ability. The old man had a vast store of knowledge. The problem with magicians, though, was their inability to produce repeatable results. That was why he didn't like to use the stuff unless he'd seen the spell worked a couple of times before.

Mandelbaum was pretty reliable although Charming didn't buy all that stuff about symbolism. Filling a grail with water, he suspected, was probably no more symbolic than putting a sword in a scabbard.

Then came the softest of knocks at the door, so soft that at first the Prince wasn't sure he heard anything. Then the knock came again, three soft raps, and the door quietly opened. Silently holding a candle, Ann slipped in and shut the door behind her.

She was a vision of loveliness.

The light from the candle highlighted her cheekbones and reflected from her shining dark eyes. Lustrous black hair fell about her shoulders in soft waves. Her lips were full, red, moist, and slightly parted, and her lashes batted gently against her smooth, perfect skin. She wore a simple white cotton nightshirt that effectively concealed the shape of her body, yet the few curves that did show through were all in the right places and richly promising. She was barefoot.

Charming's mouth went dry.

Ann put the candle on the nightstand and sat down beside Charming. "Hi," she said softly.

"Hi," said Charming. "Where's the other girl?"

"They're all asleep. I took the opportunity to come up and see you." She smiled wryly. "No milk and cookies, though. Just me."

"Well, I'm not really disappointed. Why didn't you tell the innkeeper who you are? You could have had a room to yourself."

"Silly boy." Ann took Charming's hands in both of her own. "The innkeeper wouldn't put a woman in the same wing with the men, and yet he can hardly throw Prince Charming out of his room. So he would have given me one of the backrooms to myself by kicking out the other girls."

"Then where would they sleep?"

"In the stables."

"Yeah, I get it. That was pretty nice of you, not to tell them you're royalty."

"Well, I've done enough scutt work around our castle to start seeing things from the working girl's viewpoint."

"Well, um, I still think you're pretty nice." Charming suddenly found himself desperate to keep this conversation going. "Um, well, what I mean is that it was pretty, uh . . . uh, *nice* of you to give up a room like that." He felt like an idiot. "You know, to sleep in the kitchen so they don't have to sleep in the stables is, um, nice . . . oh, heck."

"My goodness. The charming Prince Charming is at a loss for words?"

"Well, you took me by surprise, coming in here. Give me a minute."

"Oh, take your time." Ann leaned forward and rested her elbows on her knees, which didn't help Charming's concentration any. He tore his gaze away from her breasts, gently rising and falling with each breath, and looked straight into her eyes.

He said, "Ann, this evening when I went to my room, I looked out the window and there was a hedge rose growing outside. Normally, those bushes don't bloom until summer, but this one was in a sheltered location and so it had budded. The light from the window fell upon a single flower, a red rose, newly opened. The evening dew had fallen, and a few drops of water clung to the tender petals and glimmered like pearls in the lamplight. That was all I could see, Ann, a single, perfect rose, shining in the darkness, and when I saw that rose I thought of you."

"Ooh," Ann murmured. "Very nice." She snuggled up next to the Prince and rested her head on his shoulder. Charming could feel her soft breath on his neck. His blood pressure headed skyward. It was time to try out some moves.

"You know, Charming, you and I have a lot in common."

He put his arm around her waist, wondering if he could get away with touching her thigh. "We do?"

"Uh huh. We both have parents who envy our youth and popularity."

He used his other arm to brush her hair back from her face. "I guess."

"We both feel a strong sense of duty to our people."

"Uh, yeah. Sort of." He gently tightened his arm and she snuggled closer, pressing the length of her body against him. He bent his head down to her face, until his lips were only inches from hers.

Rapturously, Ann closed her eyes and let her mind drift away. Without thinking, she continued to murmur, "Both our mothers died in childbirth."

The Prince stiffened. "So what?"

"When I was a little girl, I thought of her all the time. Do you ever think of your mother?"

"Um, not at a time like this."

"It's odd growing up without a mother, especially knowing that she died as a result of your birth."

"Now wait a minute!"

"In a way, we're responsible for their deaths, almost like we killed them."

Charming's blood pressure returned to Earth with a thump. "Hey . . ." Even for a priapic teen-ager, the thought was unsettling.

"Not that I feel guilt or anything. When you were growing up, did you ever think about things like this?"

"No!" The Prince sat up and let Ann's head drop to the pillow. "No, I never thought about things like that. And I don't particularly want to think about them now. Jeez, you sure know how to kill a romantic mood."

"Romantic mood?" Ann seemed to suddenly realize where she was and scrambled out of the bed. "I'm sorry, I didn't mean to . . . you didn't think that I . . . I have to go now." She yanked open the door. "Well, I'll see you in the morning, I guess." She held out her hand for him to shake.

The Prince ignored it. "Is it cold outside?"

"Um, it's a little chilly, yes."

"Good." Charming sighed. "I'm going for a walk."

His bootsteps woke the entire floor and Ann had a devil of a time getting back to her bed without being seen.

When they rode out of the village, the sun had not yet burned off the morning's mists, but today, Charming and Wendell forswore their usual dilly-dallying, even when out of sight of the village. Wendell had caught about four hours sleep, more than enough when one has the energy of youth, and was burbling with cheerful excitement, riding his horse ahead of the group and taking off to explore side trails, then galloping back. Charming had an inner tension that came with the sense of upcoming danger; though he outwardly appeared calm, he was eager to get on with the business at hand. Mandelbaum had been up all night, yet no fatigue showed on his face; he sat stolidly in the saddle and smoked his pipe with aplomb.

Ann stared straight ahead, rode in silence, and answered all queries with "mmph." She studiously ignored the Prince. The fact that no one seemed to notice she was ignoring him, least of all the Prince, made his behavior of the night before all the more infuriating.

When they reached the thorn hedge, Wendell scouted around until he found a pile of charred branches. "Right here. Here is where it was. See, here's where we built the campfire."

Mandelbaum was studying the hedge. So was Charming. "It's perfect. It looks exactly like the rest of the hedge. See, I must have gone in here, but you'd never tell by looking at it."

Mandelbaum simply nodded. He produced a small scissors from his pocket, snipped off a twig, wrapped it in a piece of cloth, and returned both scissors and twig to his jacket. He threw his cloak back over his shoulders. "Well, to work then."

"What are you going to do?" said Ann, in spite of herself.

"Ah," said Charming, "she speaks at last."

"Shut up. What are you going to do?"

"Watch and wait."

While Charming sat under a tree and whittled at a piece of willow bark, Mandelbaum and Wendell opened two huge duffel bags and began unpacking equipment. First, they removed dozens of intricately carved wooden stakes and hammered them into the ground in a pattern that was roughly circular. Apparently the spacing was very important for they constantly measured and checked the distances between stakes with a piece of knotted string. They took out leather bags of powders and sprinkled them over the ground between the stakes. They opened up vials of foul-smelling liquids and measured them out with glass pipettes, dripping some of the fluids on the ground, some on the stakes. Then they took out fingers of metal, brass, copper and, to Ann's surprise, gold and silver, and placed them on some of the stakes.

"Aren't you going to do something?" Ann asked Charming.

"I am doing something. See, I've made a whistle."

"I mean, aren't you going to help them?"

"They look like they're doing fine without me."

"Hmmph." Ann flounced away and Charming observed that her outfit was really perfect for flouncing. She approached Mandelbaum. "Is there anything I can do to help?"

"No," said Mandelbaum testily. "You'd only get in the way. I briefed Wendell on this last night. You just sit over there somewhere."

Ann returned to the tree and sat down by the Prince. "All right. I guess I'm being silly. Actually, I suppose I ought to thank you for last night."

"What? Thank me? What for?"

"For not . . . taking advantage of me last night. I guess I got carried away. I was all ready to . . . kiss you . . . and things. Last night I felt like you rejected me, but now I realize that was wrong. But for your strength of character I might have done something that we'd both regret."

"Oh," said the Prince. He opened his mouth several times as if to speak but thought better of it. After a few minutes more of silence, he finally said, "Actually, I may as well be perfectly honest here. I didn't walk out because I'm armored in virtue; I walked out because that mother thing got me upset. I mean, really, I was really attracted to you."

"Really?"

"Yeah. I think you're beautiful. And more important than that, you're not just beautiful, you're wonderful."

"Well, thank you. You've just made me very happy."

"You're welcome. You can tell me how handsome you think I am now."

"You look okay."

He stuck his tongue out at her and she laughed and punched him on the shoulder. "Now, tell me how we're going to get across the thorns."

"Just wait. Mandelbaum's almost done."

Mandelbaum was, in fact, finished and the ground between the stakes was beginning to smolder. Wendell was packing up the duffel bags and moving them a safe distance away. The Prince and Ann stood up but didn't come any closer. Mandelbaum was muttering incantations and giving a few final taps on some of the stakes with a wooden mallet. Then he tapped out his pipe and beat a hasty retreat, his cape flapping behind him.

It happened in a matter of seconds. In one instant a small, blue flame appeared in the center of the ring, in the next a sheet of fire covered the entire circle. A second later there was a roar and a column of flame leapt twenty feet into the air, showering bits of soot and smoking embers in all directions. Within another minute, however, the conflagration died away, leaving nothing but a circle of charred dirt in the grass.

"That's it?" said Ann. "That's going to get us through the thorns?"

"Hang on."

Beneath her feet Ann felt a faint rumbling, a rumbling that quickly grew in strength. "What is it?"

"Stand back."

Around her the ground was rippling and trembling like a storm-tossed sea. The trees were shaking and raining down leaves and dead branches. A low-pitched moaning rode the wind and sent shivers down her spine.

"Here it comes," shouted the Prince.

With a mighty roar a column of water erupted from the ground and sprang into the air. Thousands of gallons per minute ripped through the soil and climbed out of sight in the clear blue sky. Somewhere beneath the clouds, the furiously rushing torrent spent its energy and the fountainhead broke up and fell back. The group found itself in a torrential downpour.

"Oh, no, I'm soaked."

Charming was laughing. "Yeah." Then he saw the way the wet cotton of her dress was clinging to her breasts and quickly swiveled his gaze away.

Mandelbaum was waving his hands and trying to get the fountain under control. Responding to his ministrations, the column of water began swaying back and forth like a palm tree in a hurricane, scattering water for hundreds of yards across the forest. Finally it bent completely over, the dense column of water forming a perfect arc across the hedge of thorns.

"Nice job," said the Prince.

"But we can't ride on that. We'll be killed."

"He's not done yet. Now comes the good part."

Mandelbaum looked at them and winked. Then he waved his hands and Ann became aware of the silence.

Charming was walking towards Mandelbaum. She followed him. A chill breeze seemed to spring up suddenly and she shivered in her wet clothes. She realized that the forest wasn't really silent, there was the same rustling of leaves and chirping of birds as before. It was only the thunderous roar of the water that no longer assaulted her ears. Yet she could still see the beautifully curved arc standing before her. Wendell came up with a towel and she took it gratefully. When she had wiped the water from her face and eyes, she took another good look at the fountain and it all became clear.

"Why, it's frozen. You've turned it into ice."

"Don't touch it," warned the Prince. "Your skin will stick to it. I have some gloves for you."

"It's very cold," said Mandelbaum. "It will maintain its structural integrity for several hours. That should be plenty of time for you to find the princess, kiss her, and get out of there providing you resist the urge to explore."

"Hmmph," said Ann.

"Why 'hmmph'?"

"Oh, come now. You're not really going to kiss this Aurora person, assuming she exists, are you?"

"Why shouldn't I?"

"Prince Charming! You don't even know her!"

"How can I get to know her? She's under a spell."

"That's just what I mean. You can't just go into a girl's bedroom and kiss her while she's asleep. She can't give her consent. It's almost rape."

"If rescuing her means kissing her, then I'll just have to kiss her. That's my job. I'm a prince."

"It's perverse."

"You're just jealous."

"Jealous? Me? Ha!"

"I can see this is the sort of pointless discussion that can drag on for days," said Mandelbaum. "Why don't you continue it while you're climbing? Two hours will pass by more quickly than you think."

"Right," said Charming. "Wendell is getting us the ropes and ice axes."

"No." said Wendell. "Mandelbaum told me not to bring them."

"I have a surprise for you," said the Wizard. "This is a little refinement I added since the last time you saw this stunt." He produced a silver teaspoon from one of his many pockets, blew lightly on the bowl, and polished it lovingly against his cloak. Holding the spoon delicately between thumb and forefinger, he leaned over to the ice bridge and gave it the most delicate of taps.

There was a tiny "ting" like the ringing of a crystal goblet. The sound broadened and deepened, taking on a dozen harmonics and undertones. The sound lasted for several minutes, fading at times, and then growing louder, racing back and forth through the frozen structure. Abruptly it stopped. Then fine shards of ice began to flake away from the arch, falling to the ground and glittering in the sunlight. When the spell had completed itself, the Prince found himself looking at an elaborate and perfect stairway carved into the mass of frozen water.

"All right!" said the Prince.

"Nice," said Ann. "Very nice indeed."

"Got me two nominations for the magician's Golden Pentaflex award," said Mandelbaum proudly. "Best New Spell and Best Special Effect."

"Right. Well, guess I better trot on over there and kiss this babe. It's a tough job, but somebody's got to do it."

He donned a pair of gloves and started up the stairs without looking back. Ann hesitated, then followed him. The ice was slippery, as ice can be, and she lost her balance on the third step. The Prince caught her arm. He was wearing hobnailed boots so he had no trouble walking, and he put his arm around her to hold her steady.

Wendell, whose boots were also hobnailed, stopped

on the first step and turned around. "Mandelbaum, was this an expensive spell?"

"Very expensive, Wendell."

"More so than the bag of smoke idea?"

"Oh, yes. Tremendously."

"Then why didn't you push harder for the bag of smoke?"

Mandelbaum glanced at the Prince, who was out of earshot. He leaned over so his mouth was next to Wendell's ear. "It's a government job, son. Someday you'll understand."

Wendell shrugged and followed the Prince up the icy stair.

Climbing the arch was not hard work, and the ice was carved roughly enough so that the footing was no more treacherous than walking, say, on a frozen winter lake. Still, the arch, at its apex, was more than a hundred feet in the air, and this was enough to keep the Prince and his party moving with the utmost caution. The thorn hedge, when seen from above, looked no more inviting than when seen from the side, and promised an unpleasant landing for anyone who slipped. It was about thirty yards wide, so the trip across the ice bridge would bring them a little to the other side of the hedge. At the top of the arch, Charming stopped and waited for the others to catch up. Ann was only some dozen steps below him and Wendell was just behind her. She came up to his shoulder, panting slightly, and said, "Oh, my!"

"It's not bad," the Prince admitted.

"I like ours better," said Wendell.

They were looking at a castle. It was an impressive sight, and clearly the sort of structure where form preceded function. It was constructed of white-glazed brick and trimmed with what was once bright blue paint but was now faded and cracked. Its design featured those high arched windows of the type that

drove upstairs maids crazy, and the roof sported a
myriad of crennellated turrets and spinnerets that
served no obvious purpose except to look cute. The
doors and shutters were of carved, polished wood and
a brace of carved stone lions flanked the front
entrance. Although the castle had suffered from
twenty years of neglect (the hinges to the front door
had rusted away, for example), it was still a relatively
new structure. The moat was apparently spring fed,
for the water was deep and clear, and no stream led
into or away from it. A wide expanse of lawn stretched
away on all sides until it met the surrounding thorn
hedge. The grass needed cutting. The tattered remains
of a flag hung sadly from the tower.

"So much for our grail quest. This place can't be
more than thirty years old."

"Oh, I like it anyway," said Ann. "It's so light and
airy. What a perfect spot for a wedding."

"Dragon," said the Prince.

"What?"

Charming had produced a small brass spyglass from
inside his tunic and was sweeping it back and forth
over the scene. "Wendell, the carriages."

"I see them."

"See what?"

There were two lines of perhaps a dozen carriages
each parked in front of the castle. They were in no
better shape than the castle, the effects of time and
weather having taken their toll on bright paint, velvet
curtains and leather harnesses. On some, a wheel or
two had rotted away, leaving the carriage canted over
at some odd angle; a few of them had toppled over
completely. Tall grass grew between the wheels.

Charming handed the spyglass to Ann. "Take a look
at those two carriages."

Ann put the glass to her eye. Upon closer inspec-
tion, the two carriages did not appear to have fallen

over by themselves. All their wheels were intact, and there were long, parallel scores in the wooden bodies. The top of the vehicle had been ripped completely off, as if by a tremendous force, leaving shattered lengths of wood protruding through the roof. It was clear that some powerful beast had broken the carriage and torn it open like the shell of a crab.

"What do we do now?"

"Keep your eyes open," said the Prince.

"Are we going to keep on?"

"You can go back, if you like."

"If you're going, I'm going."

"Fine." Charming had drawn his sword a few inches from its scabbard and was testing the edge with his thumb. "Let Wendell come up front, though. I'll need him by my side."

Wendell and Ann slid beside each other and the party started down the other side of the arch, the Prince leading, followed by Wendell, followed by Ann. The descent was slightly more treacherous than the climb up, for the ice was starting to melt and taking on a slippery wet sheen. Nonetheless, they reached the ground without mishap and stepped off the ice arch into cool, green grass that was knee high. The Prince headed immediately to the castle doors.

"But what about the dragon?" Ann hurried to keep up with him.

"Probably inside. If he was outside, we'd have seen him."

"But if he's inside, shouldn't we be outside?"

"No, we should be inside and the dragon outside. Unfortunately there are too many broken doors and windows to keep him out, so that strategy isn't going to do us much good."

"But, are you really going to try to slay him without a horse and lance?"

"Hey, let's take this one step at a time. We'll just take a look around first."

The front doors were open. Charming put a hand on one and pushed gently. The remaining hinge squealed. He pulled his hand away, faced the other two, and put a finger to his lips. Ann and Wendell nodded. The Prince eased his body through the opening and slipped inside. He waited while Wendell, then Ann, followed.

The front hall was dusty but in excellent condition. Ann expected to see cobwebs, hornets' nests, rodent droppings, curtains and tapestries chewed by mice. Instead, the fixtures and furnishings looked worn by time but largely spared by the wildlife. She whispered to Charming. "Pretty good shape."

Charming nodded. He glided over to a window. The bodies of half a dozen flies were lying on the sill. "Dead."

"Not sleeping?"

The Prince shook his head. There was a cricket in the corner of the floor and he touched it with the tip of his sword. The insect was a dried, dehydrated husk. "Dead. Some spell."

"Where are the people?"

"Gathered for the wedding? Let's look for the chapel."

They moved deeper into the building, passing through hallways and libraries and sitting rooms, moving steadily toward the center of the castle. They found the wedding guests or, rather, what remained of them. They were not gathered in the chapel, but, in the great dining hall that was to hold the wedding feast. Long tables were arrayed against the walls, heaped with gold platters and fine porcelain dishes. Crystal goblets held the evaporated residue of what was once a noble vintage. The guests were desiccated skeletons. Shreds of their fine silk garments could be seen clinging to their bones, but empty sockets stared from the well-gnawed skulls. The bones had been piled in a heap in the center of the room and on top of this heap slept the dragon.

Charming drew his head back around the corner and motioned the others to follow him. They retreated down the hall until they found a small, isolated library. High casement windows topped shelves of dusty books and knick-knacks. Charming dusted off a leather chair for Ann, sat down on one himself, and said, "Friendly looking little tyke, wasn't he?"

"Oh, my," said Ann. "Oh, it's so ugly. I've never seen one before. And it stinks, too."

"The odor of carrion. I make it to be about twelve feet long. What do you think, Wendell?"

"Fourteen, counting the spikes on the tail."

"Did you see the missing scales on the back and sides?"

"Yes, Sire. They get awfully mean when they're molting."

"Okay." Charming leaned back and rocked the chair on two legs. "Let's assess the situation. We've got a fourteen-foot green-spiked dragon, male, possibly in molt, chipped upper-left fang, missing one claw on the right hind foot, three claws each on the other feet, crested head, dorsal ridge, apparently healthy, certainly vicious. Presently asleep in a confined space."

"Um," said Ann. "That's about the way I see it, too."

"Figure a six-foot range for the flame," said Wendell. "The hall is about forty feet by one hundred feet. Double door main entrance on the south end, two doors on each side leading to hallways, two small swinging doors in the back, probably to the kitchen."

Charming nodded. "Twelve windows, evenly spaced, eight feet high and starting four feet from the floor. Lots of broken furniture and debris scattered about."

"Footwork will be treacherous."

"Right." The Prince unbuckled his sword and handed it to Wendell. "Go for it."

"Sire?"

"You said you wanted to slay a dragon. Now is your chance."

"Charming!" said Ann.

"I can do it," said Wendell. He reached to take the sword from Charming but seemed to have difficulty working his fingers. When he finally got his hands wrapped around the scabbard, he pulled out Endeavor and looked at it. The hand-forged steel, lightly oiled, gleamed in the daylight and the finely honed edge glowed like fire. He cast the scabbard aside and held the sword up, pointed toward the ceiling. "All right."

Charming was looking at him without expression. Ann was shocked. "Okay," said Wendell. "Back in a minute." In his daydreams he had always followed this up with some dashing, witty remark before going off to do battle. But now he found himself at a loss, so he opted instead to thrust out his jaw in a manly scowl before turning on his heel and striding resolutely toward the door.

Before he took three steps he felt Charming's hand on his shoulder. "Just kidding, Wendell. It was a joke. Give me the sword back."

"Oh," said Ann. "That's not funny."

Wendell gave up the sword reluctantly. "I knew it. You never let me do anything."

"Sorry, Wendell. Maybe next time, eh?"

"You always say that."

"Hey," said the Prince. He leaned down next to Wendell and spoke confidentially. "I'm only doing this one because there's a babe to impress here. Otherwise, I'd let you slay him. Really. I mean it."

Wendell glanced at Ann. "Well, I guess so. I'll carry your sword up to the hall."

Charming shook his head. "You stay back here."

Wendell was so astounded he could hardly talk. When he finally did get the words out, he was choking with indignation. "You're leaving me back with the *girls!*"

Ann said, "Well, excuse me."

"It's just one girl. I want you to stay back here and protect her. Come on, Wendell, you know how dragons are around maidens."

"Oh, yeah. Well, okay."

"Fine, then. You hold the fort here, and I'll slay this beast and be back in a few minutes. Then I guess we can break for lunch."

"All right."

Charming winked at Ann, clapped Wendell on the shoulder, and strode confidently away. Before he could reach the door, Ann ran forward. She stood silently before the Prince and then suddenly hugged him. Charming, caught by surprise, took her in his arms. "Be careful," she whispered.

"I will."

"Sheesh," said Wendell.

Charming left the two of them behind a bolted door and went back to the great dining hall. The dragon was still asleep upon its pile of bones.

Now it has been widely observed that many animals, when sleeping, display a kind of helpless vulnerability that makes them look harmless and cuddly. A big and vicious grizzly bear, lying curled in the sun, can seem as warm and playful as a cocker spaniel; the most sadistic warrior, when dozing, appears as innocent as a child, and even vermin such as toads and snakes take on a kind of cute, toylike appearance.

This is not true of dragons.

The green-spiked dragon is neither the biggest nor the most dangerous of its ilk, but it does have a qualifiable nastiness to its demeanor that is perhaps shared only by the barracuda and certain sub-species of wharf rat. This dragon, in fact, looked even nastier than most. A great row of crooked, sharp teeth protruded from its underslung jaw and there were scars around its eyes, probably from rooting some creature out of its burrow. Ticks crawled on its back and it was a good guess there were mites and fleas as well, if one cared to get a closer look. Its scales were dirty and dull, but the muscles beneath betrayed a lithe power and the claws, like the teeth, were razor sharp. It was curled in a loose ball with its nose resting on its tail and a thin trickle of drool emanating from the side of its mouth.

(Dragons tend to drool a lot. In fact, the worst thing about fighting dragons is that when they first open their mouths to flame you, you are likely to be showered with dragon spit. All knights really hate this part and it's the sort of thing that doesn't get mentioned during those romantic evenings of bragging by the fireside.)

Charming reflected on all this while watching the dragon from the doorway with Endeavor in his hand. He breathed quietly and shallowly while he took in the dragon, the room, the location of all the entrances and exits, the position of the furniture, the windows, the light, and the various obstacles scattered about that could trip up a man if he wasn't watching where he was going, like if he was preoccupied with fighting for his life. "Okay," he told himself silently. "This is not such a problem. He's asleep. I'll walk over there very quietly, being very careful not to disturb him, and put this sword through the eye socket before he knows what hit him. It's been done."

At that point, the dragon awoke.

"Time to fall back on plan B," said the Prince, but unfortunately the dragon seemed to have the same plan and charged.

Charming left the room quickly, but not so quickly that he didn't have the presence of mind to lead the dragon in the opposite direction from Ann and Wendell. The dragon roared through the door like a green flash flood, eyes bloodshot and angry, lips curled back from fangs in a vicious snarl. It caught a glimpse of Charming ducking into another doorway and followed at full speed, the sinewy body moving in a snake-like ripple, neck extended and scale-armored head held low like a battering ram. As it charged it let loose a roar, a shattering, grinding, snarl that resounded with pure animal hatred.

Dragons are very territorial.

The Prince ducked into the next room he found with a simple plan in mind. He was going to stand by the doorway and jab the dragon in the eye as its head came though the door. Unfortunately, the room he chose happened to be filled with tapestries. Not just one but several layers covered the floor and hung from all of the walls. As Charming pressed himself against the cloth, the dragon skidded to a stop outside, scanned the opening suspiciously, and filled the doorway with a blast of flame that instantly ignited the rugs on the floor and both sides of the doorway. Caught in the crossfire, so to speak, and momentarily blinded by the smoke, the Prince was forced deeper into the room by the flames. Coughing, he threw down a book case and stood behind it, ready to make his stand.

The dragon did not appear.

"Oh, bloody hell," said the Prince. The room was burning up fast and he had to get out. With three quick strokes of his sword, he cut a tapestry down from the wall and draped it over himself, using it for protection while he dashed through the flames and into the hall again. Tossing the smoking rug aside, he saw the dragon trotting down the hall, turning its head from side to side as it sniffed the air.

"Damn. He's sniffing *her* out. Why do they always go for the maidens?"

A sudden role reversal took place. The dragon broke into a full run, chasing down the female scent while the Prince followed in hot pursuit, waving his arms and yelling, trying to distract the beast from its mission. To no avail. The dragon reached Ann's hiding place with certainty, hesitating not a second as it reared on its hind legs and then brought its full weight to bear on the bolted door. The front claws shattered the wood into kindling. With a triumphant roar, the animal tore the door from its frame.

Inside, Ann was hanging from the top shelf of a bookcase, trying to open one of the casement windows. Wendell was balanced on the second shelf, maintaining a precarious foothold while both hands pushed upward on Ann's bottom. As the door came crashing down, he let go and leaped to grab one of the extra swords. It was not a well-planned move, however, for the immediate effect was to have Ann lose her grip and come down on his head. A few books sprang loose and thumped down on them, then the whole shelf toppled over, showering them with manuscripts and then burying the unfortunate couple. All this happened in less time than it takes to tell, of course, and the sudden collapse of the shelf, along with the disappearance of the intended victims, threw the dragon's feeble brain into confusion. It stopped its headlong charge, sniffed the air suspiciously, and opened its mouth to blast the area with flame. At this point Prince Charming arrived.

He was running down the hall at full speed and could only see the dragon's tail protruding from the doorway. Spying a bare patch where the scales had molted away, he bore down on it with both hands on his sword. The tempered steel bit deep into the armored flesh, stopped when it hit bone. A thin geyser

of blood erupted from the wound and the spikes on
the thrashing tail scored deep gouges in the wood of
the door frame. The animal choked off its fire to give
a blood-curdling screech, then forgetting the room's
two occupants, it whipped around in a tight arc and
galloped out the door.

Charming was waiting for it.

After chopping at the dragon's tail he sprang back,
out of the way of the deadly spikes. Now he charged
back at full speed, sword held up and angled downward, aimed where he estimated the dragon's eyes
would appear. The beast's head, eyeballs red with
rage, crooked teeth bared, came through the door like
it had been fired from a catapult. Charming ran
straight at it, striking at the malevolent eye with every
ounce of strength he could muster. He missed.

It was a difficult thrust, even for Charming, a running stab attempted under stress at a palm-sized target
emerging from a room at right angles to the attack. It
is amazing, in fact, that he was able to come as close
as he did. Endeavor's steel scored a deep groove in
the scaly plating just above the dragon's eye socket,
causing the beast to howl with rage again. The sword
then glanced off the tough hide and Charming ran
headlong into the dragon's neck.

The beast was charging too fast to stop, or even to
turn its head and fry him. Reflexively it shrugged its
assailant off and batted at him with a clawed foot, but
Charming caught and blocked this blow with his
sword. The dragon checked its charge by crashing into
the wall in front of it, fourteen feet of armored fury
piling up against the masonry, sending loosened bricks
and bits of mortar flying. By the time it got itself
straightened out, Charming had his back to it and was
leading a healthy retreat down the hall and away from
Ann. The dragon shot a lungful of flame after him,

but the Prince was already down the hall. The reptile succeeded only in setting fire to the wooden molding.

Charming found himself in a long hallway, hung with oil paintings and lined with an array of white painted doors with tarnished brass knobs. Unfortunately, they all seemed to be locked. The bare hallway offered little in the way of protection and nothing in the way of concealment. Around the corner, he could hear the approaching clackety-clack of clawed feet on the stone floor. He bounced from door to door, trying the knobs, pausing once to look at a tiny door with a keyhole. It had been meant to set flush with the wall and be almost invisible, but the door and the wall around it had been so scored with teeth and claw marks that it stood out like a sore thumb. Charming passed it after a moment and proceeded directly to the end of the hall. It held a fireplace, topped by a marble mantelpiece, over which hung a painting of a beautiful, young, blonde girl in a simple white dress. Charming glanced at it, then reached into the fireplace filled with twenty-year-old ashes, and pulled out a fire iron. It was black and heavy, and when he swung it against the nearest door, the wood splintered with a satisfying crack.

The sound of the dragon's claws at the opposite end of the hall slowed down and stopped. Having been cut once, the animal was wary. The Prince stopped and waited. The dragon's snout appeared around the corner and it sprayed the hallway with flame, igniting a few portraits and peeling the paint from the walls. Charming started on the door again. Three more good whacks with the fire iron and the bolt split from the frame. He jumped inside as the dragon began another charge.

The door did not open up into a room. Instead, it led to a narrow staircase that spiraled up to the second floor. It was meant simply to be a set of utility stairs for the servants, for the stone was rough, unfinished, and the width barely larger than the Prince's shoulders. Charming ran up the first six steps, until he was almost out of sight behind the curve of the spiral, and waited. He didn't think it was likely that the dragon would try to squeeze itself into the narrow staircase, but he could hope.

His hope was fulfilled. The dragon did indeed follow Charming. It jammed its shoulders into the staircase, filling the entrance with flame. The Prince ducked up the stairs, but he could feel the heat at his back. He got to the second-floor landing and waited, breathing heavily. He could hear the scraping of the dragon's scales on the stone as the animal slowly forced its body between the walls. He waited confidently. He would go for the eye again. It was really the only kill spot. The dragon had nowhere to go but up and the stairs were too narrow for it to take evasive action. It would be almost too easy now. Certainly nothing to brag about. He waited at the exit to the first floor landing, sword ready. When the dragon's head appeared, he drove the blade in deep.

This time he did not miss, but the results were far from what he expected. The dragon roared furiously, whipping its head from side to side, banging it against the door frame and ripping the sword from Charming's hand. The Prince backed away quickly as the wounded animal set loose torrents of flame in all directions. All in all, it appeared far from dead. It stretched out its front feet, dug the claws into the wooden floor, and began leveraging itself out of the stairwell. Charming took off.

He found the main staircase with no problem, but descended into a thick curtain of smoke, for the dragon's fire had spread rapidly. Near the library the smoke was so thick that he ran into Wendell and Ann before he saw them. Ann threw her arms around his neck and Wendell threw his arms around his waist and they hugged him. The Prince disentangled himself.

"Wendell, remember all those stories we heard about killing a dragon by stabbing it through the eye?"

"Yeah."

"They're all nonsense. Listen."

Upstairs they could hear the dragon roaring and stomping about. Downstairs the smoke was growing thicker and the crackle of flame was growing louder.

"I think it's time to fall back on plan B," Ann shouted above the noise.

"Good idea. You're getting the hang of this." The Prince grabbed a poker from the fireplace and took off. "But first, this way."

They followed him into the smoke, dashing through corridors lined with flame. After the first few corners, Ann shouted, "This isn't the way out!"

"I know." The Prince didn't stop.

"Where are we going?"

"The Princess." Charming stopped in a hallway where white paint was blistering from the walls. "Princess Aurora. The sleeping babe, remember?" He pointed to a small door with a tiny keyhole.

"Are you crazy?"

"Give me a hand here, Wendell." The page helped him insert the fire poker into the door frame. They both threw their weight on the iron bar. "They always go for the maidens. Dragons, I mean. Look at all these claw marks." The wood split and the door popped open. "He wanted to get in here badly."

"Maidens and dogs," said Ann as they started up the stairs. "You better hope this isn't the secret passage to the kennels."

This staircase was even narrower than the servants' stairs; Charming had to turn sideways to negotiate it. But the steps, instead of being rough-hewn stone, were very finely finished, so the Prince was encouraged. They went up five flights, with smoke pouring past them and the air growing rapidly hotter.

"This staircase is acting like a chimney," Wendell said suddenly. "Sire, we may not be able to get back down." The Prince pushed doggedly upward, feeling his way through the darkness and smoke, holding on to Ann's arm, who held on to Wendell's shoulder. His right hand, groping forward, found a door, then a door knob. The door was unlocked. He pushed it forward and all three companions tumbled inside, along with a billow of gray smoke. Wendell shut the door behind them and the smoke spread out and enveloped the room in a faint gray pall.

They were in one of the corner towers of the castle, a round room about ten feet in diameter. Four large windows faced north, south, east, and west, giving it a light and airy spaciousness. Charming opened one of the windows and looked down. The waters of the moat sparkled below. A light breeze cleared away most of the smoke, revealing dainty, pink-lacquered furniture, and frilly clothing scattered about the floor, or draped over chairs. A small, framed sketch of a young man stood on the vanity table along with a vase of dried and withered roses. A delicate Oriental jug and basin sat on one of the window sills, the water long since evaporated, the bright pinks and greens of the ceramic turned pastel by the thick coating of dust.

There was something on the bed.

It was a low, square bed with a pink canopy and lots of ruffles and lace on the coverlet. Ann knelt down next to it. "Look," she said quietly. "She was wearing her wedding dress."

The dried remains of a young girl lay on the bed. She was dressed in white satin, a white lace veil across her face and the train of her gown spread out around her. Cracked and blackened skin stretched across her frame except at the joints where the white bones showed through. The lips had shriveled away from the teeth giving her a rictal, death-mask grin, and the sightless, eyeless sockets still stared upward. Only the thick main of blond hair seemed untouched by time.

"That's really gross," said Wendell.

"Shut up, Wendell," said Ann. "This is the saddest thing I've ever seen." A thin gold chain looped around the corpse's neck, holding a locket that rested on her chest. Ann unclasped it. It held a miniature portrait of a handsome young man. "Her prince. I wonder if he ever came."

"Probably downstairs in the pile of bones."

"He looks like you," said Wendell.

"I'm better looking." Charming's eyes were still fixed on the corpse. His brow furrowed as though wrestling with a weighty problem.

Wendell checked the stairway. It was like opening the door to a blacksmith's furnace. He slammed it shut again. Ashes that blew in settled to the floor. "Sire, I think we have to get out of here."

"I'm not going to do it," said Charming, loudly and suddenly.

"What?"

"Kiss the girl. I'm not going to do it."

"Of course not," said Ann. "What are you talking about?"

"Kiss the girl. Break the spell. What Mandelbaum said."

"Oh, for goodness sake! She's dead. She's not sleeping, Charming. Whatever spell was cast over her is long past breaking."

"Right," said Charming, but his voice lacked conviction. "She's dead. A lifeless bag of bones. A dried-out husk. No way she's going to be revived. Right, Wendell?"

"Well," said Wendell hesitantly, "Mandelbaum said . . ."

"I don't believe you two," said Ann. "You have to be really sick even to think about kissing this . . . thing."

"Yeah, right," said the Prince. "Stupid idea. Well, I guess we better get out of here." He didn't move, though. Neither did Wendell.

"Well, what are we waiting for? Let's go."

"But, it is my duty."

"Don't be stupid."

"You never wanted me to kiss her anyway, did you? You were jealous."

"Oh, for goodness sake!" Ann stamped away from the bed. "I assure you I'm not jealous now. Go ahead and kiss the darn thing, already. This is too disgusting to argue about any further."

Charming approached the bed and knelt by its side. He leaned over the corpse. Empty sockets stared at him. Teeth grinned mirthlessly. He pursed his lips and lowered his head.

"What if it really wakes up?" said Wendell.

"This is grotesque; this is really grotesque," said Ann.

The Prince snapped his head up. "This is my job. You're not making it any easier. Suppose it was you on this bed. Would you want me to quit before I'd examined every recourse?"

"I'm not going to watch this." Ann turned away and stared out the window.

"Fine." The Prince took a deep breath and held it, closed his eyes, and pressed his lips to the corpse.

In a flash the bony arms folded around his neck and locked his head in place.

"Mmmmph! Mmmmph!" Charming flailed his arms in panic, his face still pressed against the monstrosity. He grabbed the shoulder bones and pushed, but the skeleton held him in an iron grip. "Mmmph!"

Ann still had her back to him. "Oh, you're getting

off on this, eh? I knew from the first day we met you were some kind of pervert. . . ."

The skeleton had wrapped its legs around Charming's waist and pulled him onto the bed with superhuman strength. Wendell, too, had leaped on the bed and was trying to pry the bony fingers off Charming's neck. The Prince got his hands into the ghoul's blond hair and tried to pull the face off him. Instead the jaws opened and something wet and squirmy emerged from between the teeth and penetrated his mouth. "Ooooomph!" In a frenzy of disgust the Prince rolled off the bed, carrying Wendell and the skeleton with him. The three of them landed in a heap on the floor, Wendell on the bottom, Charming on top of him, and the blond girl sitting on his chest.

The blond girl. She released her grip on the Prince and Charming sat up just in time to see the last of the restoration. The color returned to her cheeks; her eyes turned red, then white, then pale blue; her lips grew full and pink; the luster returned to her hair; the flesh blossomed beneath her dress. It all happened in an instant and Prince Charming found himself looking into the eyes of the young, beautiful, and very much alive Princess Aurora.

". . . and I suppose when you're not engaging in necrophilia you're off fondling farm animals," continued Ann. She was still looking out the window.

Charming stared at Aurora. Her eyes were bright as the day. Her teeth shone like pearls in moonlight. She ran the tip of a small pink tongue across her lips and stared back at the Prince.

Then she opened her mouth and screamed bloody murder.

Ann jumped a foot in the air. She turned around in time to see a lithe blond teen-ager leap onto the fourposter and burrow under the coverlet. A very frightened face emerged from the far corner. "Who are you?" her voice quavered. "What are you doing in my bedroom? Get out or I'll scream for help."

"You already did," said Wendell.

"Shush," said Charming. Reflexively, he started to give her the smile. Then he caught himself, conjuring up a quick mental image of what the girl was seeing. Three total strangers suddenly appearing, their clothes torn and disheveled, and their faces grimy with soot. No wonder the babe was freaking out. The Prince stood up, dusted off his hands and said briskly, "There's a fire, ma'am. King's orders; we have to evacuate. Don't worry; everything is under control." He strode forward, took her hand authoritatively and pulled her out of bed.

"Fire?" She was looking at the smoke seeping under the door.

"Don't worry about that smoke, all being taken care of," said Charming, dragging her over to the window. "Here you go, just step up onto the sill here."

"Did it start in the kitchen? We can move the reception out to the garden . . . YAAAAAaaaaaaaahhhhhh . . ." There was a muffled splash as she hit the water.

"Great, a screamer. You probably like that kind, too," said Ann.

"Don't get catty. Come on; you're next. Unless you'd like to try your luck with the stairs." Ann came forward and he hoisted her on to the window sill.

"You don't have to push me. I can jump by myself." She looked down at the sparkling water of the moat, fifty feet below, and Aurora splashing towards the banks. "On second thought, maybe you'd better push me." The Prince obliged and she dropped into the water, feet first. Wendell went next, executing a half twist on the way down. He surfaced and waved upward.

"Showoff," called Charming. He jumped after them and hit the water hard, the impact and shock of the cold water knocking the wind out of him. "Ooof." He kicked his way to the surface, shook the water out of his eyes and swam to shore. Wendell and Ann were pulling Aurora out of the water. Aurora was crying frantically.

"There's a fire! The castle's on fire! My Prince is in there! My Papa's in there! Oh, why isn't anyone doing something?"

"Time to clear out of here," the Prince told Wendell and Ann. They nodded. He picked up Aurora and began trotting toward the ice bridge. "Sorry, Princess, but you're going to have to trust us for a while."

Aurora twisted in his arms. "Let me go! We've got to help them!"

"We'll get help from the village," the Prince said. "For now, you're coming with us."

Aurora drew back her arm, closed one hand into a small fist, and punched Charming in the nose.

"Ow." The blow didn't hurt the Prince so much as surprise him and Aurora took advantage of this to squirm out of his grip. Evading his reach, she ran back towards the drawbridge, her white dress trailing behind her, shouting, "Help, fire! Help, fire!" Charming ran after her. Then the dragon came out of the castle.

Aurora suddenly reversed direction and passed Charming like a comet in a lace dress. "Aaiiiyyeee!" She caught up with and passed Ann and Wendell, who were headed towards the ice bridge at speed. Charming took up the rear, followed by the dragon. The hilt of Charming's sword still protruded from its head and blood was flowing freely down its face. It was staggering a bit, but there was still plenty of fight and meanness left in it.

Aurora reached the ice bridge and started up like a spawning salmon. The ice was melting rapidly by this time and the steps were wet and slick. They had also become rounded and irregular. She got about fifteen feet up before her feet slipped from under her and she slid back down, plowing into Ann, who had arrived at the bottom. They eventually formed a tight little group, with Ann and Aurora frantically scrambling up the slippery stairs in front, while Wendell and Charming, whose hobnailed boots afforded a better purchase, pushed up from the bottom. Thus they had progressed some thirty steps up the bridge when the dragon arrived.

Charming hadn't really believed the animal would try to follow them up the ice bridge. He had underestimated his foe. Fortunately the dragon started out by sending a prolonged torrent of flame in their direction. They were quite out of range, but the heat did have the effect of obliterating the lower rungs of stairs. The dragon made several false starts and slid back down. Charming and company put another ten feet of distance between them. Then, slowly and deliberately, the beast dug its claws into the ice. The two-inch hooks penetrated the bridge more surely than a mountaineer's ax. Slowly, a foot at a time, the animal began to drag itself up the frozen path.

Charming looked down and saw the beast approaching. He gave the girls an extra shove. "We've got company. Let's move it." Whereupon he promptly lost his footing and slipped down five steps. He scrambled back up. "I'm okay. Let's go."

They began a desperate race. Melted water from the upper steps ran past their feet. When they stumbled, as happened frequently, their clothing soaked through with icy run-off. The humans made slow but steady progress and the dragon did the same. They maintained their lead for a while, sometimes losing ground, sometimes gaining it, but the girls began to tire. The dragon seemed to have inexhaustible supplies of energy. The humans had numb feet. Little by little the beast closed the gap.

They reached the top of the arch. Charming stopped the group and looked back. The dragon was perhaps forty feet away. It glared at him with its one good eye and growled low and menacingly. Charming edged to the front of the line. "Okay, we're on the down side. Once that dragon tops the rise, all he has to do is let go to fall right on top of us. We've got to be off this iceberg before he reaches the top."

"We're moving as fast as we can," said Ann. Aurora said nothing. She just looked at the approaching dragon and shuddered.

"Right," said Charming. "So here's what we're going to do. We're going to sit down like we're on a toboggan and slide down the ice ramp. It will be bumpy, but I figure our bottoms will be so numb we'll hardly feel it."

"It's a steep drop," said Ann. "We'll be moving pretty fast."

"I'll go in front and try to break our fall. Wendell, you get behind me." Ann sat down behind Wendell and wrapped her legs around his waist. Aurora took her gaze from the dragon, now perhaps twenty steps down, and silently took up the rear. "Ready. Let's go."

Ann would long remember this ride as one of the more unpleasant experiences of her young life. They started out fast and rapidly picked up speed. Charming and Wendell tried to limit the speed of their descent by pressing their boots against the side of the bridge but this had little effect. Ice is a hard substance with no ability to cushion a fall whatsoever; each step was a bone-jarring thump that Ann could feel all the way up her spine. She clenched her teeth, afraid that she would accidentally bite off her tongue from the impact. The bumps came faster and faster, but no less jarring. Soon the surface of the ice was whizzing by in a white blur. Droplets of cold water flew up and stung her face. She held Wendell's shoulders in a death grip and felt Aurora's nails digging into her own skin. Ahead, she saw the edge of the thorn bushes, and the patiently waiting figure of Mandelbaum looming rapidly larger. The ground rushed up at them. As the wind roared past her ears, she thought she heard Wendell say something like, "Wow, this is great!" and then they hit.

Charming took the brunt of the impact, the other three coming down pretty much on top of him. Fortunate he was, indeed, that the ground, churned up at that point by the activities of men and horses and soaked with ice melt, was mostly mud. It did a lot to cushion his fall so, when the others rolled off, he was able to lay there, winded and gasping and heavily bruised, but with no broken bones. Mandelbaum, perplexed and concerned, helped drag him from the mud and felt all over for fractures. "What was that crazy stunt for?"

Charming tried to speak but couldn't find his breath. He pointed his arm up the ice bridge. The move sent arrows of pain into his shoulder. Mandelbaum, instead of looking in the direction he was pointing, began to examine his hand for injuries.

"Dragon," said Wendell helpfully, starting to recover. Charming nodded vigorously.

"Ah," said Mandelbaum.

He looked to the top of the ice bridge. The dragon was standing at the peak, four sets of claws dug into the ice, lips pulled back from snarling teeth. It cast its head about, looked straight at them, opened its mouth wide, and let out an earth-shaking roar that reverberated through the woods. Ann and Aurora, who had been sitting on the muddy ground nursing their bruises, staggered to their feet and made a half-hearted run for the shelter of the trees. The dragon lowered its head and started its slide down the ice bridge.

Calmly, Mandelbaum took the pipe from his mouth and tapped the stem against the bridge.

Instantly it disintegrated into a fine spray of water droplets.

The dragon showed not the least surprise as its foothold melted away beneath its feet. Aggressive to the last, it launched itself towards its intended victims. Then, feet flailing wildly, it descended into the thicket with a roar and a crash. All was silent.

Charming staggered to his feet. Ann came over and put her arm around his waist. "Well, that takes care of him."

She was interrupted by a roar from inside the thorn hedge. Charming sighed and disentangled her arm. "That has got to be the toughest dragon I've ever faced." He limped over to one of the duffel bags and took out some thick wooden poles. These turned out to be pieces of an oak lance, whose wooden sections fitted into hammered-metal ferrules.

Wendell nodded. "I'll get your horse."

Ann said, "Do you really think he can get out of the thorns?"

"He got in, didn't he? I guess it depends on how smashed up he is."

They could hear the dragon thrashing about inside the hedge, and occasionally puffs of smoke would drift over from where he set the thorns on fire. The thrashing and the roars grew quickly fainter, however, and by the time Wendell returned with a horse, the forest was silent.

Charming picked a dry grassy spot and sat down. "Maybe that's the end of him. I hope so. I really hate dragons. That's the worst part of this job."

"I'm hungry," said Wendell. "I'm really starved."

"Ah, excuse me," said Mandelbaum. "I think someone should be paying attention to the newest member of our little group. That, I take it, is the long-lost Princess Aurora?"

Charming, Ann, and Wendell turned and looked.

Aurora was standing some little distance away, leaning against a tree, looking very lost and forlorn. She was holding her stomach.

"Is she okay?" asked Wendell.

As they watched, she leaned over and threw up violently.

"I guess not," said Charming. "Maybe it's just nerves. Poor kid. She's been through one hell of a shock."

"She's pregnant," said Ann.

The Princess Aurora was having a really bad week.

She was descending the stairs when she was overcome by a spell of intense dizziness. "Not to worry," she told herself. "You're just overly excited. It is, after all, your wedding day." She told her maid to go on downstairs (didn't the girl look a little unwell, too, come to think of it?) and Aurora staggered back to her alcove to lay down on the bed. "I'll just close my eyes for a minute and the feeling will pass." And it did pass. She had a pleasant daydream about her wedding night in which she let her new husband do very naughty things to her and was just finishing him off with a really heart-and-soul kiss, when she awoke to find herself straddling a strange boy who looked like a chimney sweep. (A cute chimney sweep, she later decided.) What happened after that, the fire and the dragon, she didn't even want to think about anymore. In fact, she was doing her best to block out the memory right now. Several times in the last few days she had nearly convinced herself that she was still having a bad dream. There were certain things she couldn't block out, though, certain unpleasant truths that she had been stubbornly pushing to the back recesses of her brain until she felt better equipped to deal with them.

And the time to deal with them was now. She had

been riding for four days and she supposed she had better straighten things out in her mind before they got to wherever they were going. She looked at her companions. The old wizard and the young boy rode in front, the young boy asking constantly about spells and magicks, about warlocks and werewolves. The old wizard would sometimes answer at length and with amusement, but often he would simply suck on his pipe and stare reflectively into space, letting the horse follow the trail while he tuned out the world and thought. Prince Charming rode behind him, but periodically would drop back to see that Aurora was getting along okay. The Prince was dressed in all new clothes, silks and such, and with his face washed and his hair brushed, he looked very handsome indeed. He was quite friendly and personable and undoubtedly very brave. Under better circumstances, Aurora would have fallen for him in an instant. The circumstances were not better, however, and then there was the question of the girl.

At first Aurora had thought she was a maid, but then had learned that she wasn't. Aurora wasn't quite sure who she was, except that she was the most beautiful girl Aurora had ever seen, with lustrous black hair, deep dark eyes, and flawless skin. Ann was very kind to Aurora, too, helping her with her horse and inquiring solicitously after her welfare. But she stuck to the Prince like glue, Aurora noticed, and whenever he dropped back to chat with her, Ann would move in and casually include herself in the conversation. Smooth, very smooth, although with looks like that she surely didn't have to worry much about competition. "Some other time," thought Aurora, "I would have given her some competition."

All right, enough of that. Time to face facts. Time to admit the brutal truth. Time to forget the past, accept the present, and plan for the future.

Time to have a good long cry.

No, she'd done that already.

Maybe she was still dreaming.

Okay, so what were the facts? Her father was dead. Her fiancé was dead. Everybody she knew was dead. Her home was destroyed. Her kingdom was annexed. Her clothes were burned up. Her shoes were out of fashion. She was twenty years behind the times.

And she was pregnant. Can't forget that.

Try to look on the bright side.

She tried not to think of Garrison. He was dead after all. Had been dead for twenty years. Devoured by the dragon, his bones baked in the fire, while little Garrison slept inside her.

It wasn't his fault, really. Wait a minute, of course it was. It had to be somebody's fault and it certainly wasn't hers. True, she had contrived to meet him in the garden, but that was simply out of curiosity to see what he looked like. Both their parents had seen no reason why the bride and groom should meet before the wedding day. Bad for discipline. All she had known was that he was the prince of something (of course) and that he had a lot of land (of course) and they said he was attractive, too. She had declined to take her father's word for that.

And then behind the rose bushes, he had taken her in his arms and borne her gently to the ground. She had struggled—hadn't she struggled?—yes, of course she had, she must have—she had struggled but to no avail. She wanted to cry out but he just kept kissing her and kissing her and, really, she wished he would stop; she hadn't actually said no but everyone knew that nice girls like her didn't do that sort of thing. It was all his fault for being so gentle. He deserved to die. Served him right for what he did to her.

She would name the baby after him.

"Try and look on the bright side," said Ann, bringing

her horse up beside her. Aurora was a little surprised. It was the first time Ann had spoken to her without the Prince being there.

"Oh, yes. Just which bright side is that? There's been so much good news flying at me from all directions that I hardly know what piece of information to contemplate next."

"Sorry, I didn't mean to sound platitudinous. But you're alive, aren't you? You had quite a bit of luck being sealed up in that tower when the spell took hold, but it couldn't have lasted forever. Sooner or later you'd have been gnawed on by rats or something."

"How cheerful you are. I can tell you're just the life of the party everywhere you go."

"Listen, before we reach the castle we'll stop in the city and buy some new clothes. That will make you feel better. It always makes me feel better."

"I don't have any money."

"Actually, neither do I. Well, we can window shop. Oh dear, I'm going to have to show up at the castle Illyria dressed like this. I was hoping to make a better first impression."

"What? You've never been there?"

"Oh, no. The Prince and I traveled straight from my castle to yours. We were on a quest for a fertility grail. My stepmother had traced an ancient one to the site of your castle."

"Fertility grail!" Aurora laughed bitterly. "That would explain a lot, all right. We're a fertile bunch. The girls in my kingdom can hardly pop their cherries without getting knocked up."

"Um," said Ann uncomfortably. She was not used to this kind of frank talk. "Well . . ."

"You were wasting your time, though. I never heard any mention of a grail. Daddy wasn't really into cults and things, or even collecting antiques."

"Well, my stepmother has been wrong before.

When it comes to the black arts, her reach very often exceeds her grasp."

"Your stepmother, huh? Your real mother is dead?"

"She died in childbirth. My father died a few years ago."

"My mother died in childbirth also."

"So did Prince Charming's. He's kind of touchy about it."

"Everybody's mother is dead. Is childbirth as debilitating as all that?"

"Mandelbaum says it's because royal families can afford personal physicians and the very best medical care. Consequently, they die like flies."

"Ah. A cynical man."

"I don't think so. I think he was just speaking his mind."

For a while they rode on in silence. It was an uncomfortable situation for Ann. Her life had included few girls her own age and none of her own social status. Aurora was the first girl she'd ever met that she could speak with as an equal. Although her mind was surely burdened with troublesome thoughts and she had a sardonic manner of speaking, there was no doubt she was intelligent and well bred. And yet, Aurora was very wicked, the kind of girl Ann had been told she should never associate with. Sometime in the past, she had actually let a boy *do things* to her. The very idea was repellent to Ann. Also fascinating.

"So," said Aurora, looking straight ahead. "What's with you and this Charming fellow?"

"What do you mean?"

"I mean, you like him, right?"

"Of course not!" said Ann. She blushed. She could feel herself blushing, which embarrassed her and caused her face to redden even more. "I don't like him. I mean, of course I like him, but I don't *like* him."

"Sure," said Aurora. "What's there to like? Just because he's cute, smart, brave, famous, and rich is no reason to fall for a boy. I don't know what you *could* see in him."

"I'll thank you not to put words in my mouth. And he's not so much."

"So you don't have the hots for him?"

"I've never had the hots for anyone," said Ann with dignity. "That's not something that happens to nice girls. Prince Charming and I were simply thrown together for the duration of this quest by some rather special circumstances."

"I see," Aurora said and lapsed into silence.

There was something about the tone of that "I see," that Ann didn't like. But Aurora would not be drawn into further conversation. After a while Ann drew her horse away. She kept, however, a suspicious watch on Aurora from the corner of her eyes.

Her suspicion was justified for the wheels were turning in the little blonde's head and strange numbers were turning up. Her conclusions, once organized, went something like this.

I am totally without resources, she thought, until I regain the Kingdom of Alacia, which now rightfully belongs to me.

The King of Illyria has annexed my land and, historically, kings don't give up territory without a fight, regardless of the validity of their claim to it.

The prospect of an adolescent unwed mother raising an army to defeat a powerful king is so small as to be ludicrous.

However.

Aurora looked at the Prince speculatively.

Perhaps there was another path of opportunity open to her.

Wendell pulled his horse over next to Charming's. "Princess Aurora sure is pretty, right?"

"Yeah," said the Prince. "Nice tits."

"Aha! I knew it! I knew you couldn't make it all the way back to the castle without saying something about her breasts. I'm surprised you managed to hold off until now."

"Sheer will power."

"Yeah, right. Well, you wanted to meet a bad girl and now you've got one. I'll bet you're happy."

"Aurora is a nice girl, Wendell."

"But she's pregnant."

"Right. That means she's a mother and all mothers are saints. Even unwed ones, and they are always treated with deference and respect, except by other women. That's just the way it is."

"You just said she had nice tits. That's not respectful."

"So? She wasn't listening."

Mandelbaum, who had been silent for several hours, dropped his horse back and joined the group. "Your Highness, it occurs to me we had perhaps best slow our pace. At this rate, we will reach the castle well before nightfall."

"Is that a problem?"

"Well, your Highness, with all respect, you have not considered the ramifications incurred by riding into the city with a pregnant companion."

"Hey! That's not my doing."

"Yes, yes, of course not, but you must think about your image. You ride off and disappear for a month and then suddenly you ride back into town with a beautiful young woman who's just about a month pregnant. Well, certainly there will be at least the appearance of impropriety."

"Oh, come on. You were around right from the first time I even heard about Aurora. And I had Ann and Wendell with me the whole time."

"Prince Charming, I am not trying to be difficult, I am simply trying to advise you of the situation as I see it. It is not I who needs to be convinced of the purity of your intent, it is your constituency. And I am afraid that they will not consider a page and a sixteen-year-old girl to be adequate chaperones."

"How about you?"

"Wizards are generally regarded with suspicion even in the best of circumstances. Our deeds may be admired or feared, but our oaths command little respect. A chaperone, in order to command credibility, must be a middle-aged couple or a porcine adult woman."

"This is crazy. I've rescued beautiful babes all over the twenty kingdoms and escorted them home. And I've never laid a hand on them."

"They wouldn't let you," said Wendell.

"Those babes, as you call them, did not arrive home pregnant. The popular curiosity well understands the laws of cause and effect. When they see the effect on young Aurora, they will naturally look for a cause. I fear the gossipmongers will decide a living Prince makes a much better scandal than one who has been dead for twenty years."

Charming thought this over. "I think you're underestimating the people, Mandelbaum. They're not that simple-minded. But even granted that your fears are valid, wouldn't it still be better to ride boldly in broad daylight, like we have nothing to hide, which we don't, then to skulk in at night like a bunch of, uh, things that skulk?"

"I would prefer that we gamble on the possibility of scandal than confront the certainty of it."

"It won't make a difference either way," said Wendell. "All the maids in the castle and the servants and the guards and the soldiers will talk about it anyway."

"That's right," said the Prince. "I really don't think Dad's going to hide her away in a locked tower. We'll just have to brazen it out."

"Brazen what out?" said Ann. She and Aurora had ridden up beside them for this last exchange. This left five horses riding abreast on a trail meant for three at the most, so Mandelbaum and Wendell had to drop back. Their horses snorted impatiently.

The Prince explained. "We were trying to decide whether to sneak Aurora into the castle under the cloak of darkness or just ride forth in broad daylight. Do you think people will really know if you're pregnant? You don't look pregnant."

"Women can always tell these things," said Ann.

Princess Aurora tossed her hair back proudly. "I am the Princess of Alacia," she stated with dignity. "Regardless of what transgressions I may have to answer for, I am still the Princess of Alacia, and I will not go skulking about like some sort of sneak thief."

"Okay, that decides it," said Charming. "We'll just have to walk tall."

"Wait," said Ann, "Here's an idea. Why don't we just pretend she's married?"

"What?" said the Prince. Aurora looked at Ann quizzically.

"Oh, come on," said Ann. "The idea must have occurred to you, too. Look, nobody really knows what happened back there. It was twenty years ago, for goodness sakes. And the castle's a smoking ruin. If we say the spell didn't kick in until a few hours after the wedding, leaving plenty of time for the eager newlyweds to head upstairs and consummate their marriage, well, who's going to say different?"

"It'll never fly," said Aurora, but her voice left no doubt she was mulling over the idea.

"Sure, why not?" said Charming. "It's believable. I know the first thing I'll want to do after I get married is to . . ." Both girls looked at him. ". . . check to see if my wife is okay," he finished lamely.

"I don't like this," objected Wendell. "If something

like this came out, it would make the Prince look
really bad. Why should he risk his reputation to save
a girl's?"

"It's my job to save girls, reputations and all.
Besides," he took Wendell aside, "if I have to choose
between protecting my own honor and protecting the
honor of a lady, then the honorable thing to do is to
sacrifice my own honor to defend the lady's honor,
even if she has dishonored herself already. You see?"

Wendell shook his head.

"Well, take my word for it. Okay, so we don't need
a marriage certificate because that would have been
burned up in the fire. And all the people who were
there are dead, except Aurora. Yes, we ought to be
able to slip you a ring, coordinate our stories and just
bluff this one out."

Aurora was brightening up. "Do you really think
this will work?"

"I know some dwarves who can get us a pretty good
deal on a rock," said Ann. "But it will still have to be
set."

"There, you see," said Wendell. "Where are you
going to get a ring? A ring for a princess has got to
be something pretty special. You'll have to have it
made up by a jeweler. So that's one more person in
on the secret."

"What happened to your engagement ring?" asked
Ann.

"In the strong box at the castle. I wonder if it sur-
vived the fire."

"Wait a minute," said the Prince. "We don't need
an engagement ring. Those are the ones with the big
diamonds. We need a wedding ring. We'll just get a
plain gold band from the royal jeweler. He's got plenty
and any sort of story will satisfy him."

Mandelbaum, who had been silent through all this,

now coughed discreetly. "Your Highness, may I have a word with you?"

"Sure thing." The Prince and Mandelbaum rode off a little ways from the group. Mandelbaum drew on his pipe, exhaled, and contemplated the cloud of smoke as it drifted away. Charming waited patiently.

"Your Highness, it disturbs me to see a young man who has been well schooled in the practice of honesty and virtue agree so readily to this subterfuge. While I have oft noted your unwholesome proclivities toward the fairer sex, I am still surprised that you should let a pretty face turn your head this easily." Charming started to say something, but Mandelbaum held up his hand. "However, that's neither here nor there. What concerns me now is my own role in this deception. As a member of the royal court, and one who accepts the King's coin, my first loyalty is to your father. May I ask if you intend to lie to him also? And, if so, do you expect me to withhold information from him?"

"Gee, Mandelbaum, you're awfully straitlaced all of a sudden. Must be all that military support work you've been doing. I always thought you were more easygoing."

Mandelbaum said, "Hummph." Then he said, "That is not an answer."

"Mandelbaum, I'm just trying to protect the girl from being hassled. So I lie a little. I'm not committing high treason here. Besides, you were talking before about me protecting my own reputation. This gets me off the hook, also."

"I simply suggested that we ride in at night to minimize public attention. Presenting an elaborate charade to the court is not what I had in mind."

"Oh, first you tell me the public is not going to accept the truth and then you advise me to stick to it. What do you want me to do? Dress her in sackcloth and ashes and drag her through the streets?"

"There are several nunneries within a day's ride that would provide her with adequate food and shelter, as well as the opportunity to serve penance for her moral turpitude."

"Moral turpitude! Now you are getting totally unreasonable. There is no way I'm sending Aurora to a nunnery and she wouldn't go along with it if I tried. Come on, Mandelbaum. She's just a girl who made a mistake."

"How do you know she made a mistake? Have you discussed this with her?"

"Well, no. You can't talk about those things to a girl."

"Exactly. So there's no telling what sort of deviant behaviors she's been practicing. And you shouldn't let Ann get too friendly with her, either. You have a responsibility to prevent her from being influenced by bad companions."

"I'm not going to continue this absurd line of discussion any longer. All right, Mandelbaum, I'll make you a proposition. As soon as we get back, I'll arrange for Aurora to have an audience with Dad. We'll let him decide what we're going to do with her. Until then, you play along with us. How's that?"

"Well . . ."

"Come on, Mandelbaum. Think of the little kid. Do you want him to grow up under a mantle of stigma? It's not his fault."

"Oh, very well. But if his Highness asks me anything, I am telling him the truth."

"You've got a deal." Charming wheeled his horse around and went back to join the others. "Okay, ladies, the game is on. Aurora, from now on you're a widow."

"We should really stop, then, and get her some black clothes," said Ann.

"I should have known," said the Prince. "No matter

what you chose to do, girls will somehow work shopping into it."

"The clothes don't matter," said Aurora. "I just want to start rebuilding my life. Prince Charming, I can't thank you enough for all you're doing for me."

She looked up at him with eyes that were suddenly soft and devoted, putting her hand on his arm. She kept it there. Ann instantly decided she didn't like that gesture one bit.

"You sure have a nice place," said Ann, looking over the gleaming floors and woodwork, the glow of the brass doorknobs in the lamplight.

"Oh, yes," said Charming. "These are the walls, that's the ceiling. Boy, this place has everything."

It was late evening when they arrived at the castle. As planned, much of the staff had already retired and the kitchen was closed. Still, there were servants enough to prepare rooms for Ann and Aurora; Wendell, of course, saw to the horses and baggage. There was a bustle of activity as the group of travelers and servants separated and Prince Charming, returning to his own quarters, found himself walking down a deserted hallway with the raven-haired Princess.

"Did you find your room comfortable?" he asked.

"Oh, yes," said Ann. "Yes, it was fine. Very comfortable. Luxurious even. Yes, it was very nice. Yes."

"Well, that's good. I am glad you like your room. I mean, all the rooms here are pretty nice, but if you prefer another room, then you can have one. Or you can just stay where you are. Whatever you want."

"No, it's fine. Really."

"Well, good."

They continued to walk together. Charming thought his bootsteps on the wooden floors sounded unnaturally loud.

"So," said Ann. "You live here, right?" It well

ranked as one of the stupider questions ever asked and she realized it.

"Uh, right," said Charming, feeling like an idiot for not coming up with anything more clever to say. It was with some relief that he reached the door to his room.

"Well, here I am," he said, his hand on the knob. "Guess I'll see you in the morning."

"Yes," said Ann. "Well, pleasant dreams."

"You, too," said the Prince. "I'd invite you in, but of course it wouldn't look right, having a girl in my room."

"Oh, no," said Ann. "That night at the inn was an exceptional case. No, I couldn't possibly enter a man's bedroom alone."

"No," said the Prince. He pushed open the door and she followed him in. "No, there would be all sorts of a row raised."

"Right," said Ann. "Even though we aren't doing anything, of course."

"Right."

They stood in the center of Charming's bedchamber, about three feet apart, not meeting each other's eyes. The Prince made an awkward gesture with his hand. "I guess it's okay as long as we leave the door open."

"Good idea. We don't want anyone to see us together like this, but after all, we don't want to be together where no one can see us."

"That's just what I was thinking," said the Prince, kicking the door closed with his foot. Ann made no move to stop him. They stood apart in silence for a few minutes more.

"Nice room," said Ann.

"Yeah, I like it. There's a little balcony over there where you can step out and look at the stars."

"Oh, how nice. Do you look at the stars very often?"

"No, never. But if I want to, there's the balcony."

More silence.

"Well, I guess I better be going back to my room now," said Ann. "I don't even know why I came in." She took a step toward the Prince.

"Yeah, it's probably best if you don't stay any longer," said the Prince. He took a step toward Ann. His arm found its way around her waist and he pulled her close. Her breath caught in her throat. She closed her eyes and turned her face towards his.

There came a knock at the door. "Oh," said Ann and jumped a foot backward. The Prince broke away and stuck his hands in his pockets. The knock sounded again.

Charming flirted briefly with the idea of pretending he wasn't home and then said, "Come in."

The door opened and Aurora entered. "Oh," she said when she saw Ann. "What are you doing here?"

"What are *you* doing here?"

"What are *you* doing here?"

"I just came in to say good night to Prince Charming."

"Why, that's all that I came to do," said Aurora. She walked over to Charming and put her arm through his. She was wearing a nightdress she had gotten from somewhere and Charming could not help noticing the top two buttons were undone. Ann noticed this also and not with pleasure.

Aurora said, "My room is very pleasant, Prince Charming. You have a lovely castle."

"Uh, thanks."

"That's a silly thing to say to him," said Ann. "He didn't decorate it."

Aurora said sweetly. "I'm sure he didn't tailor his own clothes either, but I may still tell him he looks very handsome in them."

"Um, thanks again," said the Prince. He glanced from Ann to Aurora with a vague feeling that storm clouds were gathering. Ann had her lips set in a thin, tight line and was tapping one foot on the floor. Aurora looked like she hadn't a care in the world which was rather odd for a girl who only a few hours previously was acting about as depressed as one could get.

He said, "Tomorrow I'll see about getting you an audience with Dad. It may take a day or so, but that's okay. There's plenty to do around here, shopping and the theatre and that sort of girl stuff. Oh, and here." He slapped his pockets and produced a small ring. "I found a gold band for you." Aurora batted her eyelashes and held out her hand. Charming was about to slip on the ring when he glanced sidelong at Ann and saw a fleeting look of deep gravity cross her face. He hesitated a second and then pushed the ring into Aurora's palm. "Here you go. Don't worry about returning it. We have a million trinkets like these. Relics of past conquests and all that."

"Well, I appreciate it just the same," said Aurora. She turned to Ann. "And I appreciate all your kind words and friendship, too, Ann."

Ann summoned up her best honey-coated voice. "Why, it was a pleasure to be of help, Aurora."

"I suppose, now that your quest is over, you'll be returning to your own kingdom?"

"I suppose so," said Ann. She really hadn't thought about returning home until now. She would have no fertility grail with which to help the peasants. Being with her stepmother again was depressing enough in itself, but the idea of leaving Prince Charming left her with a sinking feeling, although she really couldn't say why.

"Well, I'm sorry you can't stay longer," continued Aurora. "But there's really no reason for you to stick around, is there? And you probably have so much to do at home."

"I suppose so."

"Oh, hey, what's the big hurry?" said Charming. "Stick around a while. Take a holiday. As I said, there's plenty to do in Illyria, all sorts of parties and balls and banquets. What's so important at home that a few more days won't matter?"

"No, really, I must be going . . ." said Ann.

"She probably misses her boyfriend," Aurora whispered to Charming. His face fell.

". . . but if you insist, I suppose I might stay a few days," Ann finished loudly.

"Hey, great, terrific! Okay, well, I'll see you both in the morning, I guess. Good night."

"Good night," said Ann.

"Good night," said Aurora.

Neither girl made the slightest attempt at movement. Aurora maintained her grip on Charming's arm. Ann stood with her feet firmly planted on the floor. The honeyed tones had dropped from their voices and they were now glaring at each other with open hostility.

"Good night," said the Prince again. "I guess you'll both be getting back to your rooms now."

Neither Princess said a word, but continued to wait for the other girl to leave first. Charming looked from one to the other, mystified. This could have gone on all night, but fortunately there came yet another knock at the door. "Come in," said the Prince with relief.

Wendell burst in. "Good evening, Sire. Oh, hello, Aurora. Hi, Ann."

"Hello, Wendell," everybody chorused.

"I rousted up one of the cooks and got him to make us a snack. There is toast and eggs and bacon and kippers and sausage. Also, there's fresh gingerbread."

"Sounds good, Wendell. I'll be down in a minute."

"I don't think I'm hungry," said Aurora. "I believe I'll turn in now."

"But there's gingerbread," said Wendell incredulously.

"Not tonight, thanks. Good night." She left with a backward glance at the Prince.

"I'll join you in a few minutes," said Ann. She left also.

"What's eating those two?" said Wendell.

The Prince shrugged.

"Girls," said Wendell distastefully. "Oh, I almost forgot. Norville wants to see you first thing tomorrow."

"Tell him I'm not back yet."

"He already knows you're back."

"Tell him I'm sick."

"He says it's real important."

"It always is. Let's eat."

"Okay. We have to hurry, though. Mandelbaum is going to mix up some new potions tonight for keeping starlings away from grain fields and he said I could help him. It has something to do with live bats. He has them flying into his tower. Won't that be neat?"

"Sounds great. You've been spending a lot of time with Mandelbaum lately, Wendell. Are you planning to go into sorcery instead of becoming a knight?"

"Oh, no. I just think magic is, you know, really neat. Mandelbaum said he'd consider me for a sorceror's apprentice, but I said no. Magic is pretty cool, but it's not as good as riding across the kingdoms and fighting with swords and slaying things, and you don't get to wear armor and you don't get a title. And it's just years and years of studying out of books and practicing self-discipline and mind exercises. Besides, when I told him how much you depended on me, he knew that you needed me to be your squire."

"Right."

"Sorcerers get to do some pretty awesome stuff, though. Maybe I could be a knight *and* a wizard. Hey, that would be wild. A knight who could also work magic. I'd be the most famous knight in the twenty kingdoms."

"Just remember there are more important things in life than fame and glory, Wendell."

"Sure. You mean like truth, justice, honor and family?"

"Actually, I meant like getting laid. But those, too."

They went downstairs and were joined on the way by Ann. She had changed out of her nightdress, back into the simple black dresses with lace trim that she usually wore. They went to a small dining alcove that spun off one of the many hallways. Charming was silent. It had been a long day and a tiring ride. He wanted simply to have a relaxing meal and go to bed. It was not to be.

When they entered the dining room, Queen Ruby was sitting inside.

To say the three travelers were surprised would be an understatement of monumental proportions. Wendell's mouth dropped open. Ann turned pale. All three were struck dumb, but it was the Prince who was the first to recover. "Ah, Queen Ruby, how good to see you again. What pleasant course of circumstance brings you to Illyria?"

The Wicked Queen was dressed in her usual black. She wore a tight black silk blouse with pearl buttons, black jodhpur pants, the spiked-heeled boots, of course, and black lace fingerless gloves, elbow length, the overall effect being both sexy and sinister. She had been sitting at the table buttering a scone, but when the Prince spoke, she rose to her feet and addressed him severely.

"Cut the chatter, Charming. I want to know where that grail is."

"What are you doing here?" demanded Ann.

"What are you doing here is more the question, young lady. I don't recall any stayovers in Illyria being part of your itinerary. Not that I'm surprised. I knew from the start you wouldn't keep your end of the bargain, Charming. I came here because I knew you'd try to keep that grail for yourself. That is, if little Ann here hasn't managed to weasel it out of you."

"Hey!" said Wendell. "You can't talk to the Prince like that."

"No one has done any weaseling that I am aware of," said Charming.

"I can't believe this," said Ann. "I am so embarrassed."

"Well," said the Queen smugly. "Those were three evasive answers. I'll try it again. Which one of you has the grail?"

"Nobody has the grail," said Ann. "There was no grail. The site is occupied by a castle of fairly recent construction. Whatever was there before must have gotten destroyed."

"Don't try to lie to me, young lady. I'll mete out your punishment when we get home. Charming, I want that grail. I've already requested an audience with your father where I intend to demand the return of my rightful property."

"The whole place was riddled with magic," said the Prince. "Dragons, sleeping spells, enchanted woods. Send in a team of archaeological magicians and there's no telling what you might find. But if there was ever a grail there, it isn't to be found now."

Ruby rose to her feet and favored Charming with a sinister smile, offset by blood-red lips. It was clear that she did not believe any one of them. She was about to speak again when Mandelbaum entered the room. "Ah, there you are, Wendell. I heard there was food in preparation and I thought I'd find you here."

"Looks like a good day for timely entrances," said the Prince to Ann, *sotto voce*.

"What have we here?" said Mandelbaum. "Scones, kippers, very nice." He spread some jam on a scone and bit into it, then his eyes caught the Wicked Queen. He swallowed hastily. "Oh, hello. Have we met?"

"Mandelbaum, this is Queen Ruby of Alacia, Ann's stepmother," said the Prince by way of introduction. The Queen haughtily held out her hand and Mandelbaum raised it to his lips. "Queen Ruby, this is Mandelbaum, Royal Sorcerer to the Court of Illyria."

All trace of haughtiness vanished from the Queen's manner. "Oh, reeeeeeallly?" She moved in closer to the magician. "You must be a very powerful sorcerer."

"At your service, Madam." Mandelbaum cast a discerning eye down the Queen's slim body and apparently liked what he saw for he let his eyes roam back up. "I do what I can to lend my humble abilities to the service of my king and country," he continued with totally transparent modesty.

"I just looove magicians," murmured the Queen. She traced a line across Mandelbaum's chest with a blood-red fingernail. "They have such power, such . . . inner strength. I'd just love to learn their deepest secrets."

"The pursuit of knowledge can indeed be very, um, gratifying," said Mandelbaum. "I take it you have some interest in the black arts yourself?"

"Oh, yes. I have long immersed myself in the science of magic." She took both his hands and looked deep into his eyes. "But I fear that, studying by myself, without an experienced magician to guide me, I have gained but a dim and incoherent grasp of the subject."

"No kidding," muttered Ann. Ruby shot her a warning look.

"One must have patience," said Mandelbaum. "These things take time. Would you be interested in a brief tour of my laboratory?"

"I'd love one," said Ruby. She put his arm around

her waist and let him steer her towards the door. "Ann, I shall wish to speak to you in the morning. Um, not too early."

"Mandelbaum!" said Wendell. "What about the bats?"

"Another time, Wendell."

"But . . ."

"Another time, Wendell." He left with the Queen. Wendell, dumbfounded, could hear their voices trailing down the hall. "Have you ever studied, I mean, really studied, the bat? An amazing creature."

"Bats fascinate me," murmured the Queen. They mounted the stairs together.

"Huh!" said Wendell. "What got into him all of a sudden?"

"Cut him some slack, Wendell. You'll understand in a few years."

"What a bitch," said Ann. "I just hate her. I can't believe Mandelbaum is such a pushover. I thought he was so smart. Can't he see she's just using him?"

"Well," said the Prince, "a guy's brain sort of fogs up when he thinks he's going to get . . . when he's with a woman. He'll do things he wouldn't do otherwise. Stupid things."

Ann gave him an arch look. "Like slaying dragons single-handedly?"

"I was thinking more like writing poems and sending flowers. But that too."

Although Charming was the Prince and heir apparent to his father's throne and also held both a knighthood and a commission in the army, he was not obligated to fill any administrative post in the kingdom. Many a young prince in many another kingdom, faced with a life of leisure and wealth, bereft of responsibility, had let himself degenerate into a wastrel, a pleasure-sodden parasite of no value to his

society or himself. Charming, however, took his role
of Paladin and guardian of justice with just enough
seriousness to avoid the temptations of sloth, drunken-
ness, gluttony and debauchery to which so many other
young men of privilege had fallen. Although in private
moments he was willing to concede that the life of a
degenerate wastrel was not without its good points.
Particularly the debauchery.

But upon returning from a long trip, there were
certainly enough of life's little details to keep even a
nonfunctionary busy. There was his tailor to see, and
the weaponsmaster, and the horses to check on (Wendell, of course, had done the bulk of the work there,
but the grooms were always flattered by a personal
visit from the Prince). There were his tutors to be
placated, the Chancellor of the Exchequer to approve
his expenses, and his father's secretary to see in order
to arrange an audience for the two princesses. There
was also, and this was unavoidable, his mission debriefing
with Count Norville. Norville had left messages with
all the maids, the breakfast cooks, and the stablehands,
stating his desire that the Prince see him as quickly
as possible. Charming had been putting him off. He
did not relish explaining to the dour and calculating
Count how a simple Slay-and-Rescue mission had grown
into a quest of such complexity.

Thus it was not until lunch that he actually got to
meet with Ann and Aurora again. They were sitting at
opposite ends of the dining-room table, eating finger
sandwiches and cucumbers in sour cream. When he
entered, Princess Aurora rose to her feet and gave
him a hug. "Prince Charming, how nice to see you
again. Did you have a pleasant sleep? I was so looking
forward to having breakfast with you."

"Hello," said Ann.

"Hi, Aurora. Hi, Ann. Yeah, I've been running
around all morning doing stuff. But I've got some

good news. We go in to see Dad this afternoon. Two o'clock. He was supposed to meet with the town council about the schools. Or maybe it was the sewers. I forget which. Anyway, it got canceled. This is really a lucky break. Even I usually don't get to see him on this short notice."

"Well, that is good news," said Aurora. "I know we have plenty to discuss concerning the disposition of my kingdom."

"Well, leave me out of that. I'm not really into the political end of things."

"Has my stepmother obtained an appointment?" asked Ann.

"Nope. She hasn't even gotten in to see his executive secretary yet."

"That's probably a good thing. If I can see the King first, I might be able to defuse the explosion she'll undoubtedly create."

"Here," said Aurora. "You just sit right down here by me and have some lunch. While you're eating, you can tell me all about Illyria."

Ann speared a cucumber viciously with her fork. "Incidentally," she said, "there is a Count Norville looking for you."

"I know. I don't want to see him. If he comes around, tell him I'm not here."

"He said it's about the slipper thing."

The Prince jumped to his feet. "What? Where is he? I've got to see him right now!"

"Relax. He said he'll be back in half an hour or so."

Charming hesitated, half standing up. Aurora put her arm around his shoulder and pulled him back down. "See, the quickest way to find him is just to wait here. Now tell me about Illyria. Is there a library here where I can find the articles of annexation for Alacia?"

"What is the slipper thing?" said Ann.

"I don't think Alacia was annexed, I think it's under some sort of protectorate. The slipper thing is . . . um, this girl lost her slipper at a ball and I've been trying to find her and give it back to her."

Ann looked at him dubiously. "That's it? That's the whole story? A girl lost one shoe?"

"Uh, yeah. That's it."

"Why doesn't she just call on the castle and ask for it?"

"I don't know."

"Well, if she's not worried about getting it back, why should you be?"

"It's just something I want to do, that's all. If we don't make an effort to keep on top of all the shoes people lose here, eventually the castle would be inundated with them."

"I see."

Aurora said, "Well, if he wants to return the slipper, I think that is very nice. The poor girl is probably wondering what happened to it."

Ann looked even more doubtful.

Queen Ruby breezed in and Charming did a double take. The Wicked Queen was dressed in black, as usual, but instead of her usual spiked heels and red lipstick, she was wearing flat sandals and pink lipstick. Her hair was tied back with a bit of pink ribbon. Ann stopped with a spoon halfway to her lips and stared at her.

"Ann, my darling, how are you this morning? Did you sleep well? You look lovely."

"What?"

"You know, as long as we are in Illyria, we should really get you some new clothes. They have the most wonderful shops here. You really should take more care about the way you dress, my dear." She kissed Ann on the cheek.

"What?"

"And while we're about it, we can have our hair done. And perhaps we'll take tea in one of those adorable little sidewalk cafes. But not today, I'm afraid. Mandelbaum is taking me on a picnic. And while we're out, he's going to show me how to find these toadstools that have the most marvelous healing powers. I just know we'll be able to use them back home. Oh, this must be your little friend Aurora. My dear, I'm so sorry to hear about the tragedy that befell you. If there's anything I can do to make your transition easier, please don't hesitate to call on me for help. Prince Charming, please convey my warmest regards to your father. Well, I must be off. I don't want to keep dear Mandelbaum waiting." And she breezed out again.

"Gosh," said Aurora. "Your stepmom sure is nice."

"What?" said Ann.

"Wow," said Charming. "I underestimated old Mandelbaum."

Count Norville entered the dining room followed by Wendell, who zipped around him and headed straight for the platter of sandwiches, taking one in each hand and stuffing a third into his mouth. Then he swallowed hastily and said politely, "Good day, Sire. Good day, Princess Aurora. Good day, Princess Ann." With those obligations finished, he resumed eating at high speed.

The Prince had his eyes fixed on Norville, nonetheless, and made a great show of remaining cool. "Hello, Norville. You wanted to see me?"

With a triumphant flourish, Norville brought a glass slipper out from under his cloak. "Your Highness," he announced, "I have found her!"

"Terrific, Norville! That's great! Are you sure she's the one?"

"Absolutely. Both the description and the slipper fit perfectly."

"That must be her then. She had very delicate feet."

"Excuse me," interrupted Aurora. "You're trying to match a girl up with a shoe? That slipper isn't that small. There must be lots of girls who can wear it."

"One would think so, but such is not the case," said Norville. "We have tried this slipper on the majority of young women in the city and not a single other woman could fit into it."

"Is that really glass?" said Ann.

"Very fine lead crystal," said Norville. "Listen." The shoe had a narrow, three-inch heel. The Count tapped it with a spoon. A faint, bell-like tone rang out and shimmered through the room. "I am surprised the heel doesn't break, but it stands up very well."

"May I try it?"

"I don't see why not, but you are wasting your time." The Count passed the shoe to Ann who slipped out of her sandals and attempted to put on the glass slipper. She continued the attempt for several minutes while Aurora watched with a growing air of condescension and Charming took the opportunity to speak quietly with Norville.

Finally Ann said, "It isn't that the shoe is so small, it's just narrow. Well, it's not so narrow, but it's just sort of narrow through the toes in a strange way."

"I believe slim is the word you are looking for," said Aurora. "Obviously this shoe was designed for a girl with slim feet. Naturally someone with chunky feet won't fit into it."

"Chunky feet!"

"Oh dear, that was tactless of me, wasn't it. I simply meant that the owner of the shoe probably has a petite rather than a matronly figure."

Ann gritted her teeth. "Okay, miss smartypants, you try it on."

Aurora took the shoe and began working her toes into it. There followed several minutes of struggling and straining. "This shoe is smaller than it looks. I think the glass has a magnifying effect."

"Yeah, right," said Ann.

Aurora gave her a hostile look and took a soup spoon from the table. Using it as a shoehorn, she was able with much effort to get the body of her foot into the slipper. "There!" she said.

"It's not all the way in!"

"Yes, it is!"

"No, it isn't. Your heel isn't touching the glass. You won't be able to stand on it."

"Of course I can. Aagggghhhh," said Aurora, attempting to stand up and sitting back down again. "This is the most uncomfortable shoe I've ever tried on. It must have been very expensive."

"I know what you mean. We have a shoemaker in my kingdom who makes women's dress shoes that are superb. They're hideously painful."

"I had shoes made for my coming out party that were absolute agony to wear. They were very expensive, but they were worth it. I couldn't stand up for two days afterward. The shoemaker later quit to become chief torturer for King Bruno of Omnia."

"Sheesh," said Wendell.

Charming, meanwhile, was talking with Count Norville in low but urgent tones. "Did you see her?"

"I did, indeed," said Norville. His voice held only the slightest inflection of distaste.

"Pretty hot, eh?"

Norville sighed. "Prince Charming, please believe me when I say I have made a serious effort to understand this obsession you have with carnal gratification. Still, I fail to comprehend how you could be attracted to such a . . . trollop, especially when there exists a plethora of pure and virtuous young women within our very borders. Even if you confine yourself to women of your own class, such as these two fine young ladies you brought home with you . . ."

"The heck with them, Norville. This girl was incredible. The moment we started dancing, she just shoved her breasts right up against me. And all the time we were dancing she never missed an opportunity to grind her pelvis into my hip. And all the time I was talking to her she kept looking right into my eyes and wetting her lips with the tip of her tongue. I thought I was going to explode. She didn't say much about herself though."

"Apparently she relies on body language."

"Yeah! That must be it! I have to see this girl again, Norville. I mean, this girl was hot for me. If I can just get her alone, I know she's just waiting for me to put the moves on her. You say you invited her to dinner tonight?"

"I thought it might be best to let this unsavory episode come to a head as quickly as possible. Provided this young woman actually consents to the sordid acts you so look forward to, I will alert the public relations staff to prepare for damage control. Oh, and while I hate to disappoint you, young sir, Cynthia will not be coming alone. Her godmother will be with her."

"Her godmother?"

"You could hardly expect the young lady to go about unchaperoned."

"Why her godmother? No, don't tell me, her real mother is dead."

"The father is also dead. Hmmm. Perhaps the lack of strong interfamily relationships has something to do with her promiscuous behavior. At any rate, she seems to be very close to her godmother. The godmother has a strong guiding influence on her life."

"I'm going to have to ask Mandelbaum if there is a correlation between good looks and dead parents."

"Apparently there is some friction between her and

her stepmother and stepsisters. In fact, the rest of the family tried to conceal the girl from us. That accounts for the delay in locating her, not that I'm making excuses for my men."

"All right. I'll scope out the godmother and see if I can figure out a way to distract her. It's probably just a question of waiting for the right opportunity."

Wendell had left the table and joined the Prince and Norville. "Sire, is this the girl you met at the ball that you really like?"

"This is the one, Wendell."

"Yuck. Anyway, I will be gone this afternoon, Sire. Mandelbaum is going to show me where to find the herbal mushrooms."

"Okay. No, wait! Uh, you can't go out this afternoon, Wendell. I'm, uh, going to practice my quarterstaff fighting and I'll need your help."

"But you never fight with the quarterstaff. We don't even carry one on our trips."

"That's why I'm out of practice. So stay around."

"But Mandelbaum . . ."

"Sorry, Wendell. I'll straighten it out with Mandelbaum."

"Yes, Sire."

"I saw Mandelbaum this morning," said Norville. "He looked quite exhausted."

"I think he was up all night, Norville. I will see you later. I'm going to escort Aurora in to see Dad."

"Ah, yes. What a tragedy to lose one's husband immediately after the wedding like that."

"Um, yes. See you later." Charming returned to the table where the girls were still bickering. "We should go in to see Dad's secretary now. The schedule is pretty tight and it wouldn't hurt to get there early." This was a signal for Ann and Aurora to both produce hair brushes and spend the next twenty minutes arranging their hair. Charming sighed and ate some sandwiches.

At long last, however, the two Princesses reached a state approaching readiness and Charming was able to lead them down the long halls and up the grand staircase that led to the throne room. They passed through a maze of antechambers crowded with waiting courtiers, lawyers, diplomats and merchants; they passed the muster of a phalanx of secretaries and undersecretaries until at last they were ushered through a side door into the throne room.

At the far end of the throne room, the King was deep in consultation with several of his lords. Charming and the girls stood to one side, awaiting their turn. "Good afternoon, your Highness," said the Captain-at-Arms. He consulted a check list. "Princess Ann and Princess Aurora?"

"Let's not stand on protocol today, Eddie. I'll announce them myself."

"Very good, Sire."

Suddenly Aurora shoved past him. She stood on tiptoe, leaning forward to get a better view of the King. His face was half turned from them, his head lowered, so that all one could see was his gray hair and the curve of his beard. Aurora was tensed, trembling, like a greyhound in the starting gate. Then suddenly the King lifted his head and looked straight at them.

"Excuse me," said Charming. "Aurora, you'll have to wait!" But she was off. To the astonishment of the court, the young girl shoved her way through the line, raced past the surprised bodyguards, and hurled herself into the King's lap. "Goopy!" she cried.

"Goopy?" said the Prince.

It was to King Garrison's credit that, no matter how busy he was (and the King of Illyria was always *very* busy), he could always open up some time to spend a private moment with his son should Charming urgently request it. That afternoon, he would be glad that the walls of the castle were stone and the oak doors were thick, for the Prince was in high ire and his voice reverberated from the ceiling. "I can't believe this! All this nonsense you've been giving me about remaining pure and celibate, about morals and virtue, about protecting my image and respecting the chastity of the girls, and now I find out that twenty years ago you were boffing blondes in the bushes!"

"All parents did the things they tell their children not to do," the King said calmly. "That's how they know to tell them not to do it."

"And now you want to get married . . ."

"Well, we're still engaged, after all."

". . . to a girl who's twenty-five years younger than you."

"Aurora is thirty-seven."

"But she's been asleep for twenty years!"

"You sleep for eight hours at night," the King pointed out. "That hardly makes you twelve years old."

"All right, all right," yelled the Prince. "Have it your way. But I've got a hot date tonight and I don't want to hear anyone laying morality trips on me. So just stay out of my way!" And he stormed out.

This confrontation still lay several hours in the future, however. At the moment the Prince was astonished to the point of speechlessness, as was the rest of the court, when Aurora hurled herself into the King's lap and began kissing him all over his face.

"Aurora?" said the King

"Goopy!"

"I thought you were dead!"

"I thought *you* were dead."

"The boys took me into town that night for a final celebration. We didn't stagger back till the next day. We tried to get through the hedge, Aurora, honestly we did. I lost two of my best men to the thorns. But eventually we had to give it up."

"Then you seized my land."

"Um, I was holding it for you."

"But you thought I was dead."

"Not until after the land had been seized ... uh, placed under a protectorate. It was my father's decision actually."

"Well, no matter." Aurora began kissing him again. "It will be *our* land after we're married."

The King hesitated for only a second, long enough for his eyes to flicker across the slim figure of the nubile teen-ager in his arms. "Of course," he said, just a little hoarsely. "Darling, in all these years I've never stopped loving you."

Aurora drew back and faced the King with narrowed eyes. "But you did marry?"

"It was a political move," said the King earnestly. "I *had* to do it. I never loved her."

"Oh, really?" muttered the Prince.

"Aurora, you are the light of my life. When I lost you, it was as if a cloud passed over the sun and I have been living my life in shadow ever since. Today, for the first time the clouds have parted and the radiance of your ..."

"Okay, okay." The Princess put a finger to his lips. "Don't try and wax eloquent, Goopy, it's not your *forte*. I believe you."

"Please don't call me Goopy in public, dear."

"Sorry, Garrison. Do you honestly still wish to marry me?"

"Of course, my darling."

"And have children?"

"As soon as possible."

"Perhaps even sooner," said Aurora. She kissed him again. "We'll talk about it."

For most of the court, unfamiliar with the history of the sleeping princess and her strange enchantment, it was a perplexing moment. Nonetheless, they recognized that something momentous had occurred and that a marriage was in the offing.

They moved in at once to congratulate the King, introduce themselves to the Princess, and otherwise ingratiate themselves with the Royal family. Only Charming and Ann stood back from the press of the crowd. Charming was still trying to sort out a range of conflicting emotions generated by the revelations of the past minutes. Ann simply leaned back against the rear wall and watched Aurora with a calculating eye.

"Hmmm," she said.

"I think there's something wrong with Mandelbaum," said Wendell. "I asked him if he found the right mushrooms and he just said, 'What mushrooms?' like he didn't know what I was talking about. What were those two doing all day if they weren't gathering mushrooms?"

Charming shrugged absently and put his hands behind his head. He was sitting on a bench in his father's secretary's office, legs stretched out in front of him, one booted foot crossed over the other. His gaze was focused on the ceiling and he seemed lost in thought. Ann sat on the desk, silent but alert.

"I got out your quarterstaff equipment and padding," continued Wendell. "I figured you'd want to start out with full padding since you haven't done quarterstaff in a long while."

"Quarterstaff?" said Charming.

"What? Is that a joke? Or is everybody suffering from memory loss around here?"

"I believe his Highness has much to think about," said Ann. "As does Mandelbaum. And his Majesty the King."

"Hah," said Wendell. "There's too many girls around, that's the trouble." He glared at her. "Guys start acting stupid when there's too many girls about."

"You may be right."

Prudhomme, the King's secretary, entered his office. Ann moved off his desk, but he quickly ushered her to a chair. "No, no, Princess, don't get up. Make yourself at home, I beg you. Well, well, that was a perfectly delightful surprise, wasn't it? To think we will finally have a queen again after all these years. How wonderful. Prince Charming, I know you must be very happy for your father."

Charming gave him a long stare. "Yeah."

"Then again, I'm sure you feel a need to remain loyal to the memory of your departed mother." Prudhomme recovered smoothly. "And I can't tell you enough, your Highness, how much we all revered her when she was with us, may her soul rest in peace. I am certain, too, that she would have been very proud of her son and . . ."

"Prudhomme?"

"Yes, Sire?"

"Drop it."

"Yes, Sire. By the way, your Highness, there is a caller to see you. I told him he needed to make an appointment with your staff, but he insisted on waiting. He appears to be a most persistent and, if I may say so, a most aggressive fellow."

"Oh, yeah? Where is he now?"

"The last time I looked, he was waiting in the courtyard below."

"I saw him," said Wendell. "It's the big hairy guy who challenged you to a fight at the Inn."

"And he's still alive?" said Prudhomme.

Charming crossed over to the window and looked down. Sure enough, it was Bear McAllister pacing the cobblestones while a few of the guards kept a wary eye on him. He had his crossbow slung over his back and under one arm he held a package, a long object wrapped in oiled cloth. Charming shrugged. "Might as well see what he wants."

He bid his leave to Prudhomme and went down the stairs, Wendell at his side, and Ann slipping in quietly a few paces behind. Outside, the big man greeted him with respect and Charming responded with all the friendliness he could muster. "What brings you to Illyria?"

"Oh, just happened to be in the neighborhood," said Bear. "And I thought I might as well return this to you." He held out the package.

"I know, it's Endeavor," cried out Wendell, leaping up and taking the bundle before Charming could accept it. He tore off the oiled cloth. "I knew it. This is great. This is such a great sword. It's my favorite of all your swords."

"Couple of the boys found it sticking out of a dragon's skull in the woods," said Bear. "They had it on display at the Inn. Charging people tuppence to see it. I sort of commandeered it back for you."

"I appreciate its return. Thank you."

"Yeah, thanks," said Wendell.

"There will be a reward for its return, of course. I'm quite pleased that your friends were able to recover it."

Bear shifted his feet. "Yeah, well, you see, that's something I really came to talk to you about. Not about a reward, but about that castle. See, we've been looking it over."

"You got through the hedge?"

"Uh, yeah. I don't know how you knew, but I guess when you burned down the castle you broke the spell. After a couple days, that thorn hedge just started drying up and dying. We started chopping at it and were able to get through with no problems. It just stayed chopped this time. The other guys found the dragon and me and my friends went on to the castle. We were going to, uh, look for stuff, you know."

"Loot it," said the Prince.

"Uh, yeah, I guess. It was a good thing we did, though, because we actually found some survivors. A couple of stewards, down in the wine cellar. They went down to bring up more wine and they fell asleep, and I guess they've been sleeping for twenty years, down there where the dragon and the fire couldn't get at them. They were pretty confused. We took them back to town. Anyway, there wasn't much left of the castle. You pretty much burned it right to the ground."

"Termites. Only way to get rid of them."

"Was that it? Anyway, we went down into the well-house."

"What well-house?"

"See, that moat is spring-fed, and where the spring comes out of the ground, there's this old well-house. The foundations of the castle are sort of built out of it."

Ann spoke up suddenly. "How old?"

"Old old, missy. Real old. Ancient."

"Go on."

"See, what I think is that castle was built on the ruins of another, older castle. You get down into the ruins, down in the dungeons and stuff, and it goes down maybe three or four different levels and stuff, there's all sorts of passages and little rooms and fallen down brick, things like that. We couldn't get into most of it, it was all blocked off with debris and stuff, but you could tell that a lot of it was real old, much older than the rest of the castle, and I don't think anyone had been down there for an extra special long time."

"Interesting."

"But here's the good part," said the Bear triumphantly. "We go into this well-house, see, basically because it's the only thing we can get into with no trouble. And on the wall there's all these pictures carved in of religious symbols, crosses and such. And in about ten different places, there's a picture of a grail!"

"Are you sure?"

"Pretty sure. It's some sort of drinking goblet, at least. Anyway, I remembered you said you were looking for a grail there, so I thought I'd pass the information on to you."

"Well, I appreciate this, Bear, but to tell the truth, that quest has sort of been wrapped up."

"Oh. So you won't be coming back our way soon?"

"Probably not. Why don't you go after the grail yourself? It might be worth something."

"It makes sense," murmured Ann to herself. "A well-house as a chapel. The grail was a fertility symbol. Water symbolizes life, birth, also baptism, symbolic birth."

Bear shrugged. "I thought about taking it. But there was rubble to clear away and the boys aren't much interested in old relics. Neither am I, for that matter. And I don't like to mess with magic stuff."

"Very wise."

"I'll take on any man alive in a fair fight or even an unfair one. But this sorcery stuff is out of my league."

"I know what you mean."

"But the village is on edge, you see. We had a nice stable situation till you penetrated that castle. Now they want to know just what happened there and what the situation is going to be between Illyria and Alacia."

"I'm really not into political stuff."

"Well, you stirred things up. You ought to see it through."

Charming gave him an irritated look. Bear spread his hands. "Not that I'd presume to tell you what to do, your Highness."

The Prince shook his head. "No, you may have a

point, Bear. Let me discuss it with the Minister of Intelligence and see if he can shed some light on the subject."

"Fair enough."

They rose and Charming clapped the big man on the shoulder. "For a tough guy, Bear, you're pretty darned diplomatic. And it looks like you're developing some village loyalty, too."

Bear scratched his head. "Well, your Highness, I guess I just figured that sooner or later, a man ought to make some friends."

"Good thinking. Thanks for the news, Bear."

"And thanks for the sword," chimed in Wendell.

"You're welcome."

"And don't forget to stop by the exchequer for your reward."

Bear grinned. "I won't."

When the hairy man left, Ann said, "Well, he certainly changed his tone."

"He's a smart man," said Charming. "He found that he couldn't intimidate us, so he stopped trying to be intimidating."

"Are you going to go back?"

"I'll think it over later. I've got other things to do tonight."

"My goodness. After all that's happened today, are you still thinking about that girl who lost a shoe? Why don't you just send it to her? Have a messenger deliver it."

"Er, it's good publicity to invite her over. Public relations and all that. It was Norville's idea, actually. She's coming with her godmother. Makes for a nice, wholesome, family scene."

"I forgot," said Ann. "You have to think about your image. After all, you're *Prince Charming*."

"Darn right."

"We've decided to continue with the story that

we're already married," Aurora told Ann. "The story has gone out and people seem to be accepting it all right. Why invite public comment by changing it now? So Garrison and I will be married in a small private ceremony this evening. It's kind of a relief, really. After the last fiasco, I've lost my taste for big weddings."

"I can imagine. Besides, why should you needlessly expose your child to the taint of illegitimacy?"

"Exactly. Anyway, Ann, I do hope you'll stand up with me at the ceremony. You've been so kind to me ever since we met and I do feel like you're my best friend, indeed, my only friend left in the world. I would be so happy if you would be my maid of honor." Aurora said this with complete sincerity, totally forgetful of the fact that only a few hours before, the two girls had been snapping at each other like rabid turtles.

"Oh, Aurora, how utterly sweet of you to ask me," said Ann, equally sincere and forgetful. "Why, of course I'll be your maid of honor. You're such a dear, dear friend; why, I almost feel like we are sisters."

Aurora hugged her. "Oh, Ann, I feel exactly the same way."

"Sheeesh," said Wendell.

The dinner guests were assembling in the sitting room that led to the dining room. Wendell went over to see Count Norville, who was nervously tugging at his cravat, and Prince Charming, who was attired in his finest silks, his hair brushed to a brilliant lustre. "We have rather limited intelligence on Alacia," Norville told the Prince. "They pay their taxes to us and never cause any trouble, so there was no need to station an agent there. Of course, now that they'll be properly under our rule, they'll become part of the information network, but it takes time to get these things set up."

"I understand," said Charming.

"Now if you're looking for a new adventure, Sire, I have the case of a rather pretty girl who was kidnaped by a brigand. She's not royalty, but she comes from a wealthy merchant family. . . ."

"Was she really kidnaped or did she run off?"

"Possibly the latter. But the point is that her family thinks she was kidnaped and, if she was returned, they would owe a debt of gratitude to the King."

"Not interested. Damn it, Norville, where is she? She's late."

"She is not late," said Norville. "It is only slightly past the hour."

"Do you think she'll like me?"

"She liked you at the ball. Very obviously so."

"Do you think she'll still like me?"

"I can only hope that if she does, she will be less demonstrative in her affections."

"Yes, well, I hope you're wrong. And the really great thing about this girl, Norville, is that I never rescued her from anything, never saved her life, never helped her out of a tight spot. She doesn't owe me a thing. Which means when she started rubbing her thighs against me at the ball, she was doing it purely out of . . ."

"Lust," finished Norville.

"Yeah. Isn't that great?"

"No. And I am compelled to point out, Prince Charming, that none of the young ladies that you have rescued owe you a thing, either. One does not expect favors simply for doing one's duty."

"But you just said," pointed out Wendell, "that this merchant family would owe a debt of gratitude to the King if Prince Charming brought their daughter back."

"Ermmmm, so I did. A good point, lad. But a political favor is not the same as a personal favor. And being a hero does not excuse one from acting within the boundaries of common decency."

"Miss Cynthia and Madam Esmerelda," announced a footman.

All heads turned. And stayed that way.

Beauty is, as a well-known poet of a later century would say, in the eye of the beholder. Women have different standards of beauty than men. Women think of beauty in the classical sense; they find it in the finely chiseled features of Greek statues, in the effortlessly flawless lines of face and form, the regal bearing, the upturned chin. Their feminine ideal is the ice goddess, ultimately desirable but totally unattainable.

When men think of beauty, they mean sexy.

Ann was beautiful.

Aurora was beautiful.

Cynthia was sexy.

Her hair was flaming red and long. In thick, soft waves it stretched to her waist and beyond, brushing up against the lush curves of her bottom, curves that were accented by the tight black silk she wore. The dress was strapless and showed the tops of her high firm breasts, with a deep V of cleavage. It dropped low in the back to emphasize the delicate curve of her spine. Her waist was narrow, and her long slim legs were made to appear even longer and slimmer by the black silk stockings and the four-inch heels she wore. Her eyes were as green as the first buds of spring and her lips were full, moist and pouting. She looked at no one but Prince Charming and to him she gave a smile that was as seductive as a siren's call.

"What did I tell you?" said Charming. "Isn't she something?"

"She looks okay," said Wendell.

Cynthia was so excited she thought her heart was going to burst. "Even if this doesn't work, it will all have been worth it," she thought. "If I never see him again, I will be happy for the rest of my life. If I never live another day, I will die in esctasy." She was here, right in Castle Illyria itself, by special invitation, to meet *Prince Charming*. It was all happening exactly as her godmother had predicted.

Just thinking about her godmother made Cynthia tingle all over. Esmerelda was so very, very special. It wasn't just that she could do magic, she was magic. She had that magical quality, charm, charisma, whatever you want to call it, that just made Cynthia fall in love with her the first time she appeared, and when she held Cynthia close and comforted her, all the girl's problems seemed to melt away and the world seemed suffused with a warm, golden haze.

She sometimes thought that things might have been different if she was an orphan. Well, technically, of course, she was an orphan, both her parents were dead, but she didn't mean *that* kind of orphan. She meant children who had been abandoned, foundlings, those who had lost their parents at a very young age and couldn't remember them at all. Such children, she knew, all shared the same dream. That someday their real parents would come back for them and they would be beautiful and rich and loving and take them away to live happily ever after somewhere else.

Cynthia had been deprived of the comfort of such illusions. Her father had hung about till she was eight years old, plenty long enough to make it clear that Cynthia's mother had died giving birth to Cynthia; she was definitely dead, no mistake about it, and she wasn't coming back. He was mightily bitter about the situation, not just blaming the woman for dying, but for dying without giving him any sons. He had eventually remarried and was planning to start a new family, a male dynasty if at all possible, but a week later he was kicked in the head by a horse and that was that.

Cynthia's new stepmother thereby found herself with another mouth to feed and no payoff. She determined to make up the difference in labor, Cynthia's labor, and the girl instantly found herself demoted to the role of household slave. As if that were not bad enough, within a few years it became obvious that Cynthia was going to grow up prettier than her stepsisters. Much, much prettier. And if the jealousy of a woman is an ugly thing to behold, the jealousy of two teen-age girls is positively fearsome.

So there was Cynthia, a beautiful girl trapped in perpetual servitude, long miserable years ahead of her, and not even much chance of escaping via a good marriage, since there was no way her stepsisters were going to let her out of the house until she was an old maid or at least until the two of them were married first, which was pretty much the same thing.

And then the night of the ball, when Cynthia was alone in the house weeping on the hearth (she wept a lot in those days, chronic depression, y'know), the room had suddenly filled with tiny, sparkling, colored lights and she heard the words that would forever change her life:

"Stick with me, kid, and you're going all the way to the top."

Now she walked slowly forward, her eyes fixed on the Prince, putting a gentle sway to her hips as she moved, just the way Esmerelda had taught her. She held her shoulders back, which had the effect of lifting her breasts and thrusting them forward, projecting a carefully calculated amount of cleavage. "The way to a man's heart starts below the waist, kid," Esmerelda had said. She also provided clothes and some of them, Cynthia had to admit, were real show-stoppers.

She continued to walk towards the Prince, fixing her gaze on his cool blue eyes. ("Keep looking into his eyes, my dear. Deep inside, all these macho types are hopeless romantics.") When she came up to the Prince, she didn't stop to curtsy, but slowly lifted her hands. Charming held out his arms and she folded herself into them, never taking her eyes off his face, pressing the full length of her luscious body against him, her lips only inches from his. "Oh, my Prince," she whispered.

"Oh, my lady," whispered Charming.

"Oh, my stomach," muttered Ann.

"Shush," said Aurora. She was staring past Cinderella with eyes as cold and fixed as rigor mortis.

"Since I lost you at the ball that night, I felt like a man wandering in the desert, without water or succor," said the Prince. "There was no life around me, only shifting desolate sands and a wind that constantly moaned your name. Now it is like an oasis has suddenly opened before me and the water of love flows from deep hidden springs."

"Since I left you at the ball," whispered Cynthia, "the sun had not risen for me and the dark nights surrounded me like wolves and prowled and snapped at my doors, and the chill wind sent icy fingers into my chest to seize my heart in a cold and unrelenting grip. Now the warm winds of springtime blow where before there was only a frozen field."

She was able to go on in this vein for quite a while because her godmother had written plenty of this stuff out beforehand and made her memorize it. Charming was able to come back with some impressively romantic lines himself, pretty good, she thought, if he was really ad-libbing. The only part she didn't like was having to be so close to him. It made her feel sort of crawly when a boy actually touched her. She had told Esmerelda this the night after the ball.

"I know, dear," the fairy godmother said. "Men are such loathsome creatures. But it's very important that you tolerate it, that you continue to pretend that you

enjoy and even encourage his caresses. It's the corner-
stone of our whole plan."

"But when I go to bed with him, won't he be dis-
gusted with me the next morning? Everyone says
that's what they do."

"Some men are like that," Esmerelda admitted.
"But not Charming. He has too much decency. You
must understand, you are dealing with a man who has
everything he wants, almost. You'll be giving him the
one thing he wants above all else, the only thing that
no other girl in the kingdom will offer him. His
ingrained sense of honor will compel him to offer you
his hand in marriage."

Cynthia nodded. She trusted her godmother in
everything.

"And remember, darling. Once the two of you are
married and we are safely ensconced in the castle,"
Esmerelda leaned forward, "you will never have to let
him touch you again."

The advice reassured the girl and now, as Esmerelda observed them across the dinner table, she was
quite pleased at Cynthia's performance. The girl was
just a natural actress; the bit when she reached across
the Prince for the salt and let her breasts brush against
him really made his eyeballs spin. He was falling for
her like a stone in water.

Esmerelda glanced down the rest of the table, plotting her next move. The page, now, he would be worth
talking to. She'd have to keep him occupied after dinner, maybe with a few magic tricks, to keep him away
from his master. The Count was a buffoon, but a mor-
alistic buffoon could be dangerous to the plan. She'd
have to distract him, too, so the Prince could get away
with Cynthia and make his play. The rest of the guests
were of no consequence. The King was fortunately too
busy to attend the dinner. The visiting dignitaries and
palace flunkies would not cause any interference and

the two visiting princesses, while attractive enough in a wholesome girl-next-door way, were clearly no competition for Cynthia. They might as well give up and go home to wherever they came from.

Esmerelda sipped her wine and smiled at Norville. "So tell me, Count, what do you think of the political situation?"

At the other end of the table, Aurora was stabbing viciously at the piece of fish on her plate. "That slut!" she hissed. "That whore! That bitch! I'll kill her if she tries anything!"

Ann affected cool amusement. "Will you calm down? Don't get so excited. What do you care if the Prince loses his head over some brassy bimbo like Cynthia?"

"Cynthia! Who cares about Cynthia? I'm talking about the godmother. That's the same fairy queen who put the spell on me!"

This statement served very well as a conversation stopper. Ann swiveled her head around and Queen Ruby and Mandelbaum, sitting next to her, leaned forward to get a good look at Esmerelda.

"She's a fairy? Are you sure?"

"Of course I'm sure. You don't forget a woman who once asked you to, um . . . never mind."

"What?"

"Well, let me put it this way. You wouldn't hire her to guard the cherry orchard, if you know what I mean."

"What?" said Ann.

"Forget it. Look, this woman's a schemer, a user and a manipulator of the first order. She always had an angle on everything in Alacia. She couldn't put anything over on Daddy, though. She kept trying to wangle some sort of political appointment out of him and eventually they had a big fight and she cursed us all."

"That was a hell of a curse," said Queen Ruby. "Her power must be substantial."

"Not necessarily," said Mandelbaum. "The spell she cast was crudely handled. She drained all the power from that fairy wood to maintain it. I suspect she only meant to leave it up a short time, but found she didn't know how to remove it. When the magic of the woods was used up, the fairies had to leave."

"But she hasn't left her scheming ways behind. Now she turns up here and she's trying to gain influence in the court through Prince Charming. She's power-mad. Well, I'll fix her wagon." Aurora suddenly dropped her fork. "Oh, my! Oh, no!"

"What's wrong?"

"What if she's still after me? After twenty years, she suddenly shows up on my wedding day again?"

"It's just coincidence," said Ann. "Charming has been searching for that girl for three months, before he even heard of you."

"Well, I'm not taking any chances. I'm going to ask Garrison to order the Prince to stay away from that girl. She's not his type anyway."

Mandelbaum looked amused. Ann shrugged. "I doubt if Charming takes orders like that. More likely you'll just push him into her arms."

"Hmmph. I don't see how you can be so calm. I thought you liked Prince Charming. How can you bear to see him hanging all over that . . . slut?"

"Excuse me," interjected Mandelbaum. "Not to be unkind, Princess, but are you really in a position to cast aspersions on another girl's moral character? I ask merely for information."

"That's different," said Aurora stiffly. "I was engaged."

"That's right," said Ann, coming to her defense. "It's okay for a couple to do it if they're engaged."

"It most certainly is not," said Queen Ruby. "Ann, I don't know where you got such an idea."

"Well, maybe it's not okay, but it's not exactly as bad as it would have been if they were not engaged. You know what I mean."

"Young lady, I can see that we're going to have to have a serious talk."

"Oh, fine! I suppose you've been the very picture of chastity."

"Mandelbaum and I are just good friends," said Ruby.

"Well, I'm not waiting around to see what happens," said Aurora. She threw down her napkin. "I'm going to tell those two gold diggers that I know just what they're up to and I'm going to make sure the Prince knows it also. I owe him that much, at least." She leaned forward to Ann. "And you don't fool me, Little Princess, with that oh-so-casual attitude. You've been cutting that piece of fish on your plate till the pieces are the size of sesame seeds and you haven't taken a single bite."

Ann looked at her plate and lifted her fork to her mouth. She put it down again without tasting from it and put her arm around the blond girl's shoulders. "Aurora," she murmured in her ear, "if you really care about Prince Charming and if you're really my friend, the best thing you can do is to get married as quickly and quietly as possible."

Aurora looked at her quizzically.

"Just trust me on this," said Ann. "Forget about this fairy godmother. It was twenty years ago. Leave it alone."

Aurora hesitated, then made up her mind. "You don't know this woman the way I do." She rose and made her way down the long table. "Count Norville, may I have a word with you in private?"

"Certainly, Princess."

"Oh, no need to be so secretive, dearie," said Esmerelda. "I'm sure I can guess what sort of little case history you plan to relate. I'm equally sure that a true gentleman will give me the opportunity to set the record straight."

"I don't see why not," said Norville, looking confusedly from one to the other.

"Straight!" said Aurora. "What a novel concept for you. Anything that you're involved in will be about as straight as a corkscrew. You and that little tramp you hired to seduce the Prince."

Esmerelda's eyes flashed but she kept her voice level. "Feeling a little cranky this evening, aren't we, Blondie. Perhaps those cramps will subside once you've fully developed. In the meantime, why don't you lie down and take a nap? A nice *long* nap. I could arrange it for you."

Aurora was shaking with suppressed rage. She spoke through clenched teeth. "Just try it, Butch. The Illyrian court has magicians that can fry you up like a piece of bacon and send your powers up the chimney like a puff of smoke. If they detect so much as a hint of spellcraft, they'll burn you to a crisp. And they can neutralize anything you put on Charming, so you can forget your little schemes."

"The spell that Cynthia casts on men has nothing to do with magic," said Esmerelda. "Perhaps you'll understand when you grow up."

"Speaking of Cynthia, where did she get to?" asked Norville.

They looked down the table. Cynthia and the Prince had quietly slipped out, leaving two empty chairs and untouched desserts.

"I believe they mentioned going out for a breath of air," said Esmerelda sweetly. "I shouldn't worry about Cynthia, Count. I'm sure Prince Charming will take good care of her."

The Castle Illyria was big. It sat on a gentle hill rising a hundred feet or so above the city of Illyria, surrounded by shops and homes, barges and warehouses, schools and playing fields, inns and churches, bars and breweries, stables, counting houses, bakeries, cafes and theatres, all that made up the largest metropolis in the twenty kingdoms. The city, in turn, sat very nearly at the geographical center of the country of Illyria, with rather good cobblestoned roads stretching off in all directions.

But it was the castle itself that caught one's eyes as one approached the city. Monstrously huge, of gray and black stone, parts of it dating back six centuries, much of it brand new, it not only housed the royal family but provided the chambers and courts for the royal government, offices for the vast numbers of civil servants required to run a country the size of Illyria, accommodations for visiting nobility, extensive quarters for servants and maintenance workers, and it housed a garrison of armed soldiers who served as guards and peacekeepers. At one time there had no doubt been some architectural consistency to the structure of the castle, some sort of rhyme or reason to the layout of rooms and hallways. But centuries of addition and remodeling had left it riddled with blind hallways, back staircases and secret rooms that were not intended to be secret but were so far from the mainstream of traffic that they had fallen from public consciousness.

"Well, this is nice," said Cynthia, as they entered such a room. "How quaint."

"Isn't it neat?" said Charming. "Queen Belinda set aside this room to look out over the city and write her poems. When they built the new south tower a hundred and forty years ago, all she got was a view of a blank wall, so she found someplace else to write. This is still just the way she furnished it, though."

"Somehow I guessed you didn't pick out the lace and velvet yourself. Did she write good poems? Were they written for a lover?"

"She wrote them for her children. They're okay, I

guess, if you like poetry. Legend has it that she gave a volume to her youngest son, who stuck it in his breast pocket when he rode off to battle. He took an arrow full in the chest, but the book stopped the arrow so that it barely scratched the skin."

"So the poetry saved his life."

"Unfortunately, the wound got septic and he died anyway. Fortunes of war."

"Mmmmm," said Cynthia hesitantly. Her godmother's scripted patter had not prepared her for a conversational gambit like this. She decided to strike out on her own. "I suppose we could draw a lesson from that story."

"Carry thicker books?"

"Don't put too much faith in good fortune. I suspect the young soldier had a good day in battle along with his narrow escape from death and he began to feel like he was invincible. He got overconfident and he neglected to put ointment on his scratch. He could have taken advantage of his luck, but instead he just let it run out."

"Uh huh."

Cynthia sat down on a love seat and spread her skirt around her. Black silk stockings gleamed on her calves. Charming sat down next to her as she knew he would. "Now suppose a girl were to go to a ball, not a Princess, but an ordinary common girl, were to go to a ball and meet a wonderful boy. That would be good fortune. Suppose this boy were to invite her for dinner. That's a good sign. It shows he's capitalizing on his good fortune. Now, I would say, this girl has got her opportunity and she, too, has to take advantage of it. It's up to her to make sure this boy isn't disappointed. Don't you think I'm right?"

"Well, that depends. How would this uncommon, extraordinary girl make sure this boy would not be disappointed?"

"By giving him what he wants."

Charming ran a finger around the inside of his collar, which suddenly felt a whole lot tighter and a whole lot hotter. Cynthia cast her eyes down demurely, batted her lashes a few times, and then slowly raised them again to Charming's face. Her pupils were wide and the green irises sparkled with hidden mischief. Her full, pink lips curved upward in a half smile. A tiny drop of perspiration formed in the hollow of her throat and gently slid down between her breasts. From the way she was dressed and from the way she leaned toward him, Charming could watch that drop go a long way down.

The candles on the table burned down to a dim glow. The room was silent except for the breathing of two people, Cynthia's breath coming abnormally fast and shallow, Charming's breath coming abnormally deep and slow. Slowly, Cynthia shifted her legs so her left thigh was pressed against Charming's. Softly, she began to rub it back and forth.

Carefully, Charming reached out with his right hand and touched the shoulder strap of her black silk dress. Slowly, he tugged it down off her shoulder. Cynthia made no objection. She placed a hand on his chest, gently twisting a button. Charming continued to pull down, until the black silk was pooled around her waist. In the flickering candlelight her breasts gleamed, full, high and round, the nipples dark and erect. With great effort, the Prince pulled his eyes up to Cynthia's face. Her eyes were half closed, her lips wet and parted, her cheeks flushed. Charming placed a hand on the small of her back and drew her toward him. Her bare breasts pressed into the thin white silk of his shirt and she made no effort to resist him. As if mesmerized, she turned her mouth up to his.

"Cynthia?"

The voice outside the door was high, shrill and

fraught with tension. Cynthia froze like a rabbit caught in the moonlight. The voice repeated itself, this time accompanied by a pounding on the door. "Cynthia, open this door immediately!"

"It's my godmother."

The Prince sagged back into the love seat. "There seems to be a recurring pattern in my life."

Cynthia pulled her dress up and unlocked the door. Esmerelda and Queen Ruby stood outside, Ruby holding Mandelbaum's mini-mirror. Cynthia grabbed her godmother's arm and dragged her inside, whispering hoarsely, "What are you doing? I had him right on the hook."

Esmerelda cast a scornful look at Charming. "Change of plans. Get your clothes on, kid. We're leaving."

"But . . . but . . ."

"I'll explain later. Forget this so-called Prince. We're going home." She turned on her heel, marched down the hall and down the stairs. Cynthia turned and cast a puzzled look at Charming, then followed her. Charming hastily buttoned up his shirt and ran after them both. Ruby took up the rear with an amused smile.

Downstairs, the servants already had Esmerelda's and Cynthia's cloaks ready. They were putting them on as Charming came down the stairs. Esmerelda ignored him. "Queen Ruby," she said, "it was a great pleasure to make your acquaintance. I do thank you for your help."

"The pleasure was all mine."

"Esmerelda," said Charming desperately. "Let me assure you that my intentions towards Cynthia are purely honorable and stem from the highest possible motivations. I admit that perhaps I was too forward tonight, but I honestly meant no harm and I do wish to see your goddaughter again."

Esmerelda gave him an icy look and grabbed the mirror from Ruby. "Mirror, mirror, in my hand, who's the fairest in the land?" The mirror clouded and cleared to reveal the image of Ann. Esmerelda tossed it to Charming who caught it with one hand. "Even your mirror is broken," she sneered and marched straight out the door.

Charming found a chair and sat down. He put his head in his hands. "What the heck was that all about?"

"Oh," said Ruby lightly. "I expect she was just upset to learn that you're not really a prince."

It occurred to Prince Charming that perhaps he was undergoing divine punishment for his sins. This argument would have held more weight if he had actually gotten to sin with Cynthia. Since their affair was not, in fact, consummated, he dismissed the higher powers from his consciousness and found instead a more immediate focus for his wrath. This happened to be Queen Ruby.

"You interfering idiot!" he yelled.

"My, my," murmured Ruby. "That just isn't a very charming thing to say at all."

"I had her right where I wanted her. She was on the couch, already stripped to the waist, just about to kiss me. It was a sure thing."

"Oh, yes. What a smoothie you are, Charming. What an effort it must have been to overcome the inhibitions of such a shy and modestly clothed child."

"For three months I've been searching for that girl and just when I finally get her alone, you have to go and tip off her godmother where we are. That's disgusting, using those magic mirrors to spy on people. It's an invasion of privacy. Then to make matters worse, you go and tell her I'm not really a prince. Now what the hell is that supposed to mean? Are you crazy?"

"Ah, you were listening. Dear boy, I really had no intention of spoiling your fun. If you want to behave like an animal with some little chippy, far be it for me to interfere, though I really should not let Ann associate with a man of such low character. No, no, I merely mentioned to Esmerelda, simply by way of passing conversation, that the Princess Aurora and King Garrison were quietly married tonight."

Charming eyed her narrowly. "That's it?"

"That is it."

"And she yanked Cynthia out of here for that?"

"Exactly."

"I don't get it. I suppose you're going to tell me that she had dreams of being the power behind the throne when I made Cynthia my queen? That she set up this whole romance as part of some manipulative scheme for social and political advancement?"

Ruby looked surprised. "Apparently I have underestimated your sophistication. Yes, of course that's what the two of them were doing."

"Well, so what? Half the princesses in the twenty kingdoms have advisors working on an expedient marriage for them. That's something you live with when you're manor born. Why should Cynthia be any different? Besides, why should having a queen make a difference to Esmerelda? I'm not going to be king for years yet. She should have figured Dad might remarry someday."

"Are you not forgetting that Aurora is carrying a child?"

"Yeah, so what? As the first-born son I'm still next in line for the throne."

"But this child will be twenty years old when delivered. Three years older than you are."

"First *born*," said Charming patiently. "Date of conception has nothing to do with it. I was born first."

Ruby pulled up a chair and sat down, crossing her legs. She was wearing her black boots again, the ones with the spiked heels, and the highly polished leather gleamed in the lamplight. She dusted one negligently with a lace handkerchief. "But you are illegitimate."

Charming, still full of frustrated energy, had been pacing up and down while they talked. Now he stopped and stared at Ruby, suspiciously, as though he expected her to reveal that all this was merely a huge joke. "Say what?"

"Garrison and Aurora were married twenty years ago. The sleeping spell didn't kick in until after the wedding. That means that the King's marriage to your mother was not legal since he was still married to Aurora. Since he was never married to your mother, you, I'm afraid, are an illegitimate child and Aurora's son is the first legitimate heir to the throne of Illyria."

"Oh, for goodness sake," Charming said heavily. "You ruined my date with Cynthia just for that?" He kicked at a chair. "I've got news for you, Queen Ruby. My father and Aurora didn't . . . uh, they weren't, um . . ."

"Yes, go on."

"Never mind."

"I suppose you're going to tell me some nonsense about how Aurora and Garrison weren't really married before the spell took effect, that you and she just concocted that story to save her from the shame and public ostracism that our society bestows upon women who engage in that sort of intimacy outside of wedlock, that you swore to keep her secret, not realizing that the father of her child was your father also?"

Charming wasn't looking at her. He studied a pair of crossed broadswords that hung on the wall. In the polished steel, he saw the face of a young man who was mired in a swamp of uncertainty. Still with his back to Ruby he said, "Suppose, merely as conjecture, that I was to claim something like that?"

Ruby leaned her head back and laughed lightly. "Oh, Charming, you are so cute. That overdeveloped sense of honor forces you to keep your promise to

Aurora even as your own life is destroyed. That prevents you from admitting the truth to me, even when you know that both girls and dear Mandelbaum have let me in on the secret. What a singular childhood you must have had, to be instilled with such integrity. I should have slept with you when I had the chance. At least you would have gotten something out of this deal, poor dear."

If there was anything that angered Charming more than the idea that he was being tricked, it was the notion that he was being pitied. He turned on his heel and fixed Ruby with a narrow glare. "Maybe I don't have so much integrity as you think."

"Oh, I think you do. But then, does it really matter? You can tell the truth now, but only by admitting that you lied beforehand. Once you've established that you will lie, why should the people believe you are telling the truth now and not then? Your motive for lying to protect yourself is certainly stronger than your motive for lying to protect Aurora."

Charming looked slightly worried, but his brow soon cleared. He rang for a servant. "Send for Prudhomme immediately!" The servant nodded and departed. "Look, Queen Ruby, I don't want to get hard-line here, but you are a guest in this castle and I think you are taking a few too many liberties, running around breaking up a guy's dates and spinning stories. As for Aurora's premature wedding, okay, maybe I did screw up by not letting her take the heat. But I'm not going to be cross-examined by a bunch of lawyers over this. In the court of public opinion, I'm still Prince Charming, who has battled half the evil in this kingdom and most of the other kingdoms as well, and my people are not going to turn against me because of one white lie."

"Mmmmmmm." Ruby tapped a blood-red fingernail thoughtfully against a front tooth. "No king, however powerful, can hope to lead without the support of his people, my dear. And no prince, however secure his claim, can gain the throne without their support, also. You know this already. But public opinion, dear boy, is such a fickle thing. The people love romance. For the King to present them with a beautiful new Queen, one who has lain in a magical trance for twenty years, oh, the people will eat that story up. It will be far more touching than yet another tale of how you slew yet another fiend somewhere. And then there's the child itself, of course. How the people love a newborn baby, especially the women. And how much fun it will be for them to watch it grow up. So much more interesting than the life of a teen-age boy."

"Get real. If Dad says I'm heir to the throne, then I'm the heir. The people aren't going to argue."

Ruby smiled. It was not a friendly smile. It was a crocodile smile. It was the smile of a woman who took a malicious delight in being the bearer of bad news. It was, in fact, the sort of smile that made it easy to understand why Ruby had been referred to as the Wicked Queen.

"Well, now," she said. "Let's consider just what the King will do. He's what, forty or so years old? Comparatively young for a ruler. In the prime of life, really. Does he have any reason to start worrying about his heir at this early age? I would think just the opposite. That he might be worried about his popular son deciding to compete with him for the throne."

"Dad knows me better than that."

"He knows you so well he sends you out of the court at every opportunity so you won't have the chance to develop liaisons or indulge in conspiracies."

"He does not. That's just stupid."

"Is it? All rulers have to be a little paranoid. It's the nature of the business. Even afraid of their own sons, perhaps. Enough to entertain the thought, not consciously perhaps, just in a tiny corner in the back of their minds, that perhaps they could breathe so much easier if the scion was killed in some dangerous mission undertaken for King and country."

"Nonsense."

"But to bear a son now, that's a different story. His Highness would be in his sixties by the time the lad reached majority, a ripe time to start thinking about retirement anyway. Until then, the whole issue can be comfortably put on the back burner. Except, of course, for Aurora. I think you will agree that there is a woman who knows how to take advantage of a situation. She will, of course, use her influence in her own child's favor. And I think it's safe to say that she will have more, how shall I put it, *access* to the King than you will ever have."

"Prudhomme!" yelled the Prince.

The King's personal secretary appeared in the doorway. His smile was as ingratiating as ever, but he rubbed his hands together nervously and furrows creased his high forehead. For some reason he seemed reluctant to enter the room, seeming to hang back in the entrance way as if seeking protection. "Er, yes, your Highness? May I be of service?"

"Access," said Charming to Ruby. "We'll see about access." He turned back to Prudhomme. "Prudhomme, I would like to see my father at once."

"Er," said Prudhomme. He glanced into the hallway behind him. "I'm afraid the King is rather busy right now. Er, too busy to be disturbed."

"Of course," said Charming understandingly. "It's his wedding night after all. How foolish of me." He glanced at Ruby. "I meant that I wanted to see him first thing in the morning."

"Um, he is very busy in the morning, also."

"Any time tomorrow. It doesn't have to be first thing. Whenever is convenient for him."

Prudhomme twisted his hands together very tightly. His voice was almost a whisper. "The King will be very busy for at least the next three weeks. Maybe longer. I don't know when I can get you in to see him."

"What? Come on, Prudhomme. He always has time to see me. You know that." Charming took a step forward. Four guards appeared from the shadows in the hall and blocked the doorway. The secretary scuttled behind them.

"Prudhomme!" yelled the Prince. "What is going on here?"

The secretary looked out from between the guards' shoulders. "I'm sorry, Sire."

Charming was seething with anger but he kept his temper under control and his voice modulated. "Now see here, Prudhomme. Enough of this nonsense. I want to talk to Dad about this baby situation. I'm not going to cause any trouble. I just want to know where I stand."

Prudhomme looked relieved. He hesitated, then stepped forward. "Well, all of this has been rather sudden, I suppose. Indeed, I've had some difficulty in accepting the idea myself. I can well imagine what an ordeal it must be for you."

"Exactly," agreed the Prince. "Just what idea are we talking about?"

"And may I say, Sire, that serving you during your tenure as Prince was most rewarding and, furthermore, that your mother, in my memory at least, will always have been the Queen."

"My mother *was* the Queen!" yelled Charming. Prudhomme scuttled behind the guards again.

"Excuse me." The tension was broken by the well-oiled voice of Count Norville. He swept his black cloak off his shoulders and strode purposefully into the room from the rear hallway. Behind him, Mandelbaum followed. From his fingers dangled a small crystal on a silver chain.

"I can see we've had some excitement generated. Well, let me assure you . . ." Norville suddenly switched conversational tracks. "Did our guests leave already?"

Ruby shrugged. "Cynthia had an appointment with her dressmaker. Something about a glass petticoat, I believe."

"Oh?" Norville gave Charming a quizzical look. "Well, where was I? Ah, yes, Charming. Well, young man, I can see you are upset by this sudden revelation of events, and quite understandably so. Let me assure you, my young friend, that we would not do something so serious as to deny you your birthright without a complete and accurate assessment of the facts. Indeed, as Minister of Information, if befalls upon me to lead the investigation of this matter. I can say with complete confidence that my report will contain nothing but the most rigorously confirmed and unvarnished truth."

"Well, great," said Charming with relief. "Because I can explain the whole thing. Now, I admit I was wrong to lie about . . ."

"Of course," Norville interrupted. "Since King Garrison and and Queen Aurora are the only two surviving eyewitnesses, the investigation can be completed rather quickly. In fact, I would venture to say the whole thing is rather cut and dried. Goodness, who am I to doubt the word of the King, particularly when it was given under oath?"

"Damn it, Norville! If Dad and Aurora were already married, what the heck did they get married tonight for?"

"Renewed their vows. Couples do it all the time."

"Mandelbaum! Tell them what happened on the ride back!"

Mandelbaum's fingers trembled slightly as he studied

the tiny crystal. He refused to meet Charming's eyes. Ever so carefully he folded up the slim silver chain and put it away in an inner pocket, all the while looking at the floor, the ceiling, the paintings on the walls, everywhere but at Prince Charming. The entire room waited. Finally he said, slowly, "As an employee of the King, I have placed myself under his command. As a citizen of Illyria, I owe allegiance to its sovereign."

"Yeah. Thanks, Mandelbaum. Thanks a whole lot."

"Now then, Charming," Norville fished into his pocket and pulled out a sheaf of notes. "Your father has compiled a list of some rather extra-special assignments that demand your immediate and personal attention. Coincidentally, all of these require that you travel outside of Illyria for an extended period. Not that you are being exiled in any way, you understand. Oh, no. Far from it. Your usual generous allowance will be forwarded to you and we expect you to remain in full contact through our diplomatic embassies. . . ."

There was a brief flash of reflected light, a slight hiss of cleaved air, and the papers, sliced neatly in two, dropped from Norville's hands. The Count took an involuntary step back, his eyes fixed on the steel in Charming's fist. The guards near Prudhomme drew their swords and four more guards, stationed in the hall behind Norville, stepped quickly into the room.

"Steady there, lad," murmured the Wicked Queen.

Charming spun on one foot until the tip of the sword grazed Ruby's throat. His face reflected the sort of uncomprehending shock generally experienced only by small animals that have been run over by carriage wheels. You!" he snarled. "You're behind all this! Well, I'm not going to stand for it!"

Ruby covered a yawn with her hand and raised a single eyebrow. Slowly, she took the point of the sword between thumb and forefinger and pushed it to one side. Her eyes fixed on Charming's, she stood up, raising herself to her full height plus high heels. Then she leaned over to Charming's shoulder and hissed in his ear.

"Listen, you little simpleton, don't blame me for your downfall. You should have seen this coming a mile away if you hadn't been playing your Prince Charming role so long you actually started to believe all that nonsense about honor and duty. Well, now you are getting a healthy lesson in pragmatism. And rule number one is this, that 'honor' is just a word that clever rulers like your father use to manipulate dumb kids like you into doing what they want."

"That's enough!" snapped Charming. He put a hand on her chest and pushed her back down into the chair. He stepped back into the center of the room and swung his blade around defiantly, pointing first at Prudhomme, then Mandelbaum, and then Norville. "All right, I'm going. Away. To think, that's all. You haven't gotten rid of me that easy. Because I'll be back. And when I return, you'll all wish this evening had never happened."

The Prince thrust the sword into his belt, walked to the great double doors and brought his heel against them viciously. Both doors swung open with a mighty crash and Charming, without a backward glance, strode off into the night. It was a most dramatic exit, so dramatic in fact that the rest of the group stood quietly for almost two minutes, expecting something to happen that would spoil the theatre of the scene. But nothing did happen. The Prince was gone.

"Well," said Prudhomme after several minutes. "That was certainly an unpleasant confrontation. You know, we don't even know if the baby is going to be a boy."

"Doesn't matter," said Norville. "By Illyrian custom the first born inherits the throne, whether a man or woman."

"It's a boy," said Mandelbaum. He took the crystal out of his pocket, glanced at it and put it back. "Still a boy."

"Yes, well, with a proper mother around to give him moral guidance, we can hope that this new prince will grow into a decent young man."

"I've always liked Charming," said Prudhomme.

"Not that Charming didn't have his good points, but his lack of respect for social mores was certainly dismaying. Particularly offensive was this unhealthy preoccupation he had with ... um ..." Norville glanced uneasily at Queen Ruby.

"With sex?" she prompted.

"Er, yes. Most dismaying. Anyone who could invite that Cynthia girl into the royal circle certainly needed a lesson in good taste. Although I must admit her godmother was extremely sensible."

"I see. Mandelbaum, dear, I will return to you shortly. I must see how my sweet little stepdaughter is getting on." Queen Ruby swept out of the room. In the hallway, a very worried Ann was waiting for her.

"Did he fall for it?"

"He fell for it indeed. The poor boy. He was very upset. And, of course, who could blame him?"

"Oh, dear," Ann twisted her hands. "I hope he isn't too shocked. Being the Prince meant a lot to him. Perhaps I should have told him myself. Broken the news more gently."

"Now, dear, this is not the time to get carried away by sentiment. You know how men tend to blame the bearer of bad news. We can't have his anger directed at you. It would spoil everything. You told me that yourself."

"Yes, I know. You're right. It just pains me to see him so sad."

"Well, you can go now and offer him comfort. And

you had better leave quickly, before he gets too much of a start."

"That doesn't matter. I know where he's going."

"Back to Alacia?"

"Right. There are some survivors who might testify that the wedding never took place. They'll be in Briar Rose."

"But will he go for the grail?"

"I think so. He's mad enough at you that he'll try to find it again, just so you can't have it."

"Good. Still, you should try to catch up with him now. You don't want to give the impression you're pursuing him."

"But I am pursuing him."

"All the more reason not to appear so. Go now. I've packed you a bag."

Ann nodded and started off. She stopped once and looked back. "You know, I always thought you were a bitch."

Ruby smiled. "I am, dear, when I don't get what I want. Now, I'm getting what I want. And I want you to get what you want, too."

Ann nodded again. "Good-bye then." And she left. Ruby watched her leave and smiled pensively.

She spent a few minutes primping her hair in a hall mirror before rejoining the men. "Oh, Mandelbaum, dear, I'm ready for that astronomy lesson now."

Aurora sat in front of her dressing-room mirror and brushed her long blond hair with a silver-backed hairbrush. She was feeling very pleased with herself. She looked at the ring on her finger, the real wedding ring, not the pretend one, and smiled to herself. Wasn't it funny how life worked out? To go to sleep one day as a princess, to awaken as a pauper and, a few days later, to become the Queen of Illyria. It was enough to make one think one was being guided by destiny or fate or kismet or that sort of thing.

In fact, even the last dreadful week was not without its advantages. Aurora was sure that if she had the time to sit down and really think about what happened to her, she would probably discover she had learned important lessons about humility, self-reliance, and that kind of stuff. And she was not one to let knowledge gained so harshly slip away. Oh, no. She would use the wisdom she had garnered to become a better Queen and help Garrison rule with compassion. And she would teach little Garrison what she had learned, too, once she figured out what it was, so that he wouldn't grow up spoiled, but would be honest and true.

Like Prince Charming.

Well, it was too bad about Prince Charming, but he would get over it. Anyway, Aurora fully intended to make it up to him. For one thing, she liked him a whole lot. For another, she owed her life to him and Illyria owed a lot to him. The new Queen was not going to see such a brave young man simply brushed aside. At least not until little Garrison got much, much older.

A happy thought occurred to her, so simple and beautiful in its clarity that she hugged herself with pleasure. She would make Charming the Crown Prince of Alacia!

It was a perfect match! Charming would get a nice little country to rule over, not too much trouble, and close enough to come for visits. Alacia, her special homeland, would get a ruler who was brave and noble. What could be better?

Aurora was so delighted with herself for thinking of this that she put on her dressing gown and ran to tell it to Ann. The Little Princess was, alas, nowhere to be found, although she did meet Queen Ruby, who was on her way up to Mandelbaum's tower with several small bags of herbs. Aurora admired the warm relationship Ruby seemed to have with her stepdaughter and decided to ask her opinion. "Queen Ruby, have you seen Prince Charming?"

"Why, no, dear. I believe he has left the country for a while. He was a bit upset about the wedding."

"Er, yes, I can see that he would be."

"I believe he said he was going to Alacia to think things over."

"Alacia?" said Aurora. It was a little disconcerting to have her wonderful idea foreshadowed. "Why Alacia?"

Ruby shrugged. "I have no idea."

Aurora furrowed her brow. It seemed a little strange that Prince Charming should decide to go to Alacia just when she was thinking of sending him there. He hadn't seemed particularly interested in the place. Still, if he liked it that much, it merely confirmed her choice of him as ruler for it. "I see. Is Ann around?"

"I haven't seen her all day," Ruby said smoothly.

"Princess Ann?" said Norville, coming up behind them. "My reports say she rode off to Alacia last night." He bowed. "Good morning, ladies."

"Alacia? Really?" said Ruby.

"Oh, ho," said Aurora. "So Ann is on her way to Alacia, also. She's chasing after Prince Charming. I knew she was just playing hard to get."

Norville rubbed his temple. "There seems to be an uncommon interest in Alacia of late, your Highness. This morning I received a report that Madam Esmerelda and Miss Cynthia were both on their way to Alacia in a carriage."

"Charming must have impressed that girl, too."

"No, they left before he did."

Aurora frowned. Why was everyone going off to Alacia? "Well, the farther that woman is away from me, the better, as far as I'm concerned. If she wants to go picking around the ruins of the castle looking for relics and grails and things, let her. But if she tries to come back to Illyria, I'm going to teach her a lesson."

"Grails?" said Ruby. "Did you say grails?"

"Esmerelda always claimed Daddy was hiding all sorts of magical stuff that she wanted. It was one of the things they fought about all the time. Prince Charming was also looking for a fertility grail," she explained to Queen Ruby. "That's how he found me."

"Really," said Ruby weakly.

"I must see that we get some extra intelligence from Alacia," said Norville. "In the meantime, your Majesty, I should like to review the security arrangements for your reception this evening."

"Of course," said Aurora, drawing him down the hall. "Queen Ruby, have a nice day."

"Um," said Ruby. "Thank you."

In fact, it took longer than Ann expected to catch up with Charming. It is usually treacherous riding at night, but it was a full moon, and a sure-footed horse and skilled rider could cover much ground. Charming was a skilled rider and took the fleetest horse in the stable. Ann was not so skilled and had to choose her mount essentially at random. On the first night, the Prince outdistanced her quickly. And although she had ridden back from Alacia with Charming, her memory of the roads was not perfect and in the following days she got sidetracked more than a few times. On such a diversion, Wendell passed her in the early hours of the morning. Even when back on track, she quickly lost hope of catching up with the furiously riding prince. She reassured herself, however, that she knew his final destination and kept her horse at a steady pace.

Wendell had no idea what Charming was up to.

There had been a brief reception following the wedding, nothing fancy, just champagne and cake and a plethora of toasts from the castle's inner circle; Wendell had ignored the champagne and concentrated on the cake. As the reception broke up, he descended from the second floor with a piece of cake in each hand and greeted Mandelbaum and Queen Ruby coming upstairs. Mandelbaum asked how Charming was getting on and Wendell said fine, why do you ask and Mandelbaum looked uncomfortable and said oh, never mind and the Wicked Queen was watching Wendell so sharply during this exchange that he decided to seek out Charming immediately. The Prince was not in his room and he was not downstairs and he was not even in the old Queen's studio that Wendell wasn't supposed to know about. One cannot, however, make as vociferous an exit as Charming made without alerting a whole bunch of the castle servants and Wendell soon got the idea that the Prince had been evicted from the castle without quite learning just why. He threw together an assortment of weapons and clothes, grabbed the second-fastest horse in the stables and took off.

A night watchman pointed him down the southern road. At dawn he reached a village that had been terrorized for the last fortnight by a large wolf. The villagers reported that Charming had ridden the beast down, dispatched it and galloped off without even waiting to be thanked. The next day another set of villagers explained that a gryphon had been depleting the spring's birth of lambs; the Prince had walked right up without a thought for his own safety, sliced the damned thing's head off, then mounted his horse and departed without a word to anyone. Just over the border into Alacia he heard an even stranger tale. A band of outlaws had raided a trading village and were dividing up their loot when a wild young man, clothes torn, hair disheveled, eyes wide and staring, had walked fearlessly into their camp, pommeled their leader severely about the head with the hilt of his dagger, and told them all that he would be back to finish them off later. He was gone before any of the astounded mercenaries dared reach for their swords. It wasn't until several hours had passed that they realized they had just encountered the legendary Prince Charming.

All this had Wendell very worried.

He caught up with Charming on the outskirts of Briar Rose Village. It was late in the afternoon. Charming was walking his horse and carrying the saddle. The horse was exhausted. Its flanks were soaked with sweat and it was blowing foam. Charming had taken off the halter, too, and was leading the horse with a hand in its mane.

The Prince did not look much better than his horse. His clothes were dirty and torn, and his hair was matted with sweat and blood. He was even more exhausted than the horse and, while he wasn't foaming at the mouth, the sight would not have surprised Wendell. His boots were muddy and scuffed and his sword belt hung low on his hips, so the tip of the scabbard dragged in the dirt. He greeted Wendell with tired eyes. "Oh, hello, Wendell."

"Never mind hello." Wendell grabbed the Prince by the arm and led him to a nearby stream, where he dug a bar of soap out of his saddlebag, handed it to Charming and pushed him in. "Why did you go off without telling me? You know you can't get along without me." He took Endeavor from the Prince, examined the blade disgustedly, and set it aside. "I was really worried." He set out fresh clothes for the Prince. "What are we doing here anyway?"

"Going back to the castle."

"What for?"

"Aurora forgot her toothbrush. We're going back for it."

"What?"

"Just kidding."

"Boy, are you acting strange. So I guess Cynthia must have turned you down, huh?"

Charming was holding his head underwater while he scrubbed his hair. He looked up. "What?"

"I said you must be all upset because Cynthia turned you down."

"Something like that."

"You've been turned down plenty of times before and you didn't get this weirded out. What made her so special?"

"Must have been the high heels. Spikes really turn me on." Wendell was about to object to this when Charming waded ashore. "Have we got anything to eat?"

"Bread. Pickles. Cheese. Wine. And cold chicken."

"You're a good kid, Wendell. I'll see you get a royal citation for this."

"What a thrill. So why are we going back to this castle? I thought you lost interest in that grail thing."

"Well, Wendell, I just felt, for various reasons that I'll tell you about later, that I had to get out of Illyria for a while. The thing with Cynthia isn't going to play out, Dad is going to be on his honeymoon, Mandelbaum is preoccupied with Ruby . . ."

"I'll say."

". . . and with one thing or another I just wasn't going to get much done in town. So I thought I'd come back to Alacia, check out this story of Bear's, ask some questions, straighten up a few loose ends I'd been meaning to get to. Does that sound reasonable?"

"No. Now tell me what's really going on. Do we spend the night at that inn again?"

"Nope. I've already been there. I wanted to talk to

those two wine stewards Bear found in the castle. But they couldn't say for sure whether Aurora's wedding took place."

"That's too bad," said Wendell, who didn't quite see the point of this.

"Yeah. But I did learn something pretty interesting. Esmerelda and Cynthia arrived here last night. I thought I made pretty good time, but somehow they passed me."

"You got sidetracked on a few Slay-and-Rescue missions," Wendell pointed out.

"Right." The Prince was silent for a few minutes. "Pretty odd coincidence that Mandelbaum suddenly showed up the first time we were here. He's hardly left the castle in years."

"He came to help us out."

"Uh huh. And he said the fertility grail wasn't worth much, either. Then Esmerelda learns that the wall of thorns is down and suddenly she takes off for Alacia."

"Well, that's lucky for you. You can make another play for Cynthia. What do you care if Esmerelda is here? She's just an old lady. You hardly spoke to her."

"I should have checked her out more carefully." The Prince spoke thoughtfully and very slowly. "Bear says Esmerelda is the fairy Queen that put the curse on Aurora."

"Oh," said Wendell and then, "Wow!"

"The villagers of Briar Rose are very upset to see her back."

"I can imagine."

"I think I'll pay her a visit."

"At night? We're going to visit an evil fairy in an enchanted chapel at night? That's when all the evil sorcerers work their worst magic."

"Well, then she'll be awake. If we went by day, we'd wake her up. That would be impolite."

"You won't be able to see anything."

"We have lanterns. It's all below ground anyway."

Wendell crossed his arms stubbornly. "Sire, with all due respect, this sounds like a pretty risky venture just for a crummy old relic. It's not like there's a maiden in there to be rescued. You always said we didn't do quests."

"*We* don't. I've got a different angle on this one, Wendell. I'm going in alone."

"Oh, come on. You know I always fight by your side."

"Not this time."

"My Lord and Prince is not going into some demon-infested cave without me."

"Well, that's something we need to talk about right now, Wendell. I may not be your Prince any longer. Now, listen carefully . . ."

The sun was setting when Ann reached the edge of the thorn hedge. She shivered. The fading light fell on the thorn branches and the shadows were twisted into gruesome patterns, the thorns themselves showing up like rows of pointed teeth on evil, grinning mouths. She tied up her horse and approached the gap where Bear and his men had chopped a passage through the hedge. Here the barricade looked far less formidable. The bushes had been chopped off low to the ground and the branches trampled into the dirt; broken and hacked-off limbs hung forlornly to the sides. The passage stretched off into the gloom, big enough for several men to walk abreast and high enough to lead a horse. It looked quite safe, but Ann remembered how quickly the thorns had grown back before.

She didn't want to go through with this, really she didn't, but she was certain that Charming had returned to the grail castle. Probably, he was inside the hedge right now. In a moment, she had convinced herself that Charming *was* inside the hedge checking out the ruins of the castle. Suddenly, the inside of the hedge seemed much more comforting than the outside. She looked at the setting sun. There was still enough light, she told herself, to run inside, look for the Prince and still return to Briar Rose Inn if he wasn't there. It would be a terrible shame to come all this way and miss him. She wanted to find him when he was still emotionally vulnerable, still on the rebound, so to speak. After he got the stupid grail, of course.

She gave her horse a final, reassuring pat on the nose and stepped into the passage. She hesitated after the first step, waiting for a thorny tendril to grab her from behind, but nothing happened. Taking a deep breath and hitching up her skirt, she started down the passage. Although gloomy, it grew no darker, with enough light filtering through the branches to see by. When she could see the light at the end of the passage, she walked quickly and with more confidence, certain that she would see the Prince in a few minutes. She would be very glad to see him, she decided. She didn't really care if he had the grail or not. She walked faster. Probably he would be glad to see her too, she thought. After the debacle in Illyria, he'd want someone to talk to and she could comfort him. She looked over her shoulder. The sun was setting faster than she expected. It was quite dark inside the thorn bushes. She quickened her pace . . . and stumbled.

When she lost her balance, Ann also lost her composure. The floor of the tunnel was littered with chopped-up thorn branches and they jabbed her hands as she tumbled down on them. "Ow!" She was back on her feet in an instant, but the thorns clung to her dress and she scratched herself even more as she frantically tried to brush them off. It was not quite dark in the tunnel and Ann simply panicked. Her heart pounding, her breath coming in short gasps, she ran full tilt the last yards to the end of the tunnel, almost crying in fear at the thorny branches that plucked at her skin and hair.

Once she was outside she felt like a total idiot, of course.

The sun had set and the murky twilight had turned into a clear, starlit night. A warm, clean breeze was blowing; the deep grass, soft beneath her feet, swayed gently and made comforting whispering noises. Ann sat down on the grass and let the rapid beating of her heart return to normal. "Great," she told herself. "Just great. That was an impressive display of fortitude. Try to remember you're too old to be afraid of the dark." Gripping the twigs between her fingernails, she carefully pulled the remaining thorns away from her clothes. She inspected her arms. They were crossed with light scratches, some of which were beginning to form welts. Not the sort of look one went for when one was trying to attract a boy. Well, it couldn't be helped now. She shrugged, stood up, and looked around.

The castle of the Sleeping Beauty looked different from the way she had last seen it. For one thing, it was now night. For another, it had burned to the ground. Even though it was largely built of stone, much of the masonry had fallen in when the timber pinnings had burned away. There were still the bases of the towers to be seen, though, some reaching as high as twenty feet, and the intact remains of some walls and stairs. But mostly it was just great piles of rubble, with the moon rising behind.

There was no sign of Charming.

She felt a sharp stab of apprehension. She had been sure he would return to Alacia, seeking evidence to discredit Aurora, and that his natural thirst for adventure would lead him to seek out the grail while he was here. The ruins not only seemed deserted, but the grass between the castle and the thorn hedge showed no sign of having been trodden by man nor beast, at least, not recently.

"Maybe I've misjudged him," she thought. "Maybe he's stretched out somewhere on the bank of a river, fishing pole in his lap, happy to be relieved of the responsibility of being Prince Charming." On second thought, that didn't seem likely. Well, it was too dark to go back through the hedge. She decided to take a closer look at the castle.

The moat was still intact, the icy clear stream still flowing. The drawbridge had burned part way through and fallen into the moat, but someone, Bear's men probably, had found some charred beams to lay across the sunken part, so it was still passable. She crossed it and climbed to one of the higher piles of rubble from which she could survey the whole of the ruins in the rising moon.

Nothing conveys a feeling of loneliness and desolation more thoroughly than a burned-out ruin, except a burned-out ruin at night. The stark blackness of the charred beams, the tumbled, soot-covered stones, the broken pottery, the pools of oily rainwater, and here and there the fathomless pits and dark, yawning chasms where the castle structure had collapsed into several layers of basements and sub-basements, all combined to create an atmosphere of despair and mind-numbing weariness. Ann's heart sank. A small animal scurried among the stones with a sinister rustle and she clutched at her skirt nervously. Her own decrepit castle seemed quite warm and comfortable now, her downtrodden peasants friendly and protective, and she wished quite seriously that she had never left home to pursue this stupid scheme.

Then, close to the center of the ruins, she saw the dim glow of a fire.

Her heart leapt. "It's Charming! I knew it!" and she was about to call out when she caught herself. It might not be Charming. She remembered childhood tales of warlocks and witches. She also thought of ghosts, goblins, trolls, ogres, bandits and one-armed maniacs with hooks for hands. She thought that she was a defenseless young girl alone at night. Finally, she thought she had better take a closer look before she revealed herself.

It was a task easier said than done. When she climbed down from the mound of rubble, she lost sight of the fire's glow. She was able to maintain a good idea of where the center of the ruins was as she picked her way through the wreckage, but it was hard going to avoid falling into the sub-structure as she clambered about in the darkness. It took an hour of detours and false trails to approach the fire. There she found a small, flat clearing, with a small fire cheerfully burning in the center and an extremely pretty girl, dressed in black, sitting crosslegged on the ground training a flock of crows.

At least, that's what it looked like. The girl held a six-inch length of polished wood in one hand and the half dozen black birds that sat on the ground in front of her were watching it intently. She would move it to one side and they would all turn their heads. She would move it to the other side and they would turn their heads back. She would tap it on the ground and they would all take a little jump, fluttering their wings slightly. Finally she tossed the stick in the fire and all the birds formed a line and marched around the fire in a circle, bobbing their heads in unison. It was very strange, but also comical and Ann, hiding among the rocks, had to smile.

Eventually the little parade ended. The black birds dispersed, not flying, but hopping off into the darkness of the rocks surrounding the fire, except one of them, a large magpie, fluttered to the top of a pile of stone and stood there with its head cocked, watching the girl. She stood up, stretched, yawned, and then looked over at Ann and said, "Well, hi there. You can come out now."

Ann came out, feeling a bit foolish. "Hello. I don't think we were actually introduced, but your name is Cynthia, isn't it? We met a few nights ago at the Castle Illyria."

"Hi. Yes, I remember. You're Ann, right? A princess? Princess Ann."

"Um, yes."

"Good, good. We've been expecting you. Nice night, huh? I guess you're looking for Prince Charming. He's not here yet. Awful cute, isn't he?"

"What are you doing here?" said Ann, getting right to the point.

"Getting the grail, same as you. Oh, you mean with the birds? Just a little magic trick Esmerelda taught me. She knows a lot of stuff like that. Of course, she lost all her real power, but she still knows a lot of cute little spells and stuff."

"No, I mean . . ."

"Of course, a lot of this magic stuff is pretty useless anyway, in my opinion. Most of it is things like throwing hexes on your neighbors and making their livestock infertile. And talking to animals."

"Um . . ."

"I mean, what's a cat got to talk about anyway? They've got a brain maybe the size of a walnut. Not exactly much room there for intellectual dissertation."

"Uh huh . . ."

"Got any cows you want sterilized?"

"Um, not really."

"Nobody does. Useless. Political power, now that's a different story. When you've got political power augmented with magical power, now you're getting somewhere. That's why Illyria is so strong. I learned all this from Esmerelda. She's my fairy godmother."

"I know."

"Of course, when you start out poor it's tough getting any sort of power. If you're male, you become a soldier and slash your way to the top of the heap. If you're a woman, you have to rely on your looks. You probably never had to think about all this, since you're already a princess."

Ann glared at her. "I . . ."

"I was going to marry Prince Charming, but that's all off now. He's not really a prince, you know. Not a legitimate one."

"Is that so?"

"Yeah. But fortunately this grail became available, so we still have an angle on magical power. This is really important to Esmerelda."

"Uh huh," said Ann, since it seemed as though Cynthia was waiting for a reply.

"Oh, yes. And she's really interested in meeting you. Which we might as well do right now."

"Well, I'm rather afraid I'm waiting for a friend."

"Prince Charming, yeah, right. You said that already. Don't worry about it. He'll be along in a little while." Cynthia picked up a torch that was resting on a flat rock and lit it from the fire. She took Ann by the arm. "Let's go."

"Where are we going?" Cynthia seemed to have a bit more depth then when Ann last saw her, and she was getting a bad feeling about this encounter. She really wished Charming were here.

"We're going to the grail chapel. It's underground. This whole hill has all been pretty much hollowed out. It's all underground rooms and passages and stuff. It's kind of spooky."

"Hard to believe."

Cynthia did not seem to be the type who reacted to sarcasm. She held the torch to the edge of one of the dark pits and revealed a set of narrow stone stairs carved into the rock. She started down them. "Watch your step. The rock is kind of damp and there's a lot of rubble and stuff like that. So be careful."

"Well," said Ann. "It's very hospitable of you to offer this tour and all, but I have not the slightest intention of entering these catacombs or whatever they are. Thank you, but I believe I'll just sit tight until Prince Charming arrives."

Cynthia marched back up the stairs. She stood in front of Ann, legs apart, torch in one hand, the other hand authoritatively on her hip. "Look. Esmerelda told me to bring you to her. Now we can do this the hard way, or we can do it soft, but either way you're coming with me."

Ann felt a sudden chill. There was steel in Cynthia's voice and a glint in her eyes that was a little bit strange and not at all pleasant. Around the two girls the night settled in like a velvet cloak and the torch offered a flickering circle of light that spared only a few rocks from the darkness.

"Actually, I suppose I can wait for Charming just as well inside as outside."

"That's the ticket. Just stay close to me. It's not that bad."

Cynthia held the torch in front of herself and descended into the interior of the hill, Ann following on the step just above her. The air got immediately damper and cooler, but the stone stairway spiraled down only about thirty feet. Ann found herself standing on a dry, level passage, dimly lit by scattered candles set in nooks in the walls. Tunnel entrances led out from the main passage. A few were curtained off, but most had thick wooden doors with iron hinges set into the stone. The caves looked as if they had been formed naturally, then worked over by generations of masons to form smooth walls and squared-off portals.

"Not bad," Ann said.

"We've cleaned up quite a bit. It was filled with centuries worth of rubbish. I should say, I cleaned up. Esmerelda would live in a pigsty if left to herself. Too obsessed with magic and scheming to attend to the day-to-day details of living."

Ann shrugged.

"There's the grail passage." Cynthia pointed down a dark hallway.

The grail passage was elaborate indeed. The entrance was surrounded by a frame of heavy, thick and very dark wood, every square inch of which was intricately carved with tiny runic symbols. The frame looked very, very old. The wooden frame was in turn surrounded by a marble frame, only slightly newer and just as intricately carved. A set of double wooden doors, also carved with incredible detail, hung from the wooden frame, but now they were stopped open. Inside, the passage was dark, damp and musty. The light from the candles penetrated only a few feet into the gloom.

"Don't stick your head in there too far," Cynthia warned Ann. "You're likely to get it lopped off. There's nothing but a bunch of skeletons in there anyway. Only a knight who is pure and chaste, which means one who's never got his wick dipped, can enter the grail chapel."

"Got his what?"

"Skip it. The knight has to be a virgin, that's all."

"I'm a virgin."

"Too bad. It only works for men."

"Unfair."

"Just as well, I think. Do you really want to fight a disembodied arm with a sword?"

"What?"

"Don't look at me like that, I didn't set this up. The wrong person steps into that chamber, a ghostly arm swoops down and lops his head off."

"That," said Ann, "is really stupid."

"Yeah, well, these ancient priests and sorcerers, they had a lot of power, but they weren't all that sophisticated."

"But someone like Prince Charming would be able to walk right through the chapel and grab the grail with no problem?"

"Nope. Everybody still has to fight the arm with the sword. But only a guy who is pure and chaste can defeat the dumb thing. If he's good."

"Charming's good. Well, suppose two knights entered the chapel. Even if they weren't pure, it would still be two to one against the arm."

"Nope, wouldn't work."

"Well, suppose one was a virgin and the other wasn't?"

"Who cares? Look, this isn't exactly the treasure of King Solomon in there. It's just a crummy little fertility grail that will cause your sheep to put out a few more ewes and your peas to sprout a few more pods and maybe a barren woman will get pregnant. Maybe it's kind of nice for a sheep farmer, but it's hardly the sort of thing to die over."

"There are people," said Ann, "for whom the birth or death of a single lamb can mean the difference between starvation and sustenance."

"Tough break," said Cynthia unsympathetically, "because the kind of people who can really use a grail like this are magicians who can tap into its power. Like Esmerelda. Once she understands from where its magic originates, she can use it to power her own spells. Her sphere of influence will be expanded, her power will be undefiable, and she'll be able to crank up some really, really neat spells and they won't run out at midnight, either. She has some great clothing spells."

"Uh huh. How thrilling. Well, this has been absolutely fascinating, Cynthia, and I really appreciate the tour, but if there's nothing else, I should really be going now. It's past my bedtime and all that."

"Oh, we're just getting started," said Cynthia. She seized Ann's wrist in a grip that seemed unnaturally strong and dragged her down the passageway. "Here we go. This is where Esmerelda has her laboratory set up."

Ann, however, was not the hothouse flower Cynthia expected and she didn't go far. The red-haired girl found her grip twisted away. Ann stared her down with narrowed eyes.

"I," said the Princess, "will wait outside. Do not try to stop me." She turned with dignity and walked away.

Cynthia hit her on the head with a rock.

She knocked once on the door, then pushed it open without waiting for an answer and roughly dragged Ann inside. "Hi, Esmerelda. I've got her."

Charming dismounted outside the thorn hedge and examined the horse he found tethered there. It was undoubtedly from the Royal stables. One of Norville's agents, perhaps? The stirrups had been cinched up high, so the rider must have had short legs. Charming shrugged and tied up his horse beside it. Whoever it was would show up eventually.

Taking a lantern from his pack, he quickly traversed the tunnel, entered the ruins and, after a bit of scouting around, found the entrance to the underground passage without too much trouble. He lit the lantern and drew his sword, descending into the cavern cautiously but quickly. The entrance to the grail chapel was easily found and still open. He ignored it.

"Hello, Esmerelda," he said.

The fairy Queen was standing beside the open doors. She looked the same as when Charming had last seen her, but Charming had not paid much attention to her then. Her hair was dark brown streaked with gray and cut close to her head. She wore a green velvet cloak that reached from her shoulders to the floor and she had at least one ring on every finger of her hands, including the thumbs. Her mouth, as she looked Charming over, was pursed in a frown of disapproval, but her voice was calm and reasonable. "Good evening, Charming. I realize you are surprised to see me."

Charming was not at all surprised, but he nodded. "I should say I'm more impressed than surprised. I had no idea when I invited you to dinner that you were responsible for the deaths of an entire castle's household and a country's nobility."

"Dear boy, surely you do not hold *me* responsible for that catastrophe. I had no intention of letting anyone die. King Stephen's wizards were all off duty, enjoying the wedding festivities, and I took advantage of their distraction to lay a sleeping spell over the castle. It was to be purely temporary, I assure you. Just long enough for me to enter and help myself to the grail and a few other artifacts."

"So what happened?"

"I'm afraid I can only speculate. Stephen's wizards, I believe, kept a back-up defense spell at the ready. When all three of them were disabled, the spell went into place automatically and raised a wall of thorns around the castle. I was unable to enter. The spell drained so much power from the fairy wood that I could not even lift my own spell. Nor could your father break it by kissing Aurora, for he also could not enter. Thus, you see, it was only the most unfortunate chain of errors that caused that tragedy."

"Very neat story," said Charming. He tested the edge of his sword with his thumb. "I'm not sure I believe it, though. I've suddenly become a lot more cynical."

"I am not surprised."

"But," said Charming, "then you knew that Dad was outside the hedge when the spell took hold. So he couldn't have made it to the wedding."

"Correct. And you are the legitimate heir to the throne of Illyria. I can provide evidence to refute the King's story. So, are you willing to bargain with me?"

"Nope. No, I think I'll just kill you, grab the grail, and be on my way. I've been in kind of a bad mood lately, anyway."

"And I don't blame you. When a healthy young man's natural physical desires are thwarted by a repressive and hypocritical society, small wonder that he seeks release in acts of violence against . . ."

"Oh, shut up."

"Well, that's beside the point anyway." Esmerelda raised his voice. "Oh, Cynthia! Are you ready, my sweet?"

"Coming, Esmerelda."

"Queen Ruby had me misinformed," explained Esmerelda. "We were halfway to Alacia before we put the whole story together. So I'm giving you another chance with Cynthia as part of the bargain. I think you'll be very pleased with this, Charming."

"Don't hold your breath."

One of the heavy wooden doors opened along the passageway and Cynthia came out into the hall. She had changed clothes. Charming had to admit he was intrigued.

She wore a dress of thin red silk that clung to her body as though it were wet. Her eyes were outlined in mascara that made them look even deeper and greener than they were, and her skin had been rubbed with oil that gave it a soft, almost luminous glow in the candlelight. Her hair and throat were heavily perfumed with a rich, damp scent that was traced with musk. Her lips were wet and faintly parted. She looked very, very sexy.

"Okay," said Charming. "I'm impressed."

"I thought you would be," said Esmerelda. "You want your position back and I can help you get it. You want to sleep with a beautiful girl and now one is available for you."

"Yep," said Charming, looking Cynthia up and down. "You got it."

"You need magical power to hold your position and I will place mine at your disposal. All I ask is that eventually you give me a place in your court and that you listen to my . . . advice."

"Advice?"

"Guidance, let's say. So this is the bargain. Take Cynthia for the night and leave the grail for me."

"That's it?"

"That's it."

"You get this magic cup and I get a single roll in the hay?"

"I assure you, Charming, that this will be much more than a roll in the hay. Cynthia is quite skilled . . ."

Cynthia closed her eyes to narrow slits and ran a smooth pink tongue lightly over her teeth.

". . . and she will provide for you a night that you will remember for the rest of your life."

Cynthia ran her fingers lightly down the inside of her thighs. Charming swallowed hard. "I thought only a man could work the power of the grail. The Fisher King."

"There are ways around that. For a certain type of woman. But I cannot guard the grail at all times. After you sleep with Cynthia, you will have to leave it be, but that is not enough. You must also report back that it was not here, that someone else carried it off first so that others will not seek it from me."

The girl shook herself lightly, her body rippling beneath the clinging red silk. Charming watched every motion. "If I leave you alive with this source of power, you're going to do terrible things to the people of this valley."

"I will do what I feel is necessary. But you've defended the common people quite enough already, Charming. Let them find another hero. Or better still, take responsibility for their own defense. It's time to start thinking of yourself a little. And this night with Cynthia need not be a one-time event. You can take her as your Queen or, if you do not wish to marry a commoner, as your consort."

"You're asking me to sell out my public trust," the Prince said hoarsely.

"I'm giving you the opportunity to stop being a slave to an ungrateful populace and start being your own man."

Cynthia ran her palms up across her smooth belly, cupping her breasts in each hand and squeezing them lightly. Closing her eyes, she threw her head back and moaned.

"Okay," said Charming. "I'll take the babe."

"He went for it; he went for it!" The fairy Queen was dancing around her makeshift laboratory, chortling with glee. This woman's voice was probably the most disgusting sound Ann had ever let past her eardrums. She rattled her chains helplessly, then let her arms fall to the scarred wooden table. A large bruise had formed on the back of her head.

"I've been tracking both of you ever since you got within range of my new magic mirror. It's the best bargain I ever made. I got it in the bazaar at Sarcasia for only thirteen hundred gold royals."

"So what?" snapped Ann. "I bet you got stiffed on the financing."

"Ha! Seven and a half percent interest and no payments for ninety days! I went through the evil fairy's credit union." Esmerelda glared at her, then continued smugly, "And look how quickly it paid off. Prince Charming in my clutches and a princess on my dissecting table. Amazing what one can do with a little advance notice. It's like the old saying goes, 'You can catch more flies with honey than with vinegar.'"

"Hmmph."

"And what a honey that Cynthia is. I should have thought of this years ago. Charming can slash his way past an army of bodyguards, but set him up with the right girl and he goes soft in the head."

"She's a slut," said Ann. "Charming doesn't really go for her type at all. He's just upset because of some family problems and that's clouded his judgment."

"You," said Esmerelda, "have no understanding whatsoever of teen-age boys. And, alas, you are not going to live long enough to learn about them. The blood of a princess, slaughtered at midnight with a silver blade . . . well, I won't bother you with the necromaniacal details. A sacrifice is simply necessary to convert the power of the grail over to me."

"So you must have been planning to sacrifice a princess twenty years ago, too. You were going to kill Aurora."

"I considered it. You understand now why King Stephen was so adamant about hiding the grail from me. But you, my dear, will do just as well. In a way, it's a pity. Tonight's seduction, you see, is only the beginning. Once the Prince has strayed from the straight and narrow path of virtue, only the gentlest push is required to keep him on the long, downhill slide to degradation. It would be so nice to force you to witness his gradual corruption. Mental torture, I think, can be almost as satisfying as physical torture."

The more frightened she was, Ann decided, the cooler she had to act. "I think you're expecting a lot from one roll in the hay," she said coolly.

Esmerelda waved a hand casually. "He'll be back

for more. Always the same with these chivalrous types; they abstain for so long, then they fall in love with the first woman who gives them a piece of ass."

"Nonsense. Boys aren't like that. They want *nice* girls."

"Ah. Missed your chance with him, eh?"

"Certainly not!"

Esmerelda glanced at an hourglass that was set into the wall. A thin trickle of sand was forming a neat pyramid in its bottom half. "A little time, a little time," she murmured. She flipped open a wooden box and removed a gleaming knife with a short, bone handle and a narrow, wickedly curved blade. "Silver is such a soft metal," she observed. "So difficult to put a proper edge on it. You don't mind being carved up with a slightly dull knife, do you?"

Ann closed her eyes.

Cynthia closed the door behind them and turned the key in the lock. The heavy bolt slid through the wood and set itself into the stone with a quiet "snick." She casually fluffed her hair, then turned toward the Prince. He was sitting on the edge of the bed, running one hand over the smooth rock wall.

"What are you doing?"

"Dry as a bone," murmured Charming. "But this cavern is below the water table. I expected at least some seepage."

"It's the grail. The power of the grail holds the water back. Remove it and this place would fill right up."

"Oh, really?"

Cynthia studied him. Had he said that just a little too casually? He was a very cool customer and hard to read.

She sat down next to him, the two of them sinking into the down-filled mattress. It was draped with satin sheets; they rustled as she slid next to him and put her arm around his waist. "Is this really your first time?"

"The very first." Charming put his arm around her waist. She snuggled closer.

"Esmerelda says boys are a little nervous the first time."

"Are *you* nervous?"

"What's there to be nervous about? You know what to do, don't you?"

"Of course." She kissed him and, after only a second, he kissed back. The kiss was long and lingering, and her lips were warm, soft, moist and slightly parted. He felt the soft angel's breath of her hair against his face and the briefest sensation of her tongue, probing for an instant against his mouth. Then she pulled away and leaned her head on his shoulder, sighing with satisfaction. "Oh, Prince Charming, I've waited so long for this moment."

"Me, too."

"I guess I just didn't think you'd be so easy to seduce. I thought you'd have all sorts of idealistic notions of honor and virtue that I'd have to overcome."

"Oh, that. Actually, I did. But, um, from the first moment I saw you, Cynthia, all other thoughts were swept from my mind and I could think of nothing else but being with you."

"Really?"

"Really," said Charming, grabbing a lush handful of thigh. Cynthia responded by wrapping her legs around his waist and pulling him down on top of her. They locked lips for another, oh, three or four minutes. Charming came up gasping.

"Uh, listen," he said between pants. "What do you say we go topside and, uh, take a walk under the stars and make love in the moonlight? Wouldn't that be romantic and stuff?"

Cynthia's nipples were straining against the red silk

of her dress, protruding through the fabric like cherries. She pulled herself up and pressed them into Charming's chest. Her arms snaked around his neck and she took the lobe of his ear between her teeth.

"Silly boy," she whispered, nibbling gently. "You don't have to stall. If you need more time, just relax. We've got all night."

Charming held the squirming girl close to him and instinctively caressed her back and bottom. He glanced toward the door, noted the key in the lock and forced himself to look away. "I think you'd be surprised at how much time we have," he muttered.

"Hmmm?"

"Nothing."

Cynthia drew back and faced him. Her cheeks were flushed, her lips swollen, and her eyes were hot and shining in the darkness. She looked at him searchingly a moment, then ripped open his shirt with a single motion. She began licking his chest, her tongue tracing wet circles on his skin.

Charming's vision blurred. He got her dress down off her shoulders and her breasts, high, round and firm, sprang free. He closed his eyes and cupped a hand around each one. It was like nothing he ever felt before. A long, drawn-out breath escaped him. "Oh, wow."

Cynthia moaned softly. "Mmmmm." She had kissed her way down his chest and her manicured fingers had found the buttons on his pants. Her breath was hot on his thighs. "Oh Prince Charming, I've waited so long for this night. I'll treat you so much better than she does."

"Mmmm?"

"For three nights, I've watched you in Esmerelda's magic mirror. Day after day you grew closer, while my heart beat faster at the sight of you. Eagerly I've awaited your . . . you . . . wait a minute!" She sat bolt upright. "Where's your page?"

"Page?" said the Prince innocently. "What page?"

Wendell slipped into the darkness of the grail passage, using his most catlike movements to avoid making any noise. He stood still for a minute and listened as hard as he could, expecting to hear the sound of blows or scuffling, or the clash of swordplay, or some other diversion that would indicate Charming's presence. But the rock walls of the cavern and the heavy oak doors effectively masked all sound. The page gave himself a mental shrug. Charming was clearly doing his job of diverting attention from the grail, now all Wendell had to do was snag it.

In his right hand he carried a single-edged sword of Nordic steel, slightly curved in the style of the far east. It was one of Charming's favorite swords and he had coated the blade lightly with oil and dusted it with soot before giving it to Wendell. "So it won't reflect the lamplight. Makes it harder to see in the dark." In his left hand he held a dark lantern. He was strongly tempted to slide back the cover and shine it down the passageway, but he decided against that. The light from the lantern would give away his presence and there was still enough torchlight shining through the open door to find his way.

He moved stealthily along the tunnel with the sword in front of him, arm held high and blade angled slightly downward. This, too, was Charming's advice. He had told it to Wendell when they made their plans that afternoon. "Go for technique, Wendell. It will be some sort of ghost. A disembodied arm with a sword, the legend goes. Possibly the sword will be flaming or the arm will be flaming or both. The point is, it's already dead. Don't try to batter it down. You'll have to disarm it."

Wendell nodded after replaying the conversation in his mind and continued to explore the cave. The walls were about four feet apart and the ceiling six feet high, plenty of room to move around, although it could get cramped fast if he had to fight in here. The rock walls were pretty smooth, although one could feel the marks left by chisels and hammers. It must have taken centuries to make this place; it was clearly very old. The floor was smooth also and, although it was coated with a thick layer of dust, at least it presented no obstacles for him to trip over. He went around a corner and into complete darkness, so he opened up the lantern. The light played on the walls and ceiling, revealing carved and painted runic symbols. He knelt down and studied the floor, looking for booby traps. His search found nothing but smooth, bare stone.

As he moved forward, the floor took a sudden slope downward and the passage narrowed until there were only a few inches of clearance on either side of his shoulders. A few feet later, it opened up again and Wendell entered the grail chapel.

It must have been a large cavern, for when Wendell aimed his lantern around, the light dissipated without reaching the walls or ceiling. He took another step and his foot brushed something. He knelt down and held the lantern to it.

It was a human skull.

He swung the lantern slowly in a small circle. There were, he estimated, a dozen skeletons scattered about. Some wore armor. Most had carried weapons, which now lay tarnished among their bones. The skeletons were very old. No trace of flesh remained. For some reason he found that a relief.

In the center of the room was the altar. A small, nondescript object sat on top of it.

The altar, at first, confused him. It was the focal point of the chapel and the object of his quest; why had he not noticed it immediately? Then he realized it was too far off for his lantern to reach. He could only see it now because it was back-lit.

The altar was outlined by an eerie green light. It hadn't been there when he entered, he was sure, but now it grew steadily brighter. As he watched, a ball of green flame, like ball lightning on the masts of a sailing ship, rose from behind the altar and hovered above it. The flames began to swirl and shimmer and take on shape. A few seconds later they suddenly solidified into the definite image of an arm. A glowing, green arm.

An arm with a sword.

"You jerk! Let me go!" Cynthia's sultry voice took on a most unpleasant screech when she was angry.

"What?" said the Prince. "I thought we had a date."

"It doesn't count." Cynthia was squirming and struggling in Charming's arms, but the Prince held her firmly around the waist and leaned back on the bed. "You liar! You made a deal with Esmerelda. You only get to have me if you leave the grail alone."

"I'm not touching the grail."

"Your page is. It's the same thing!"

"It is not."

"Is too!"

"Is no . . . OWWWWWW." Cynthia had scraped down his chest with the fingernails of both hands. Charming's grip involuntarily loosened and, in a second, she had wiggled free and leaped clear of the bed. She was still wearing her high heels, though, and a momentary loss of balance had her tumbling to the hard stone floor. Immediately, Charming grabbed her shoulders and held her down. She slipped out from under him and once again made a dash for the door. Charming managed to get a handful of her dress as she fled and it tore away leaving her naked but for her stockings. She hit the door and bounced off it, pounding on the wood with one hand while the other twisted the key in the lock.

"Esmerelda," she yelled at the top of her voice. "They're after the grail!"

"Give it up," said Charming. He came up behind her and clamped his hand over hers. Effortlessly he turned her wrist until the key locked again, then pulled her hand away and pried the key from her fingers. "That door is four inches thick and the walls here are solid stone. She can't hear you." He put the key in his pocket.

"You rat. Esmerelda was going to make us both great. Now you're taking away her source of power."

"That's life."

"You cheated. You weren't supposed to bring a back-up virgin."

"I guess this means you won't go to bed with me?" Cynthia glared at him.

The Prince shrugged philosophically. "I'm getting used to it. Well, in that case, I think I'll give Wendell a little more time and then we'll bug out of here. Send me a bill for the dress."

Cynthia stopped glaring and looked at him thoughtfully. He had outsmarted them, but he still didn't know the whole story. If she could delay Charming long enough, Esmerelda could still recapture the grail. And Cynthia still had one trick left.

She started to cry.

"Okay," said Ann. "I'm willing to bargain with you."

Esmerelda looked surprised. "Well, that's a new twist. The usual reaction of young girls in your position is to cry a lot or scream their bloody little heads off. Either that or beg for mercy. I hate it when they beg. Well, actually I rather enjoy it, but I still think they shouldn't do it. It's so degrading. They should have more dignity."

"Oh, yes," said Ann. "Take Cynthia for instance. I can tell dignity is real important to her."

"However, I'm afraid you are hardly in a position to bargain. Your life is in my hands and you have nothing to bargain with."

"I'm very rich. I can offer you treasure beyond your wildest dreams of avarice. The wealth of a nation is at your disposal."

"Your country is impoverished."

"Magical secrets, then. My stepmother is a powerful sorceress who can weave powerful incantations that even you, with all your knowledge, would yearn to master."

"Queen Ruby has the skill level of a good apprentice, nothing more."

"How about a couple of season tickets to the jousting matches?"

"Forget it," said Esmerelda. "I never bargain with my victims."

"You bargained with Prince Charming."

"That was different. Charming is a vicious son of a bitch. I had to have him on my side. He took out Magellan, one of the most powerful wizards in the twenty kingdoms, without suffering a scratch. And two of his bodyguards besides. Have you heard that story?"

"Yes," said Ann. "I mean, no. No, I haven't heard that story. Why don't you tell it to me now, withholding no detail, no matter how trivial or unimportant? Take your time."

"There you are, trying to stall again. Why don't you just quietly accept the inevitability of your fate with calm resignation and good graces? Then you can start crying and screaming, too."

"I'm not going to scream," said Ann without much conviction.

"Spoken like a true princess." Esmerelda took a leather strap, wrapped it around her hand and began stropping the silver blade against it.

Strangely enough, Wendell did not feel the least bit frightened. Charming had been utterly confident that Wendell would be up to the task he was set and the page shared that confidence. What he felt now was excitement, a strange elation that came not from the prospect of a dangerous fight, but from the vague realization that he was undergoing a rite of passage, an entry exam into the exclusive world of heroes and adventurers. After tonight he would not merely listen at the fireside to tales of great battles fought and great beasts slain, he would have a tale to tell of a mystical foe vanquished. Wendell gripped his sword and stepped forward cautiously but with assurance.

The arm had risen a little higher and now hung in the air over the altar. It burned, with a cold green light that provided little illumination. It was normally sized, as big as a large man's arm and muscular, although Wendell couldn't really make out much detail. It ran from a broad shoulder to a thick wrist and the sword it held was short, broad-bladed and flat. It was of bright metal but otherwise seemed to be a perfectly ordinary sword. Wendell moved in closer, holding up his lantern to throw more light on the altar. In the dimness he could see a flat brown object on its top. Nothing that looked like a grail.

He kept his attention on the arm. It was still hanging motionless and he wondered if he was going to have to make the first move. Perhaps it was expecting him to fall into a trap. He swept the lantern around, looking for a pit or deadfall, but all he found was smooth flat stone. At least there was plenty of room to fight.

He was less than two sword's lengths away when the arm made its move.

It moved suddenly and without finesse, the point of the sword simply taking aim at Wendell's heart and bearing down at him very fast. Despite the speed and the suddenness, the blow was easy enough to parry. What did surprise Wendell was the force of it; it deflected from his sword with a force that made him stagger.

The arm tore past him in a blaze of green light. The sword itself disappeared into the darkness, but the arm circled around in a wide arc, glowing like a green comet. It came back at top speed and he caught the blow with his sword. This time the impact drove him to his knees. The arm sped off, made another circle and came back faster than ever. Wendell make a quick strategic decision.

He picked up his lantern and ran.

"Remember this," Charming had said. "Whatever it is, it's going to be old. Hundreds, maybe thousands of years old. Sword fighting was pretty crude in those days. They didn't have the kind of tricky moves we know. Keep your head and you should be able to chop anything you meet into mincemeat."

Wendell ran back to where the tunnel opened into the cavern, stopped about four feet from the cavern wall and turned around. With the wall at his back he felt a lot better. The sword came at him and this time he simply sidestepped the blow. Driven by momentum, it carried on straight into the wall and the crash of steel on stone rang through the cavern. It bounced off the wall and hung motionless for a second. Wendell stepped up and swung at the ghost arm. His sword passed clean through it without the slightest effect and the arm drew away again. Wendell was not too surprised. He decided to ignore the arm and concentrate on the sword.

The arm followed a simple pattern. It simply drew the sword back and then drove it straight in. Time after time it attacked and each time Wendell deflected the blow, but letting it work him deeper into the tunnel, so he had only to defend a narrow front. It became a fairly repetitive game, but the arm was indefatigable and there was a limit to how long an eleven-year-old boy could keep warding off its blows. Wendell was tiring and had to make his move.

In the end it was simple. Wendell had once seen Charming use the same trick against an ogre.

When the arm made its thrust, he didn't ward the blow completely off. Instead, he let his own blade slide up the sword until the hilts locked, then threw all his weight to the side, pushing the sword up against the tunnel wall with his shoulder. With his left hand, he dropped the lantern and reached for the sword's hilt. He had to put his own fingers right through the green fist. When he did they burned like fire, but he ignored this, grabbed the handle and pulled with all his might. All this happened in less then a second. The ancient blade snapped cleanly at the hilt.

The arm dissipated in a green mist. Wendell stood up straight and let the broken blade clatter to the stone floor. The hilt he tossed aside. "Well," he said out loud, breathing hard. "That wasn't such a big deal." He looked around, half wishing that someone could have seen him in his moment of triumph. A girl, maybe. But there was no one else in the cavern. Being a hero is a lonely business.

He approached the altar again, this time without incident. On the altar lay a crudely shaped wooden bowl. Very old, very worn, very shallow. He picked it up in disbelief. "This is it? A piece of wood?"

In the darkness he heard a rumbling sound and a sudden inrush of water.

Wendell put the bowl in his pocket and ran for the exit.

"Hey, look, let's have none of that," said Charming uncomfortably. He hated to see a woman cry. Of course, he hated to see a man cry, but it wasn't the same thing. If for some reason a man started crying, you just patted him on the shoulder, bought him a beer or two and made sure to avoid him in the future. If a woman cried, though, you were supposed to give her aid and comfort which was very difficult if you were the reason she was crying in the first place.

"Come on, it's not as bad as all that." He patted his pockets for a handkerchief to offer her but came up empty. Cynthia continued to sob. "You're going to ruin your make-up." The sobs came louder. "I didn't hurt you, did I? If I did, I'm sorry." He stepped closer and tried to take her hands. Instead, Cynthia threw her arms around him and buried her face in his neck, letting hot tears wet his skin.

"You don't understand," she sobbed. "All my life I have been scorned and abused. My stepmother and my stepsister hate me. Before Esmerelda I was nothing. And now that we've finally got the chance to be someone, you're taking it away from us." She squirmed against him and let her hand drop casually to his pocket.

"Take it easy," said the Prince, patting her back in a not quite avuncular fashion. "It's not like we're going to destroy this grail. It'll still be around. If you two want to work some magic, I'm sure we can work something out."

"But Esmerelda . . ."

"Forget Esmerelda. She's bad news for you. Look, I know plenty of magicians who can spell rings around Esmerelda. They've got their own sources of power too. If you want an apprenticeship, I'll give you an introduction to a couple of them. And if you still need a grail, you can use this one on loan."

"No, you won't," sniffed Cynthia. "Your little princess friend wants the grail for herself to restore her kingdom. You'll give it to her, and once she has it, she'll never let it get away."

"Don't be silly. Ann doesn't tell me what to do and I have not the slightest intention of turning over the grail ..." He stopped in mid-sentence and Cynthia felt him get very still. Her fingers slipped into his pocket and found the key.

"Ann," said Charming slowly. "She must have followed her here. That was *her* horse outside the thorn hedge." He grabbed Cynthia by the shoulders roughly and stared into her face. "She's here. Where is she?"

Cynthia kneed him in the groin.

Charming saw stars. When they cleared, Cynthia was standing at the far end of the room, laughing wildly. She held up the key for him to see.

"Ann," he croaked. "Where is she?"

"With Esmerelda. She's dead meat now, Charming. With the blood of a princess, Esmerelda will have all the power she needs." She sneered. "With or without the grail."

Charming lunged at her. She popped the key in her mouth and swallowed it.

"Damn you!"

"Wish your girlfriend godspeed, Charming."

Charming gave the door a calculated look. He put his shoulder down and ran into it full tilt, putting every ounce of force he could muster into the blow. The door did not budge.

Cynthia was laughing again. "That door is four inches thick, my Prince, and the walls are solid rock. We're in here until Esmerelda lets us out."

Charming didn't reply. He rubbed his shoulder and limped over to the bed.

"I'm glad it worked out this way, Charming. I wasn't sure I could keep up that wanton woman act for much longer."

Tossing aside the sheets, he found his sword in its

scabbard. Slowly, he turned and held it up for her to see.

She stopped laughing. Her eyes got very big. "You wouldn't dare," she whispered.

Charming looked at her sadly. "I really hate to do this," he said and pulled the sword from its scabbard.

Esmerelda had cut off all of Ann's clothes with a large pair of scissors and was drawing cabalistic symbols over her body with a piece of green chalk. Occasionally she would mark a small x over an artery with a piece of red chalk. Apparently, this meant a spot where cutting was to be done, for after chalking each limb she placed a large bucket at the end of the table. The whole experience was the most humiliating, disgusting and altogether frightening thing that ever happened to Ann and the fact that Esmerelda was humming off key while she worked didn't help one bit.

"The table has blood grooves carved into it," she explained. "The blood will run down the grooves the length of the table and collect in this bucket."

"Isn't technology wonderful? What will they think of next?"

"Ah, a bit of sarcasm there. Good, good. I admire a girl with spunk. One who's willing to spit in the face of death."

Ann looked interested. Esmerelda quickly put her hand over the girl's mouth. "That's not an invitation to spit, lass. If you do, I shall simply have to gag you these last few minutes until the cutting starts."

Ann nodded and Esmerelda took her hand away. The girl said, "You're going to need another bucket to hold your own blood after Charming cuts your head off."

"Prince Charming," said Esmerelda, "is humping

his little brain out right now and does not want to be disturbed."

"He'll find out eventually and then he'll avenge me. You'd better let me go."

"I think not. I know what strings to pull to manipulate Charming. After tonight I will be the most powerful sorceress in the twenty kingdoms."

"Haven't you ever thought of using your skill to benefit people instead of hurting them?"

"No. I never have." Esmerelda picked up the silver knife again. "Take a deep breath, dear."

Ann clamped her mouth shut and held her breath. Her eyes were tightly closed. She waited for the first touch of the knife, determined not to scream. She waited for the chilling touch of the cold metal, the pressure of the tip against her skin, the agonizing feel of the blade slicing through her flesh. She waited for . . . good Lord, what was taking this idiot so long anyway? She opened her eyes. Prince Charming was smiling down at her, grinning like a little schoolboy. He held up his sword.

"Hey, Ann. Did I tell you I finally figured out what this little twisty thing in the handle is? It's a lock pick."

"I," said Ann, "am very happy to see you."

"I should think you would be." Charming turned Esmerelda's body over with his foot. The woman's face still wore an expression of surprise, the sudden shock of feeling Charming's sword pierce her heart from behind. "Never knew what hit her," the Prince murmured. "What a slime ball. Why does a woman with mystical gifts dedicate herself to a life of evil? What does she get out of it?"

"She mentioned something about low-interest loans."

"Mmmmmmm. Not good enough. Fairies are strange. Ann, what are you doing here anyway? I thought you were back at the castle, celebrating with the happy couple."

"Say, um, you don't happen to see a blanket around here, do you? I'm getting kind of chilled like this."

The Prince looked around. "No. Here, I'll get Esmerelda's cloak off."

"Don't you dare!"

"Oh, all right." Charming took off his shirt and draped it over her, then started going through the dead woman's pockets. "You didn't happen to see where she put the key to those things?"

"No. Can't you get them with your lock-pick?"

"I'm not so good with manacles. Door locks are the main obstacle in the Slay-and-Rescue business." The Prince made a quick search of the shelves in the room. "Tell you what. I'll get some tools from Wendell and we'll pound those things off. I'll only be gone a minute." He went to the door and paused with his hand on it. "Don't go away."

Ann raised her head and looked at the chains. "Right."

"Just kidding." He turned the door and handle. A two-foot-high surge of water forced the door open and poured into the room.

"Water?" said Ann. "Something must have happened to the grail."

"Wendell snatched it." Charming pulled Endeavor from its sheath and unfolded the lock-pick. He applied it to the cuff on Ann's left wrist, his mouth set in a grim line. "At least we know Wendell got out okay."

"Uh huh. Can you get these things off?"

"Hmmm? Oh, sure. Not to worry. Have them off in a jiffy. No problem. Relax. Nothing to it." The pick made a scraping sound beneath his fingers. "Damn."

The water was coming up awfully fast. It swirled up past Charming's knees and poured in the tops of his boots. It soaked through his trousers and was past his hips by the time he got the first cuff off. The second cuff went a little faster because he already knew what to do but, still, the water had topped the table by several inches and Ann had to prop herself on one arm while he worked on it. He helped her to her feet and she stood on the table, letting the water cover her feet while Charming worked on her ankles. The water was too muddy to see into and he worked by feel, with his hands underwater, while the water came up past his chest, then his neck.

"Charming," said Ann. Her voice quavered. "I don't think we're going to make it. You'd better leave me."

"Don't be ridiculous." The Prince took a deep breath and ducked his head underwater. Seconds later, Ann felt the first ankle cuff pull away. Charming surfaced and shook the water out of his hair. "There, see. I'll have that last one off in plenty of time."

He ducked back under the water. Ann could feel his hands working around her ankle. She waited, watching the water level rise against the stone wall. Charming came up again, gasping for air. She said, "You have to leave me. In a minute the water will put out the torches and then you won't be able to see your way out."

"Almost have it," Charming promised. He took a deep breath and sank down again.

Ann was breathing in short, hysterical gasps. The torches went out quickly, snuffed by the icy water, leaving her in oily blackness. The water topped her shoulders and she stood on her toes, keeping her head as high as possible. She wondered briefly if drowning was really as bad as everyone said it was and she was suddenly glad that Charming had stayed with her. She hadn't wanted him to die with her, but she didn't want to die alone, either. The Prince surfaced beside her, choking and coughing in the darkness.

"Prince Charming," she shouted above the rush of

water. "I have something to tell you. Something very important. I should have told you sooner. I don't know why I didn't but I have to tell you now."

"Oh, for God's sake! You're not going to tell me you love me, are you?"

"Yes, damn it! That's just what I was going to say!"

"Well, save it!" There was a splash and then he disappeared again. Ann tried to say something, but water poured in her mouth and she coughed it out. It rose past her face and she tried to tread water, splashing with her hands and kicking her free leg. She felt Charming grab her free ankle and rest it on his shoulder. Her other leg was stretched to the limit of its chain. When her face rose out of the water once again, she took one last, deep breath before the water covered her once more. Suddenly her ankle came free and she rose to the surface with Charming.

"Okay," said Charming. He was struggling to get his boots off. "Deep breath, now. We'll have to swim for it."

They were in the rapidly disappearing air space between the top of the water and the ceiling. "Swim where?" said Ann. It was pitch black.

She felt Charming grab her hand. "Just hold on. I remember the way."

And he did. How he found his way she never figured out. He pulled her along through the black water, several times banging her against the stone, but always finding an air space just when she thought her lungs would burst, until finally they surfaced again in the stairwell, the same one she had climbed down hours before. Overhead, stars were shining. They clung together in the muddy water, getting their strength back, then crawled up the remaining steps. There was a cheerful fire blazing in the clearing and Wendell sat beside it, cleaning his sword.

He shook his head when he saw them. "For a guy

who is always complaining about his love life, Sire, you sure have a lot of women stashed around the place." He pulled a blanket out of a kit bag and brought it over to Ann. "Hello, Ann."

"Hello, Wendell. Thank you."

"Cynthia came out of that cavern, too. I gave her the other blanket, so you'll have to stay wet. She didn't have any clothes on, either."

"That girl is a fox," said Charming. "I really hated to give her up."

"I guess we know his type now," Ann told Wendell. "Obviously he goes for redheads. What happened to her?"

"She went off with Bear. Bear was guarding the entrance while I went inside."

"Wendell," said Charming. "Did you get the grail?"

"Sure did."

"Good work. Any trouble?"

"An arm with a sword. It was no big deal."

"It will be by the time the minstrels get through rewriting the tale. Is that it?"

"Uh huh."

"A piece of wood?"

Ann examined it. "Olive wood. This is a fertility grail, all right."

Charming sat down on a rock. "We should have grabbed the magic mirror. At least that had some resale value."

"This has what we want," said Ann. "Wendell, are the horses still tied up outside the thorn hedge?"

"Yours are. I led mine through to carry the gear."

"All right. Take the grail and leave us alone for a while. We'll meet you back at the Inn by daybreak."

"Have fun," said Wendell. He tucked the grail back in his tunic, buckled on his sword and left, picking his way carefully between the stones in the darkness. Ann waited till he was out of sight, then walked over to Charming and sat in his lap.

"Well," said Charming, "How about explaining what you were doing mmmmmmphh . . ."

Ann kissed him. The kiss was long and warm and deep. Once Charming got over his initial surprise, he enjoyed it thoroughly. When she finally came up for air he said, panting a little, "I thought you were supposed to be sweet, pure, chaste and innocent."

"It's okay," said Ann, kissing him again. "We're going to be married. I'll tell you about it in the morning."

It was a warm, sunny morning five days later. They were back at the castle Illyria, sitting on one of its many terraces.

"That's all?" said Charming. "It was okay? Just 'okay'?"

Ann had Charming's shirt unbuttoned and had been biting his chest. She looked up. "It was fine. I liked it. The kissing is really the best part. I really don't see why we can't have more kissing and do away with the rest of it."

"Well, we can't. Skip the rest of it, I mean. We can have more kissing."

"Good," said Ann. She squirmed in his lap and wrapped warm arms around his neck.

"I didn't mean right now." She put her tongue in his mouth. He decided not to argue.

Ten minutes later she broke away and rested her head on his shoulder. "Aurora says she picks a spot on the ceiling to concentrate on and just lets her mind go blank. It's over before she knows it."

"Arrrgh," Charming lay back and put his face in his hands. "No! Don't do that. It'll get better, I promise you."

Ann climbed on top of him. "I think you're just

wonderful now." She began nibbling on his ear. "But there's one thing you can't do," she whispered. Warm breath caressed his ear. "You can't put your hand up my dress today."

"Oh?" murmured Charming, letting his hand slide up her thigh. "Why is that?"

"Because I'm not wearing panties," breathed Ann. She took the lobe between her lips and gently tugged on it. "So it would be very, very naughty if you were to put your hand ... oooh ... there." They grappled for long minutes before Ann pushed away and hastily pulled her dress down. "Aurora's coming."

Charming buttoned his shirt and gathered up a pair of books. Although he was still wearing his sword, he looked very relaxed and casual. He kissed Ann once more on the cheek and then stood and bowed to Aurora. "Good morning, your Highness."

"Good morning, Charming." Aurora set down her purse. "I won't take too much of your time as I know you two want to be alone. Ann, I just wanted to review with you the plans for the ball. I'm afraid, Charming, that your little red-haired friend will not be invited this time."

"I can't say I'm disappointed. But actually, I expect I'm going to be rather busy. . . ."

"Aurora is giving the ball in our honor," interrupted Ann.

"Oh. Well, yes, it would be a pleasure to attend."

"You're very gracious. Er, Charming, could you have a word with Wendell? He's very upset."

"Oh, yeah. I've been so busy I haven't had a chance to talk with him since we got back. Come to think of it, I haven't even seen him."

"He's been avoiding you since he was filled in on the news. In fact, he'd been avoiding everyone."

"He probably just wants some time to himself."

"He skipped breakfast this morning." said Ann. "And dinner last night."

"Hmmmm. That's serious all right. Well, Mandelbaum will straighten him out."

Ann looked at Aurora. "Mandelbaum seems to be preoccupied these days. Wendell really needs to talk to you."

"Hmmm, okay. Do you know where he is?"

"Down by the river, fishing. Here." She gave Charming a parcel. "I made some cookies for you to take to him."

"Thanks." He kissed her again. "See you later. Good-bye, Aurora."

He found Wendell at a secluded spot, fishing from the river's banks, and sat down beside him.

Wendell ignored him.

"How's the fishing?"

"Fine." Wendell did not look up.

"Catch anything?"

"No."

"Okay."

Pause.

"Want some cookies? Ann made them."

"What kind?"

"Oatmeal."

"Figures."

They sat in silence. The silence stretched out. Finally Charming said, "Look, I guess you're upset, right?"

"What do you think?"

"Come on, Wendell, it had to end sooner or later. We can't just spend our whole lives running around the country seeking adventure. Sooner or later you've got to settle down, take responsibility."

Wendell sat in silence for another minute while his face got redder and redder. Finally he leaped to his feet and flung the fishing pole into the river. "Is that what you think I want?" he shouted at Charming. "Is that all you think I care about?"

"Well, what?"

"I care about you. Look at you. You were the greatest Prince this country ever had. You were admired by everyone. You were my hero and the hero of every boy in the twenty kingdoms. And now you're nobody. You were Prince Charming and you were going to be King Charming and you let them take it all away from you. You didn't even put up a fight. Now you're just another knight and you don't even care!"

"Wendell!"

"And you don't care about me, either! Look at me. I'm the seventh son of a Duke. You know what that gets me. Nothing! No land, no title, no inheritance. I won't even get a gentleman's education. Last week, people respected me because they knew I rode with you and someday I'd have a knighthood of my own. Now I'll be living as a guest in my brothers' homes and laughing at their jokes so they don't get mad at me and cut off my allowance." He picked up a stone and threw that into the river also.

"Wendell, you know I care about you. What did you want me to do?"

"We could go to war!"

"What?"

"I'll help you!" Wendell ran to Charming and threw his arms around him. "We'll go south. We'll raise an army. Bear has some men. He'll help us. There are at least seven kings who will support you! They'll give you money and arms and men. And when we're ready, we'll march on Illyria!"

"Wendell!"

"You'll force your father to recognize you as the true Prince and heir to the throne. You'll make him give you back your birthright. And if he doesn't, we'll take the throne from him. We can do it. I'll fight by your side, Sire. I'll never let you down."

"Wendell, I already am a king."

"What?"

Charming disentangled himself. "Wendell, Ann and I were married last night. I'm now King of Alacia."

Wendell sat back down. Charming could see that he had trouble digesting this. "Alacia? Why?"

"They need a king, Wendell. The people love Ann, but the country has real problems and she can't do it all by herself. Ruby has always been too wrapped up in magic to be a good leader. She tried to rule through spellcraft and simply botched things up. But she did learn about the grail."

"The grail again."

"It really is a fertility grail. Remember how lush that valley was. Remember when Aurora said the girls in Alacia got pregnant real easily. That's all because of the grail. But, like Mandelbaum said, it's a male thing. It needs a king to work it."

"But you're giving up Illyria for a mudhole!"

"Illyria doesn't need me, Wendell. Dad's only forty years old. With luck, he'll rule for another twenty years or more. I'd just be sitting on my hands.

"But Alacia is in big trouble. It's a blighted land. The soil is poor and the crops aren't producing, the trees are dying, and the cattle are barren. They really need help. With hard work and the fertility grail, Ann and I figure we can turn that country around."

"Ann isn't queen, though. Queen Ruby is queen."

"Ruby is abdicating the throne to Ann. She's going to stay here and study magic with Mandelbaum. Magic is what she really cares about anyway."

Wendell thought long and hard on this. "So the women actually planned this whole thing right from the start. Queen Ruby didn't just want the grail, she wanted you and the grail. I'll bet she planted that story about wanting to kill Ann just to get you over there."

Charming sat down beside him, putting his books on the ground. He plucked a blade of grass and split it with his thumbnail. "I don't know, Wendell. I guess I'll never know for sure. Maybe Ruby knew about Aurora and Cynthia all along, maybe she plotted out the whole scenario. Or maybe Ann had her own agenda and was moving things along, making new plans as the situation changed. She's pretty smart."

"She knows what she wants, anyway. And she's loyal to her people. That's good. I guess you could have done a lot worse."

"I'm sure she'll appreciate that vote of confidence, Wendell." Charming flipped the blade of grass into the river. "I think Grandfather knew about the grail and he wanted it left alone. So he never let Dad go back with a team of magicians and take out the hedge. I think Mandelbaum was keeping tabs on the grail, also. He wanted it left alone, too, until he thought someone like Esmerelda might get it.

"And then sometimes I just tell myself that nobody knew anything, that it was all just coincidence and random chance."

"Maybe you just have a destiny to get in adventures. What are the books for?"

Charming showed them to him. "Economics and Political Theory. Dad's having his ministers give us a crash course in how to rule a country before we go back. There's a lot to it. Basics of agriculture, finance, diplomacy, and military strategy. Illyria will guarantee Alacia's borders so we won't have to sink any money into an army for a while. And Dad's happy about getting a buffer state to the north."

"Then the King is happy, too. Everybody is getting what they want."

Charming grinned and stood up. "So are you, Wendell."

"What do you mean?"

"Alacia is full of trouble, Wendell. Especially with bandits hiding out in the mountains. Plus, they've got a persistent problem with mandracores."

"Oh, come on. Even I can handle a mandracore."

"Glad to hear it. Because a King is busy all the time with affairs of state. He can't go running around chasing after bandits and mandracores. He needs a paladin to fight for him."

"Sire! You really mean it?"

"Of course. You'll start your training when you come back with us to Alacia and you'll be knighted when you turn fourteen. And . . ." Charming unbuckled his sword belt. "You'll need a good sword."

Wendell took the sword with awe. "Prince Charming! I mean, King Charming! You're giving me Endeavor?"

"I know you won't dishonor it, Wendell."

Wendell hugged him. "I don't deserve all this."

"Sure you do, kid. Come, let's get out of here. The fishing is terrible in this spot anyway."

"I threw my pole away," said Wendell, looking out at the river. "Oh, well."

"I need to take a break from studying this stuff. What do you think we should do?"

Wendell considered this and nodded thoughtfully. "I think we should eat."

BUILDING A NEW FANTASY TRADITION

The Unlikely Ones by Mary Brown

Anne McCaffrey raved over *The Unlikely Ones*: "What a splendid, unusual and intriguing fantasy quest! You've got a winner here...." Marion Zimmer Bradley called it "Really wonderful ... I shall read and re-read this one." A traditional quest fantasy with quite an unconventional twist, we think you'll like it just as much as Anne McCaffrey and Marion Zimmer Bradley did.

Knight of Ghosts and Shadows
by Mercedes Lackey & Ellen Guon

Elves in L.A.? It would explain a lot, wouldn't it? In fact, half a millennium ago, when the elves were driven from Europe they came to—where else? —Southern California. Happy at first, they fell on hard times after one of their number tried to force the rest to be his vassals. Now it's up to one poor human to save them if he can. A knight in shining armor he's not, but he's one hell of a bard!

The Interior Life by Katherine Blake

Sue had three kids, one husband, a lovely home and a boring life. Sometimes, she just wanted to escape, to get out of her mundane world and *live* a little. So she did. And discovered that an active fantasy life can be a very dangerous thing—and very real.... Poul Anderson thought *The Interior Life* was "a breath of fresh air, bearing originality, exciting narrative, vividly realized characters— everything we have been waiting for for too long."

The Shadow Gate by Margaret Ball

The only good elf is a dead elf—or so the militant order of Durandine monks thought. And they planned on making sure that all the elves in their world (where an elvish Eleanor of Aquitaine ruled in Southern France) were very, very good. The elves of Three Realms have one last spell to bring help ... and received it: in the form of the staff of the New Age Psychic Research Center of Austin, Texas....

Hawk's Flight by Carol Chase
Taverik, a young merchant, just wanted to be left alone to make an honest living. Small chance of that though: after their caravan is ambushed Taverik discovers that his best friend Marko is the last living descendant of the ancient Vos dynasty. The man who murdered Marko's parents still wants to wipe the slate clean—with Marko's blood. They try running away, but Taverik and Marko realize that there is a fate worse than death ... That sooner or later, you have to stand and fight.

A Bad Spell in Yurt by C. Dale Brittain
As a student in the wizards' college, young Daimbert had shown a distinct flair for getting himself in trouble. Now the newly appointed Royal Wizard to the backwater Kingdom of Yurt learns that his employer has been put under a fatal spell. Daimbert begins to realize that finding out who is responsible may require all the magic he'd never quite learned properly in the first place—with the kingdom's welfare and his life the price of failure. Good thing Daimbert knows how to improvise!

MERCEDES LACKEY

The Hottest Fantasy Writer Today!

URBAN FANTASY

Knight of Ghosts and Shadows with Ellen Guon

Elves in L.A.? It would explain a lot, wouldn't it? Eric Banyon is a musician with a lot of talent but very little ambition—and his lady just left him lovelorn in a deserted corner of the Renaissance Faireground, singing the blues and playing his flute. He couldn't have known the desperate sadness of his music would free Korendil, a young elven noble, from the magical prison he has been languishing in for centuries. Eric really needed a good cause to get his life in gear—now he's got one. With Korendil he must raise an army to fight against the evil lord who seeks to conquer all of California. And Eric's music will show the way....

Summoned to Tourney with Ellen Guon

Elves in San Francisco? Where else would an elf go when L.A. got too hot? All is well there with our elf-lord, his human companion and the mage who brought them all together—until it turns out that San Francisco is doomed to fall off the face of the continent. Doomed that is, unless our mage can summon the Nightflyers, the soul-devouring shadow creatures from the dreaming world—creatures no one on Earth could possibly control....

Born to Run with Larry Dixon

There are elves out there. And more are coming. But even elves need money to survive in the "real" world. The good elves in South Carolina, intrigued by the thrills of stock car racing, are manufacturing new, light-weight engines (with, incidentally, very little "cold" iron); the bad elves run a kiddie-porn and snuff-film ring, with occasional forays into drugs. *Children in Peril—Elves to the Rescue.* (Part of the SERRAted Edge series.)

HIGH FANTASY
Bardic Voices: The Lark & The Wren
Rune could be one of the greatest bards of her world, but the daughter of a tavern wench can't get much in the way of formal training. So one night she goes up to play for the Ghost of Skull Hill. She'll either fiddle till dawn to prove her skill as a bard—or die trying. . . .

Also by Mercedes Lackey:
Reap the Whirlwind with C.J. Cherryh
Part of the Sword of Knowledge series.

Castle of Deception with Josepha Sherman
Based on the bestselling computer game, *The Bard's Tale*. (Available July 1992.)

The Ship Who Searched with Anne McCaffrey
The Ship Who Sang is not alone! (Available August 1992.)

And watch for **Wheels of Fire**, Book II of the SERRAted Edge series, with Mark Shepherd, coming in October 1992.

To join the Mercedes Lackey national fan club send a self-addressed, stamped, business-size envelope to: Queen's Own, P.O. Box 43143, Upper Montclair, NJ 07043.

A SIMPLE SEER

In a display he had never before witnessed, the Stone threw off rays of red and purple light, erupting like gobbets of liquid rock and sparks from the vent of a volcano. Amnet felt the heat against his face. At the focus of the rays was something bright and golden, like a ladle of molten metal held up to him. Without moving, he felt himself pitching forward, drawn down by a pull that was separate from gravity, separate from distance, space, and time. The heat grew more intense. The light more blinding. The angle of his upper body slid from the perpendicular. He was burning. He was falling. . . .

Amnet shook himself.

The Stone, still nestled in the sand, was an inch from his face. Its surface was dark and opaque. The fire among the twigs had burned out. The alembic was clear of smoke, with a puddle of blackened gum at its bottom.

Amnet shook himself again.

What did a vision of the end of the world portend?

And what could a simple aromancer do about it?

The Wizard thinks he's in control.
The gods think that's funny . . .

It started in the 12th century when their
avatars first joined in battle. On that occasion
the sorcerous Hasan al Sabah, the first and
Chief Assassin won handily against Thomas
Amnet, Knight Templar and White Magician.
There have been many duels since then,
and in each the undying Arab has ended
the life of Loki's avatar. But each time the
avatar is reborn, and the Assassin tires. . . .

It is now the 21st century. Loki's time
approaches, and Ahriman, Lord of Darkness,
must fall.

Continuing the tradition of *Lord of Light*
and *Creatures of Light and Darkness,* a new
novel of demigods who walk the earth. . . .

THE MASK OF LOKI

Roger Zelazny & Thomas T. Thomas
72021-X • $4.95